JERÉ ANTHONY

Edited by Olivia Kalb

Cover by Bailey McGinn

For my best friend, Natalie, who basically handed me the tampon/shark scene on a silver platter.

CHAPTER ONE

Gwen

"And that's how I know Big Foot's out there, just walking around among us, yet to be discovered. You can mark my words; I'm going to find him if it's the last thing I do."

Why are the pretty ones always the weirdos?

This always happens to me—I meet a hot guy, we flirt back and forth, and things seem promising. But the minute I agree to a date, it's like the switch flips, and they bring out their inner weirdo, which I have to suffer through just to get laid.

I drain my martini and sneak a glance at my phone, conveniently located in my lap underneath the table. I know it's bad date etiquette, but it's not as if Preston's giving me a lot to work with here. Call me crazy, but I'm a bit of a workaholic, so it's going to take more than a Big Foot story to keep my attention ... But if you want to get laid, sometimes you have to pay the price, and tonight, that price is lending an ear to his god-awful story.

I close my email and check the time. Shit, it's only seven-thirty. I've only been listening to Preston's childhood Big Foot encounter for an hour.

We haven't even gotten our food yet, and I'm already bored. He's attractive enough, in a pretty boy, conventional way. Tilting my head, I study his tall frame, letting my eyes roam up his khakis; they've been pressed *properly* with a crease down the middle, heavily starched. I crinkle my nose. Starched pants just don't give me that rugged throw-me-against-the-wall vibe I'm looking for tonight. Letting my gaze wander higher, I see a slight bulge, and I'm pleasantly surprised. Maybe I'll give him a second chance? Who knows, maybe he took his clothes to a new dry cleaner? Though, he's wearing his long-sleeve button-up shirt—with crease—tucked in and with the sleeves fully down to his wrists. I'm disappointed by the lack of forearm action, but maybe he's got a tattoo sleeve and doesn't want to scare me away?

A girl can dream, right?

"What about you, Gwen. Are you superstitious?" Preston's question breaks me from my internal assessment of his clothing until he pulls out a rabbit's foot from his pocket and lays it on the table. "I've carried it with me since I was a kid. This was actually my pet rabbit, Buster. When he died, I was so upset that my grandfather cut off his foot and made it into this token to protect me—it's like he's always with me everywhere I go." He pushes the foot closer to me just as the server brings our food.

"Pet him. See how soft he is."

I close my eyes and take a long, slow inhale, calming myself. *It's not weird to keep your pet rabbit's foot in your pocket and show it to someone on a first date. Nope, that's not weird. Just look at his eyes. They're moody blue, and his eyelashes are long and thick. Plus, he's tall. You know how much you love tall guys. You can do this, Gwen. You need this.*

Okay, so maybe "need" is a bit of an exaggeration, but I could certainly use the distraction of a one-night stand, considering I've worked over sixty hours this week alone. I deserve to have a little fun, and why should I not let Preston here blow my back out? I mean, haven't you ever experienced post-coital clarity? Orgasms offer the best stress relief, plus I need to be on my A-game for tomorrow's meeting if I want to stand any chance at earning that promotion.

I stifle a yawn and sit up a little straighter with a newfound determination. If I can just get past the small talk and move us toward the dirty talk...

"You know, I don't really like animals... especially their detached appendages, so I think I'll pass. To answer your question, I'm not superstitious. I just work hard and trust that good things will follow because I've earned them." I push the foot across the table, making as little contact as possible, and I hate to admit it, but the foot *is* surprisingly soft. "Why don't you tell me about your job. What is it you said you do again?" I force myself to take a bite of my chicken, though my appetite's taken a hit after the foot bit.

"Oh, I own a taxidermy shop outside the city. I specialize in deer and elk heads, but every once in a while, I get to work on a bear for a special project. Bears are my favorite." His eyes widen in excitement, and the chicken forms a lump in my throat as I try to swallow. It's like he knows my vagina is desperate for a suitor to call on her.

Is this a test from the universe? Either way, it's not funny.

I grit my teeth and force out a smile. "And what size shoe do you wear?"

"That's a funny question. Um... a thirteen but sometimes a twelve. It depends on the brand. Why do you ask?"

"No reason." I force down another bite of chicken and order a second martini. It seems like I'm definitely going to need it.

"Wow, you're really strong. Hey, that kind of hurts," Preston whines as my teeth slide down his jaw. We're riding the elevator back up to my apartment, where I plan on finding out if his shoe size is an accurate predictor. Who am I kidding? I'd dry hump a man with a micro-penis at this point. I'm desperate, so desperate that I'm actually going to let a Big Foot-hunting taxidermist into my panties for the night. I'll have to do a whole vagina cleanse tomorrow. Maybe I'll get Maggie to bring over a sage bundle, and we can hit the factory reset or something.

"Shut up and take off my bra," I order once we're inside my apartment. I shove him into my now-closed front door as I set my purse and keys aside. He obliges, though his hands shake as he unclasps my bra and yanks my shirt over my head. Once I'm undressed from the top up, his eyes seem to pop out of his head, and I let him take in my delectable breasts in all their glory. At first, he hesitates, but after a little more encouragement, he lunges toward me in a frenzy. Preston's hands roam my body frantically as if he can't get enough. He grips my ass as I climb up him, wrapping my legs around his waist and moaning into his ear. "Yes, I like it rough," I whisper.

Yes, ok, I may be putting on a bit of a show, but if I can turn myself on enough, then I'll hopefully be able to chase down my big O tonight, which is all I'm after.

"You like it rough, do you?" He carries me through the apartment and kicks open my bedroom door. *Wow, maybe I underestimated Mr. Khaki's after all?*

He drops me onto the bed, and I bounce on the soft mattress. "Do you like it dirty, Gwen? Do you want me to fuck you?"

My heart skips a beat, and a grin spreads across my face. Who could've predicted this? Surprise overwhelms me. "Yes, I want you to fuck me," I say, trying to lose the crazy grin. I don't want him to lose whatever act this is.

Preston unzips his khakis, and I lean back on my elbows for a better view, my heart racing in anticipation. I may be a master vibrator operator, but every once in a while, I need a good dick-down to reset my operating system. The big reveal is my second favorite part of the equation. His khakis fall to the floor in a crumpled mess, and I can't help but think of how noticeable the wrinkles will be when he walks out of here tonight.

I almost miss the sight of his extremely long, extremely thin penis before he pounces on top of me, wearing only his white crew socks. The force knocks the air from my lungs, and I cough several times to regain my breath.

"You want dirty; I'll give you dirty," he growls.

As a final cough leaves my lungs, I hear him hock up something in his throat. Before my mind can register what he's planning, Preston spits a thick wad of phlegm into my open mouth. "Yeah, baby. I like it dirty, too."

Repulsion rips through me, and I launch myself off the bed with the strength of twenty men. I don't care that my tits are on full display or that Preston's pencil dick is out at attention. I run past him straight to the bathroom and proceed to hurl everything back up.

He pokes his head around the corner, "Come back in here, you nasty little bitch. I want to show you just how dirty I can be."

"Stop. Do not come anywhere near me, you fucking lunatic. Get out of my apartment before I cut off your dick and you have to carry it around in your pocket as your new good-luck charm!"

Mouth agape, he blinks several times and covers his penis in a protective stance. "You, um, you said you liked it dirty ... I was just trying to be dirty for you. I've actually never done this before. I just watch a lot of porn, and the women seem to enjoy that. Let's start over. I promise I won't spit on you again. I'll do better."

"OUT," I scream, pointing to the door.

"Yeah. Ok. Let me just go grab my pants." He waddles away, his head hanging in defeat, as I crawl toward the shower to turn on the scalding stream. There isn't a shower hot enough to wash away the shame I feel, but it's a start.

I hear the door open. "I'll, um, I'll call you, ok?" he calls before closing it behind him.

"Yeah, I wouldn't hold your breath on that one, buddy." I grab the entire tube of toothpaste and my toothbrush and climb into the shower, where I proceed to wash every orifice until the water goes cold.

The things I do in the name of stress relief. I guess it's me and BOB once again tonight.

The next morning, I drag myself into my office, not nearly as spry as I hoped to be, and make my way up to the eleventh floor. My office building is sleek and professional, with a strong feminine influence. Mauve and lavender geometric murals cover the white walls, and colorful rugs bring warmth to every conference room. We've got pastel pink leather sofas in the common areas and a full-service coffee bar on each floor. The whole building was designed with the motto, "Make pretty choices," which flows over into our company culture. Éclat is known as the leading PR agency in Chicago. Celebrities, influencers, and brands line up for our services, especially when shit hits the fan, and I don't mean to brag, but I'm the very best at cleaning up shit—metaphorically speaking, anyway.

Monthly meetings are the bane of my existence, especially when we're starting a new quarter. My boss, Sandra, seems to get off on inflicting as much pain and fear onto all of us as she can; I think she gets off on the drama. She's got that whole Miranda Priestly from The Devil Wears Prada vibe.

Starting as an entry-level billing clerk straight out of college, I've worked my way up at her company, and now, I'm one of her top two performing PR specialists. Sandra hasn't made it a secret that she's considering me for the VP role opening up in the near future. In fact, she's all but promised me the role for the last three years after I almost took a job offer from a competitor who sought me out. She's dangled the promotion in front of my face like a carrot, and I just need something big to push me over the edge. Then she'll have to promote me.

My mouth practically waters at the thought of having those infamous two letters following my name on my office door. I can already see it now: *Gwen Pierson, VP.*

I want to prove to Sandra—but mostly to myself—that I've finally made it all on my own and I'm good enough to sit among the best in the industry. That I earned a leading title on my hard work alone, not because anything was handed to me. This promotion would provide me with a solid, stable income and plenty of clout to go with it.

I've worked my ass off, representing the most difficult clients, spinning their horrifying fuck-ups into solemn apologies that somehow make them more lovable and approachable than they were before. Every one of my clients has left me with a better reputation and because of my track record, I'm known as the crisis-intervention queen around the office. After I've worked my magic, spinning their story to reflect whatever positive outcome I can manage, I hand them off to one of my co-workers to maintain, rinse, wash, and repeat.

I glance over at Pantone Brown, my arch-nemesis. If anyone beats me out of this promotion, it'll be her. Pantone is a couple of years older than me and has the reputation of a snake. She's one of those people you have to keep a close eye on. I wouldn't put anything past her when she's trying to get ahead. She comes from a powerful family with plenty of money and prestige. Every job she's gotten has been handed to her by her daddy—be it her biological or *sugar*. Honestly, even having her as my direct peer is insulting.

We take our seats in the cushy conference room around a large, crisp white table with views overlooking the cityscape of downtown Chicago. Sandra sits at the head of the table facing an oversized TV monitor, showing all our clients' information. Today's meeting is primarily focused on assigning new clients.

"Laura, what do we have on the horizon? Do you have any rocks you're working on this week?" Sandra peers over the top of her delicate designer glasses and scribbles something in her notepad.

Laura, the newest team member fresh from her internship, clears her throat. "Actually, we've just picked up a new client who'll need a little help. His name is Wombat Willy, and he's an adventure tour guide turned YouTuber. He recently had an incident on one of his guided tours where a man lost his hand from a caiman bite. His sponsors have insisted he seek a PR agency to repair his image. Apparently, the accident happened on a live stream."

"How many followers did you say he has again?" I chime in as the wheels in my head start turning.

Laura flips through the deck until she finds what she's looking for. "1.3 million followers. All organic within the last five years–"

"I believe we can all read the slide deck, Laura," Sandra interrupts.

I feel a bubble of excitement in the pit of my stomach, and my fingers itch to pull out my phone and Google him myself, but I resist. There's nothing Sandra hates more than seeing someone on their phone during a meeting. It's a total oxymoron considering that's most of our job, but it's one of her pet peeves.

Laura takes a shaky breath before she continues. "We've also got the Thorstein sisters who've recently decided to split up their shares of their businesses. There will be a lot of handholding for the middle sister. We need to get her out and break away from her shy image. VIP parties, house tours, we need to appeal to a younger audience. Maybe we set her up with a B-level celebrity to get some coverage? Their mother is sick about the dispute and wants to make sure all the girls are on an equal playing field."

I wipe my sweaty palms against my pants and blurt out, "I'll take Willy," before I think better of it and change my mind. It's a risk, something completely out of my comfort zone, but with the limited information I have, I think I can spin this. This could be exactly what I need to show Sandra just how valuable I am here at Éclat.

Sandra's eyes widen, then narrow as she searches my face for something only she can see. "Interesting. That's quite *ambitious* of you, isn't it?"

I swallow the lodged lump in my throat, "I'm up for a challenge. Besides, if his sponsorships reflect his following, this could bring Éclat to the next level." I steady my shoulders and hold eye contact.

"Great. It's decided, then." Sandra slaps her notebook closed. "Gwen will be onsite with Wombat Willy while Pantone takes Pheobe Thorstein.

"Whoa, whoa, whoa." I hold up my hands as if I'm a watch guard directing traffic. "What do you mean when you say *onsite?*"

Sandra scoffs. "Gwen, do I really need to give you a basic vocabulary lesson?" She grabs the clicker and scans through the slides. "It says right here in the agreement that the Public

Relations Representative is needed in-person to help aid Wombat Willy during his next filming session in Costa Rica." She tosses the clicker and stands, brushing non-existent lint off her jacket. "For someone so good at their job, you're really off your game this morning." She pulls her glasses down and peers over the top of them as if she's staring straight into my soul. "I suggest you take this assignment seriously if you even want to be considered for the VP role in the fall. Meeting adjourned. Good luck, ladies!" Then she turns on her heel, leaving me wondering what I've just agreed to.

"Ooh, that doesn't sound fun at all." Pantone's nasally voice pierces my already aching head. "Have fun with your assignment, though. Maybe you'll embrace a whole new lifestyle and finally stop trying to be something you're not." She flicks the rogue coffee stain on my blouse. "I think you and the wild man may have more in common than you think."

I grit my teeth, forcing a smile because VPs generally don't punch their colleagues. *It's just a two-week assignment. I can do anything for two weeks, right?*

CHAPTER TWO

JACK

"Ready, set, action!" Pedro, my film guy, calls from behind the camera, and I slowly inhale and exhale, calming my nerves. You'd think by now I'd be used to leading groups of rich pricks through the wilderness, but after doing this for five years, I still get a rush of nerves every single time. Rich men are the absolute worst, especially the trust fund college kids on spring break. They never fucking listen.

"Hey there, Dubbies! Welcome back to our live stream in the jungle of Costa Rica. Today I'm giving a tour to these interesting gents—" I gesture to the rowdy group of men behind me. This group's particularly feral, and I wouldn't be surprised if someone snuck in drugs without my knowing. I sigh and roll my eyes, not caring in the least that I'm mocking my paying clients on a live stream.

I slap my hands together and press them to my lips, signaling for Pedro to focus the shot on me. "We've just spotted a Great Green Macaw in the tree behind me, and this is a super rare creature." I point over my shoulder. "As you know, this is a survival channel, but it's always cool to see rare endangered species in their natural environment. Come on, let's get a closer look."

Pedro follows me to the shoreline, and I call over the group of guys to come closer as I spew all the facts I know about the endangered bird. "Now, just a reminder, it is spring, which means you need to watch your step for any baby animals, especially the caimans, which are in the water here because when there's a baby, there will almost always be a mama close behind."

No sooner have the words left my mouth than I hear.

"Hey, watch this!" one of the douchebags announces as he grabs a stick and pokes a freshly laid nest of caiman eggs.

Oh, fuck.

"Stop! Those are—" I shout just as the protective mother caiman jumps from its camouflage in the water and locks its jaws around the guy's arm... ripping it completely off as she falls back into the dirty water.

My heart falls into my stomach as I lunge into action, pushing everyone away from the nest and, more importantly, away from the arm-snatcher as the man's bloody arm-nub shoots blood straight in my eyes like a water hose.

Panicking, I wipe the sticky hot liquid from my face only to find my camera lying on the ground with its red light blinking, indicating we are indeed still live. I squint my eyes, catching sight of Pedro running for the hills several hundred yards away.

"Fuck." I grimace, trying my best to wipe the fresh blood from my face as I pick up the camera. "Sorry, guys." Then I end the recording and yank off my belt to make a tourniquet.

"I don't think I've ever seen so much blood in my life. I bet he'll think twice next time someone tells him to leave the wildlife alone." I take a sip of my beer and sit it down a bit harder than necessary, the harsh clank of the metal chair reverberating through the crowded tiki bar. My manager, Landon, flinches in response, momentarily distracting him from doomscrolling through his contact list.

He sighs rather than answering me.

I had to listen to his exaggerated moans and complaints about his stomach ulcer during the entire flight to Miami. He even told me that I made him nervous before we landed as if I'm some amateur pilot.

I've had my pilot license for six whole months and have made at least ten trips to Costa Rica, where I do most of my tourist expeditions. Besides, it's not rocket science. Yes, flying a plane is sexy as hell, and yes, I worked my ass off to pass the test, but sometimes people just have a natural talent for things, and piloting is definitely one of mine.

It's Friday night, and we should be celebrating another successful adventure, but thanks to the douche-canoe who thinks rules don't apply to him, I'm sitting here with my manager, who's on the verge of a conniption. What was supposed to be a normal wildlife tour turned into a complete and utter mess. On the bright side, I'll be able to fly back home in time for my buddy Benjamin's engagement party tomorrow night.

Benjamin popped the question to his now-fiancée, Elliot, last week. I'm so damn happy for them. I can't wait to stand by his side when he says "I do" to the love of his life. He hasn't *explicitly* asked me to be his best man yet, but I know it's coming.

So now I get an unexpected night off to celebrate with my crew before I have to hit the ground running in recon mode.

I take a swig of my beer and shiver at the memory. "Did you see the tendons in his arm? They were just dangling in the wind. It was gnarly." I scrunch up my nose at the memory and chance a glance at Landon. His face is as white as a sheet. He pins me with a death glare, mirroring my grade school headmaster, Sister Maria.

I swallow a gulp and grab a menu to distract myself.

I realize this may seem like a really big deal, especially since the man in question was in my direct care ... but I have the entire thing on film, including the part where I specifically told him not to go near the caiman. Plus, everyone signs a waiver before we depart. So, as far as I'm concerned, mother nature is to blame, not me. This is the fucking jungle. Anything can happen. That's kind of the point.

I haven't always led excursions for rich, delicate men through the jungle.

Ten years ago, after graduating college with a biology degree and a minor in marketing, I helped Benjamin start his marketing firm. I learned a lot about the trade, but mostly I learned that the daily grind of the nine to five wasn't for me. I craved adventure, so after leaving the corporate world behind, I set out to discover myself. I traveled the world and started a vlog. Pretty soon, white-collar CEOs and other high society folks began asking to accompany me on my travels. One thing led to another, and now I own the fastest-growing nature channel on Youtube. People from all over the world spend thousands of dollars for week-long trips to exotic locations led by yours truly.

While it pays well, the main purpose is to create content for my YouTube channel. Over the last five years, I've been able to take my hobby to a global scale and turn it into a thriving channel where I teach my audience real-world survival skills.

So I split my time between leading tours where I film real people learning survival skills and going at it solo. For my solo trips, I poll my audience quarterly and let them choose where they want to see me rough it. Then I set out alone with only my video camera and what fits in my backpack.

People love living vicariously through the lens of my handheld camera, and I get to make a living doing what lights me up. I really am living the dream. I never imagined I'd make a living doing what I love, but here I am. So, while Landon is having an aneurysm over a mere flesh wound, I'm not sweating it. Money's not my end all be all. If I lose a couple of sponsorships because some dumbass didn't want to listen, so be it.

I sneak another look at Landon, who's hunched over his phone with a finger in his ear, shouting over the techno music blaring through the speakers.

"Just hear me out–" Landon's plea comes to a sudden stop, and I assume the person on the other end of the line hung up on him.

He rolls his eyes and slumps in his seat in defeat.

"Landon, my man, you sound too desperate. You can't beg like that. You're showing all your cards."

"Jack, could you just shut up for one minute while I rack my brain and *try* to fix this! They're calling you the Johnny Knoxville of the Wilderness. It's on the front page of Google, for Christ's sake!" he hisses.

"I feel like it could definitely be worse..." Landon doesn't take the bait. He just rolls his eyes as he dives back into his contact list, putting the small phone up to his large sweaty head.

"Alright, it's your evening at stake." I hold my hand up in surrender.

I really hope he remembers to hydrate because at the rate he's sweating, the poor guy will need IV fluids by the end of the night.

"You're lucky you have me around to clean up your messes.

Do you know I've single-handedly talked you out of three sponsorship drops? If we don't do something quick, you're at risk of being demonetized," he snaps.

"I already told you. I have the footage." I pull out my phone and show him the clip, pausing it the moment after I told him not to go near the caiman.

"Do you really think your sponsors care that he didn't listen to you? Jack, they're dropping like flies over this." He drops his voice lower, pinning me with his angry gaze, "Someone got their arm bitten off—"

"It was closer to being ripped off. The caiman bit it, but the death roll was what actually tore his arm off," I correct him.

Landon shakes his head and continues, "On a live video where over fifty thousand people were watching."

"So maybe we can spin this into a lesson? Maybe the message needs to be: *don't be dumb*." I try my best to sound hopeful, but Landon doesn't bite.

"I don't have time for this right now." He pushes away from the bar, dabbing his forehead with a napkin, "I'm going to step outside for some fresh air and clear my head. Please don't post anything on social media until I give you direction. I'm waiting to hear back from Sandra at Éclat. Her people are the best in the business." He keeps his eyes trained on me, making me even more uncomfortable under his scrutiny, "Jack, I need you to listen to me. If you want to salvage this and keep from losing everything, you'll have to do whatever they tell you to do. This isn't a game. Your career is on the line." His voice trails off, turning to leave.

Well, isn't Landon just a ball of sunshine? I roll my eyes and gesture for the bartender to pour me another beer as he walks away.

The truth is maybe I should be freaking out right now, but everything in me knows things will work out. I know it may seem naïve or lazy even, but I live my life guided by my gut, and my gut tells me this isn't over.

Now I get to work with some PR agency and bullshit my way back into the good graces of my sponsors. I feel like a scolded child. I've got one night of freedom, and then I'll be flying back to Costa Rica, this time accompanied by some high-profile babysitter who's supposed to help "clean up my image."

I take Landon's dramatic exit as an opportunity to order some chili cheese fries from the bar. And since he wants to give me the cold shoulder, I'm only sharing if he asks nicely.

CHAPTER THREE

Gwen

"Elliot, I'm so happy for you. You look absolutely stunning!" I take in my gorgeous bestie, and a prickle of jealousy stabs at me and catches me off guard. It's been a weird day. After the events of last night, maybe I'm just so penis-starved that I'm actually jealous of my best friend's engagement even though there's no chance I'm locking down the same D for the rest of my life. Nope, that's not how this girl rolls.

I met my best friends, Elliot and Maggie, in college, and they've been my ride or dies ever since. While Maggie's the mom of the group, making sure everyone feels seen and heard, Elliot is the chaos. I'm not going to lie; she's a good time and seeing her finally find herself has been the most amazing thing. I'd like to think she did it all on her own, but I know her fiancé, Benjamin, made a huge impact on her. I'm so happy they have each other.

"Gwen, you look stunning. I have a table for you and Maggie right next to the bar. Come on, let me show you your seats!" Elliot drags me across the dance floor of the hip ballroom. My mind flashes back to the moment she caught her big break in this same place. Though the job didn't work out quite how she'd planned, I'll never regret making that introduction. My, how things can change in just a year.

I scan the room and spot Maggie talking to Elliot's mother, and the knot in my stomach finally relaxes. I love these girls, and there's no one else I'd rather spend time with before leaving the country.

Today was a whirlwind of a day, and I'm so exhausted. I've been up to my eyeballs in paperwork and forms, preparing for tomorrow's excursion. Éclat even mandated I receive three different vaccines before I could leave.

I rub my achy arm and grab a fresh glass of champagne, pushing all my work thoughts out of my mind. Tonight, I'm here to celebrate my best friend. Even though it goes against everything in me, I suppress my control issues and force myself to be present for her. I'll just have to worry about Wombat Willy on my flight first thing tomorrow morning.

"Here's to Elliot and Benjamin! Now, let's have some fun, shall we?"

"I'm swearing off men. I can't handle the disappointment. He actually spat in my mouth! You know I can't even handle someone's breath in my face, much less a wad of phlegm." I shiver at the memory that will haunt me for the rest of my life. "I don't know what it is, but every guy I've attempted to hook up with in the past year has left me utterly disappointed. Maybe this is the universe's way of telling me I'm supposed to be a lesbian." I shove a french fry into my mouth.

"Gwen, we all know you'd be a shit lesbian partner. You'd

be jealous of your girlfriend rather than in love with her." Elliot laughs.

"You're right. We all know I have great tits. I don't know what I'd do if my girlfriend had better boobs than me. Besides, there's just something about having a super-masculine man wrapped around my finger that gets me going," I add.

"Personally, I'm more concerned that the rando-spitter guy knows where you live," Maggie scolds, "Gwen, you can't just bring random men back to your apartment like that. What if he's a stalker and he planted a recording device in your bedroom or something?"

"I'm not going to lie, Mags. My vag just lit up when you said the word stalker. I guess I do still have that exhibitionist fetish..."

"I can't with you right now! And you're leaving tomorrow morning going where exactly? When did you find all of this out?" Maggie takes another pull of her beer.

"I'll be on a flight to Costa Rica first thing in the morning. I volunteered to babysit some high-profile wannabe Steve Irwin. I'll be trading in my LBD for DEET for the next two weeks." I shrug.

"Why would you do that? You hate the outdoors?" Maggie asks.

"I just had this gut feeling in the meeting today. I can't explain it. I know this client is completely out of my comfort zone, but I really think I can do this. And if I pull it off, there's no way Sandra can deny me that promotion. Besides, it's Costa Rica." I take a long sip of my champagne. "At least I'll have great views from my room. I'm going to treat this time away as a break from reality, get some work done, and come back rejuvenated and ready to ask Sandra to make me a VP finally."

"Well, I'm so glad you could make it tonight. You may want to take it easy on the champagne, though. I'd hate for you to be hungover on your flight." Elliot wraps her arms around me, pulling me into a tight hug.

"I love you, girl, but you know I can handle my liquor. Besides, who knows when I'll be able to get my hands on a fabulous glass of champagne again? It may be Mai Tais and Sex on the Beach for me for the new few weeks." I pull away and offer my drink. "Cheers!"

"Cheers," they say in unison as Maggie gives Elliot a side-eye.

Over the rim of my drink, I see a tall, dark, and mysterious piece of man-candy lounging at the bar. His long brown hair is pulled up in a messy bun, and his biceps are practically crying to be freed from his suit jacket. He's not my usual type, too rugged, but my vagina seems to have her own ideas.

"Who's that?" I casually ask Elliot.

"Who's who?" She looks around.

"The bearded hottie talking to Benjamin at the bar." I nod toward the group of men.

"That's Jack. He's one of Benjamin's best friends... Why do you want to know?" She tilts her head in suspicion, and then she realizes. "No, Gwenneth, don't even think about it. Benjamin's friends are strictly off-limits until *after* the wedding. You know the last thing I need is for him to spit in your mouth or breathe on you with his morning breath and you ghost him in the middle of wedding planning." Elliot slaps her hand on the table. "Maggie, could you please keep an eye on her? I've got to make sure my mother stays away from the jungle juice that Jack so generously contributed."

After she walks away, I turn on Maggie. "I haven't had jungle juice since college. It would be so sad if I missed my only chance to taste it again." I wink.

"Gwenneth Peirson, now is not the time to get a wild hair!"

she hisses as I shimmy out of my seat with only one thing on my mind.

"I hope you know what you're doing..." She drains her beer and stands, rubbing her palms down the front of her dress. "Fine, I'm going to help Elliot keep her parents in line. You can think again if you think I'm not going to cash in this favor at a later date."

"I love you..." I coo.

"Yeah, I know you do." She takes off just as Elliot's dad makes his way to the dance floor.

I set my eyes on the handsome brute. Maybe I was a little too abrupt in swearing off men for good. Jack looks like fun, and boy, do I need to blow off some steam.

Jack's leaning against the bar, wearing a tailored navy suit, and talking to Benjamin. I glance around for Elliot and see she's dancing with her father, so I make my move. I give the girls a proper adjustment and calm my nervous breath before I approach.

I walk up behind him and tap him on the shoulder, "Excuse me, Jack? Elliot was telling me you brought something a little more exciting to drink tonight? I was wondering if you could pour me a glass?" I lean forward, giving him a prime view of my cleavage.

"Baby Spice, is that you?" He waggles his eyebrows. "Damn, you clean up nice." He cocks his head to the side as his eyes trail up my body. "I'd love to share some of my juice with you." He winks.

Confusion washes over me. There's something vaguely familiar about this man that sparks my memory. I tilt my head to the side. "Have we met?"

He laughs. "I guess you were pretty wasted that night you told me off. You don't remember the purple-nurple you gave me when you educated me about calling dibs on a woman in front of her?"

A faint memory flashes through my mind. I do remember something about that. Maggie and I were having drinks at Terry's when I caught sight of Benjamin. I marched over to tell him off in my drunken state, and that's when Jack called dibs on me in front of everyone.

I straighten my shoulders and lift my head, "Well, I'm happy to hear you learned your lesson. You're a smart boy, Jack." I wink. "Now, where's this jungle juice everyone's talking about?"

Jack's mouth momentarily drops, then he's grinning like the Cheshire Cat. "It's in an ice chest outside. Benjamin wouldn't let me bring it in, said it was an eyesore. Would you like to accompany me?" He tucks a strand of hair behind my ear, and a bolt of electricity shoots straight to my crotch. Yep, I was right. The sexual chemistry is strong with this one. I desperately need to quench my thirst. It's been a long time ... too long. My poor vagina needs a tune-up. She hasn't been serviced in about ...six months? No, that can't be right, can it? I think back to Sandra's twentieth-anniversary party and count back in my head... Yep, six whole months, I'm afraid my virginity may have grown back.

I lean into him so only he can hear me, more determined than ever. "You know, I think I would. I can't wait to taste your juice."

Jack blinks several times but doesn't miss a beat, "I see. I must warn you, once you've tasted my juice, it's going to be hard to forget it." He ushers me through a door on the other side of the bar. I glance over my shoulder and catch Maggie's eyes, giving her a little wave before I follow him.

"You know, that's not something I'm too worried about. You should probably watch out for yourself, though." I tease as I step through the doorway.

As soon as the party's behind us, I turn on Jack and pounce, wrapping my legs tight around his waist, the force of my attack sending him crashing into the wall. "I don't have a lot of time, and you look like a capable man." I let my fingers trail down his chiseled forearms. "I'm not usually this forward, but this is an emergency," I say between our frantic kisses. His scruffy beard scratches my face as my lips trail down his neck. Jesus, he smells delicious, like cedarwood and honey, and I think I could get off right here in this hallway from his scent alone. Just as the thought crosses my mind, he adjusts my pelvis over his rock-hard erection. Any thoughts of orgasming without penetration melt from my mind, and my mouth waters in anticipation. I've never been this worked up, much less by someone I've just met.

"Well, it looks like you've crawled up the right tree. Though I hate to break it to you, this won't be fast if that's what you want. It's not in my nature." Jack smirks and hurls me up higher, holding onto my ass with his massive palms before glancing around for somewhere a little more private than the middle of the hallway.

He carries me to the only other door in the hallway like I'm no bigger than a kitten and swings it open. "There's no bed, but it could be worse." He steps into the tiny janitor closet and closes the door behind us, leaving us in the pitch-black dark.

The music starts to pick up from the party across the hall. Good, at least I won't have to worry about keeping quiet. Not that I could help myself if I tried. The feel of Jack's corded muscles carrying me around like I weigh nothing and his smell alone have me writhing for relief.

I hike my dress up and kick my thong away into the pit of darkness that is the bottom of the closet, and I catch a faint whiff of bleach as my back bumps against a carton of chemicals. "Here, I brought a condom just in case." I reach my hand down my bra and pull the foil packet free.

"Are you always this prepared to get fucked in a janitor's closet, or is it just my lucky day?" He takes the condom from my hand with his teeth, and even though it's so dark I can't see his eyes, I feel them burning into me.

Jack reaches under my bare ass and pulls me up his body with little effort, wrapping my legs around his neck. "Oh my God, what are you doing?"

Somehow he manages to balance me with just his arms and the wall. "I told you I don't like to rush. Calm down, Baby Spice. This is my favorite part. Don't rush me while I enjoy my dessert." Then he slides his tongue gently over my soaking wet center, and I mew in response. My head falls back, but I'm careful not to lean too much. The last thing I want is to break this delicious contact by throwing off our balance.

Heat pools in my stomach, and my toes start to tingle as my impending orgasm works its way through every cell in my body. Jack's tongue licks slowly, finding sensitive places I never knew existed. My eyes roll back in my head, and I'm thankful he can't see the look on my face in this raw, carnal moment.

"Fuck, Gwen, you taste so good. I don't know if I want to stop. I think I could eat you all night." He pulls me tighter against his face, and I melt as my orgasm courses through my body. I lose all composure and ride his face to the finish line. He holds me tightly until my heart rate slows and I catch my breath. Then he places me down gently on my legs made of noodles. "Now turn around and grab the wall. You're going to want to hold on to something for this."

I hear the rip of the condom, and my breath hitches when I feel him at my base, bracing himself before pushing into me. "I have a feeling this pussy is going to ruin me," he whispers into my neck before I feel his long thick cock push inside me. My eyes roll back in my head, and it takes all my strength not to collapse into a puddle.

Jack's penis must be the mold for the perfect-sized dildo. I brace myself against the door and let him wreck me like a savage. His thrusts are deep and slow, keeping the perfect rhythm. When he hits a spot that makes me see a new color, tears well in my eyes from the pleasure. "Oh God, don't stop. Right there!" I moan.

He pulls my hair along the base of my neck and tightens his grip as he licks his way down my neck. "So fucking tight." He gives my hair a final tug before gripping my hips and pushing my back forward ever so slightly, giving him a better angle. My legs begin to shake as I feel a second orgasm rising in me. "You like that, baby? Cum for me, gorgeous. Cum for me all over my cock."

His words are my undoing, and a second orgasm rips through me as he steadily pounds into me. I don't even try to keep quiet. He grips my waist tighter, and his thrusts begin to slow. "Oh God, yes, Jack. Yes. Yes. Yes," I moan as his hands pull my head to the side, bringing my lips to his. I taste myself on his tongue, and it's strangely alluring.

He turns me in his arms, and my legs are like Jell-O. "You are a goddess. Let me take you on a proper date as soon as I get back from my work trip in two weeks." He plants a kiss on my forehead, and my body falls into his strong embrace as he steadies me. I don't know how I'm going to walk out of this closet and act like I didn't just have the best sex of my life.

"With a performance like that, how could I resist?" I pass him my phone, so he can plug in his number. I know Elliot's going to be pissed when she finds out, but we're all mature adults. There's no reason I shouldn't be able to have a repeat performance. After all, this orgasm is going down in my vagina's history books. I'll dedicate a whole scrapbook page to Jack and our special time in the janitor closet together.

Hell, I'll even make a playlist.

"I'm actually leaving for a two-week work trip in the morning, so I guess we can catch up when we get back?"

He hands me my phone and helps me straighten my dress. After several minutes of searching, my panties are nowhere to be found. There's zero chance I'll walk out of here not looking freshly fucked, but I'm in such a good mood that I don't even care. I'm feeling lighter than I have in months, and there's a spring in my step that I haven't felt since college.

"Why don't we grab some of that jungle juice before I make my way back to the couple of the hour?"

"I'll get you some, but I'd rather keep your taste in my mouth for a little while longer," he whispers as he ushers me out of the closet. "Right this way."

CHAPTER FOUR

Gwen

My head is pounding as I close my eyes, trying to pretend I'm anywhere but sitting in a cramped airplane. What was in that jungle juice? I wince as the cabin lights flash brightly, indicating our arrival, and everyone stands up to retrieve their luggage.

So much for the meditation technique. I'll be sure to inform Maggie that her woo-woo ways stand no chance against my hyper-vigilant work brain. I suppose I can rest when I'm dead.

In just a few hours, I'll be sitting on a beach in Costa Rica if I can just get through this next connection, though I'm cutting it extremely close. I sigh and check my watch. If I get off right this second, I could make it ... if I sprint.

I sigh. I hate seeing people run through the airport. It's so obnoxious, but this is the only flight out today, and if I miss it, I'll be stuck in the Miami airport overnight.

I swipe to open the weather app to triple check the forecast. Just like the last three times I checked, it shows a huge tropical storm coming in overnight.

The last thing I want to do is fly over the ocean in a hurricane. Nope, I'll take my chances sprinting through the terminal like an idiot before I put myself through that torture.

It's not that I'm afraid of flying. It's not the flying part at all, really., I have an irrational fear of deep water, and I figure water doesn't really get much deeper than the ocean.

A shiver works its way up my spine, and I shudder at the thought.

As soon we're cleared to exit, I grab my carry-on and force my way to the front of the plane. I have a clear path, and just as I pick up my pace and see the exit sign, an elderly gentleman stands up and steps into the aisle ahead of me.

I all but crash into him as I wait for him to grab his luggage from the overhead compartment.

"Jill, I don't see my bag," he tells the little old lady sitting in the seat next to his.

"Well, Bruce, I don't know what to tell you. It's the black bag. You put it up there yourself," she says, looking up at him into the aisle.

"Well, shit, Jill, there's a sea of black bags up here. How the hell am I supposed to know which one's mine?" he barks as he ever so slowly ruffles through the luggage.

If I were a good person, I'd offer to help the old man, but I think it's clear that level of patience isn't exactly my virtue, so I tap him on the shoulder, "Excuse me, sir, I'm in a hurry, and you're blocking the way to the exit. Could I just get by you? Real quick?"

"Huh?" he yells, then turns to continue looking for the bag. "Jill, did you say it was the red one?"

"Christ, Bruce, it's the black bag. You packed it yourself. Where are your glasses?" she screams. He ignores her, still looking for the bag.

My breathing starts to hitch, and a thin sheen of sweat forms on the back of my neck. Glancing down at my watch, I see it's ten minutes until my next departure. "Sir, I really need to get by you, so I don't miss my next flight." I realize the only way I'm getting off this plane is if I push Bruce out of the way and risk breaking his hip—which is actually quite tempting at the moment—or help him find the damn bag.

I open the compartment on the other side of the cabin and stand on my tiptoes. I see a black carry-on rolling bag with a tag that reads *Bruce & Jill Tanner*. I pull the bag down and pass it to him. "Here you go, Bruce. Now I need you to pick up the pace before you make me late."

He takes the bag reluctantly and turns to his wife. "Well, no wonder I couldn't find it. That angry lady behind me had it. Damn luggage pirates! Jill, I told you someone would try to steal from us. These airplanes aren't safe. They'll let anyone on a flight."

I roll my eyes and resist shoving him out of the way, my threadbare patience fueled solely by last night's riveting encounter, as I tap my foot incessantly and wait in the now full line for my turn to get off the plane. I check my watch and see it's five minutes past my next departure.

Great, the old bastard made me miss my flight. I supposed there's no rush now. I throw up my hands in defeat. I'll be hanging out in the airport all night long. At least I've got a hell of a highlight reel to pass the time.

An hour later, I've finally gotten my new flight sorted out. I drag my suitcase behind me as I make my way to the gate where I'll be spending the night until my next flight at 6 a.m., roughly twelve hours from now. Normally I'd get a hotel room, but all the rooms close enough are booked for the night, and I don't want to Uber across Miami for four hours of sleep. I pull out my phone and text Maggie, letting her know I'm safe.

Ugh! Some old fart caused me to miss my connection to Costa Rica so I'm roughing it tonight in the Miami airport. My head is killing me!

Remind me to never drink questionable alcoholic juice from an ice chest ever again!

MAGGIE

I hate to say I told ya so… but…

Too soon, Mags, too soon.

MAGGIE

Well, I hope your shenanigans last night were worth it. I'll have you know, I had to run interference with Elliot… I had to lie to her, Gwen. You know I hate lying!

What did you say, you know, just so we're on the same page?

MAGGIE

I told her you had a female emergency and spilled your menstrual cup blood down your leg which required the hour-long cleanup and explained your disheveled appearance when you returned.

Eww, Mags! Could you think of anything more disgusting?

Did she believe it?

MAGGIE

Yup. She, Benjamin, Sam, and her parents were all very concerned. Then I had to explain to Mr. James what a menstrual cup was. It was an enlightening experience for all of us.

I hate you.

MAGGIE

I put my phone in my pocket and dig for my charging cable in my bag. Then I plug my phone into a nearby wall socket and pull my hoodie over my eyes. I may as well get some rest, then maybe once my head stops pounding, I'll actually be able to get some work done.

Willy Wonka will just have to wait.

———

A persistent poking stirs me from my slumber, and I wake with my neck in agony, crooked to one side. I blink away the sleep from my eyes and try to focus my blurred vision. A tall, muscular figure hovers over me. "Gwen? Is that you?" I hear a familiar masculine voice, and it takes me a moment to gather my thoughts.

"Jack? What are you doing here?" I jump in my seat and shift my head from side to side to work out the kinks.

"I could ask you the same thing. I'm flying out at six, headed to Costa Rica to shoot some videos for my Youtube channel." He sheds his backpack and takes a seat next to me.

"Oh, no, you don't. I just woke up, and my breath probably smells like a dragon fart." I shield my face, and then his words sink in... "Did you say you're shooting a Youtube video in Costa Rica?"

"Yeah, I guess we didn't really have a lot of time to get acquainted the other night. I'm a YouTuber Adventure Tour-guide. You may have heard of me by the name Wombat Willy. I'm headed on my first ever solo flight. Well, my manager just called me to let me know I'm supposed to be meeting some PR person from Éclat. Apparently, she missed her connection, and I'm all that'll depart in time." He grins, "Are you impressed?

I nod in disbelief. He continues, taking my stunned silence as a cue to keep talking.

"I mean, usually, I don't like to brag that I'm multitalented, but I think we both enjoyed ourselves last night." He waggles his eyebrows. "I'm sorry I haven't texted. My manager's been riding my ass, making me clean up my image for my stuck-up public relations agent. Apparently, she's a real bitch. Landon says she's known for having a giant stick up her ass. I tried everything I could to get out of this, but at the end of the day, if the sponsors aren't happy, I make a helluva lot less money," He shrugs. "How about you? Where'd you say you were headed?"

Oh my God. This has to be a joke. Please let this be a horrible joke. I look over my shoulder, praying to see Maggie doubled over in laughter, but there are only a few locals and a family of five.

"Fuck." My mouth falls open, and I let my head fall back onto the seat. *Of all the penises in all of Chicago, you let the only one who you are literally forbidden by contract to touch give you a vaginal tune-up.* "Looks like I'm your PR bitch..." I say through gritted teeth. "Did I hear you correctly? You said that *you* were piloting the plane?"

Jack's lips curl in a devilish grin. "Oh, Baby Spice, are you doubting my skills? I don't remember you complaining last night." He winks and rubs his hands together. "This is awesome! I mean, I've always known I was lucky, but getting to

33

show off my flying skills firsthand and my epic nature skills... It's like that movie *Serendipity* or some shit."

I drag my hands down my face, peering between the gaps in my fingers. This can't be happening to me right now. "It's Gwen to you, and this is nothing like *Serendipity*. This is a nightmare." I stand up and pace back and forth, "I can't get on a plane with you! Even if I thought you were a competent pilot and I wasn't your guinea pig, I can't do this! It's against the company's covenant. It's against my own personal covenant!"

I throw my hands above my head as I attempt to calm my frantic breathing. "That was the best dick I've had in... in..." I snap my gaze and meet his dark green mischievous eyes.

"Please continue. You know, my ego really enjoys being stroked every now and again." He stands up to approach me, but I push him away.

"No, Jack... or Willy... whatever your name is! How could you do this to me? Why would you have an internet persona named Willy when your name is Jack?"

"Well, my favorite animal is a wombat... and I liked the idea of using alliteration in my name, so Wombat Willy just kind of worked? What does my name have to do with anything?" His puzzled expression is so sexy, the way his brows are pulled up like he's trying to solve a problem.

"Your name could've at least given me a semblance of an idea of who I was actually fucking in the janitor's closet!" I scream. The father of the family of five shoots daggers at me and pulls his small children toward him. I try to smile through clenched teeth as I wave an apology. I suppose it's not common decency to shout obscenities at five in the morning in an air terminal, but I'm beside myself with this news.

I plop down and throw my head between my knees as I work through my panic.

Ok, Gwen, maybe you accidentally slept with your client last night. Do the rules really count when it's not done on purpose? Surely not. Besides, this doesn't mean this whole promotion is doomed. You can do this. You're just two professionals on a work trip together, and the past is in the past.

I shake my fist at the sky because although Jack seems to think this is some kind of fucking Hallmark-movie-kismet-shit, this is actually my worst nightmare come true.

"I'm confused. What's the problem exactly? The way I see it is, we've already established we've got an amazing sexual connection, and now we're being paid to go off to one of the most exciting and romantic places on the earth together. We'll explore the great outdoors, hump it out, and get paid while we do it? This is the best news I've heard since our last World Cup win." He places his large hand on my shoulder to comfort me, sending a rush of chills down my arm.

"Nope. That's not going to happen!" I shrug him off and cross my fingers in an X in front of my face. "I'm sorry, Jack, but even the best sex of my life will always come second to my career. This is a non-negotiable for me." I extend my hand for a shake. "From here on out, this will be strictly a platonic working relationship. Please forget how my vagina smells, tastes, and feels because, from now on, it's off-limits." I set my shoulders and pull my bag toward me as they announce our plane is ready to board.

"Well, now that you put it like that... I guess I do like a bit of a challenge." Jack rubs his beard, reminding me of just how amazing that beard felt pressed between my thighs.

"Nope, not a challenge. Just a hard limit. This cannot happen. You know, on second thought, maybe I should just call Sandra and ask her to send someone else—"

"No! Don't do that. I promise I'll be on my best behavior. I really need this sponsorship. Without your help, I'll have to hang up my camera gear for good. I know you're scared, but once my manager found out they were sending you, the guy finally unclenched his jaw for the first time in a week. He said he's heard nothing but good things about you, and you may just be my only shot at spinning this shit show."

He extends his hand in a truce, "I solemnly swear to keep my hands to myself until you tell me otherwise."

I stare at his hand, pondering all my options. It appears that Jack Manning knows exactly what to say to get his way, punching me right where it hurts, my ego. I take his hand reluctantly and give it a firm shake. "Ok. You've got yourself a deal, but no funny business. I'm a woman of my word, and nothing gets in my way when it comes to my career. I've given up a hell of a lot more, and I don't intend on screwing things up just because some wild man came along and made me forget who I was for one night." I give his hand one final squeeze, using every bit of strength I can muster.

"Ah, shit, ok, She-Hulk. That's my flying hand." He shakes his hand out, and I stifle a laugh. "I'll see you in a few." When he turns to leave, he glances back over his shoulder, "Oh, Gwenny, I don't think I'm the one you'll have to worry about. We'll see if you can keep your hands off *me* after seeing these babies in action." He holds up his hands and wiggles his fingers, and I swear my panties spontaneously combust at the motion.

I collapse into my chair and throw my arm over my eyes. How will I spend two whole weeks in paradise with Tarzan and not let him ravage me like his own personal Jane?

Shit, this is going to be harder than I thought.

Jack's plane—if we're really going to call it that—is a measly four-seater that looks like an old Chevy someone repaired in a garage with their grandfather. It's mostly white, with a few rust spots that he's cleverly tried to hide with hand-painted images of busty women. Really, the paintings look more like something you'd find in a cave illustrated by the first man... He made sure to get the parts anatomically correct anyway, and it appears Jack Manning is a boob guy if I had to make a wild guess based on the name of the plane—Betty White, The Tits of the Sky. I roll my eyes at the pun. Let's just hope his flying is better than his sense of humor.

Out of the corner of my eye, I see him attempt to polish a rust spot. After a moment, he spits on the hem of his shirt and throws a little more elbow grease into it. "That'a girl, I can't have you dingy-looking. We've got company today."

A large raindrop lands on my forehead, rolling down my face, and I look up at the dark gray sky. "Cute, you talk to your plane." Another raindrop falls, and slowly, they turn into a constant stream. "Uh, Jack, do you think we should wait until the weather clears up?" I point to the rust spot he failed to remove with his spit-shine attempt, "Are you sure it, er... She," I clarify, "can hold up in this storm?"

"I don't call her Betty White for nothin'. She's survived a hell of a lot more than this. Trust me. Besides, it's just a little shower. Once we get above the cloud level, it'll be smooth-sailing." He winks. "Hey, if you want, I could even let you take the reins for a few hours once we're up there." He yawns, stretching his arms above his head. "You know, I was pretty keyed up last night, didn't get a lot of sleep."

I swallow a gulp, and a lump forms in my throat. I like to think of myself as fearless, I'm a go-getter in the office and even in the bedroom, but I'd be lying if I said I wasn't scared shitless right now.

My hands begin to tremble, so I clench my fists to mask the movement and purse my lips tightly. "Jack, if you think you're going to try some of that Johnny Knoxville shit while you have me thousands of miles in the air during a tropical storm, you don't know who you're messing with." I fling the creaky door open and climb into the passenger seat, "Let's just get this over with. The sooner we get to Costa Rica, the sooner I can get drunk on the beach. We'll start working on repairing your image first thing tomorrow morning."

Jack throws his head back and laughs, running around the other side of the plane to climb in. His long legs make it look easy. "Baby Spice—I mean, Gwen." He corrects himself. "I'm sensing some nervous energy." He gestures to me as I fight to put the seat belt on with my shaking hands. "Here." He takes the belt from me and clips it with ease. When his hand brushes against mine, it sends a tingle up my spine. Then he pulls the strap tight, pinning me comfortably into my seat, and I sigh in relief. My body feels like I'm engaging in some sort of game of chicken, but with sexual tension, and all he did was buckle my seatbelt.

This will be a long two weeks.

Jack grabs his headset and places a spare on my head before I can stop him. "You look sexy as hell in that. It's going to take every ounce of strength I have to keep my eyes off you through this whole flight."

My cheeks heat in arousal before I remind myself that Jack is a client. I shake the feeling away and focus on the raindrops beating down harder and harder. My stomach turns, and I reach for my emergency anxiety meds. I'm usually able to work out my frustration with sex or spin class, so I haven't ever had to take them.

I throw my head back and swallow a pill. There, in just a few minutes, I'll be cool, calm, and collected. Maybe I'll even start to build his profile on the way.

Jack fiddles with knobs and buttons, checking safety

features, and I'm thankful he at least *seems* to be halfway competent.

"You all set, sweet cheeks?"

We begin to move forward, and I close my eyes, digging my fingernails into the side of my legs and waiting for the pill to kick in.

Jack seems to notice my nerves. "Oh, shit, are you afraid of flying? Don't worry. I've got you. Betty White and I have flown this trip five times together already. This is the first time on my own, but I've got this. Just trust me, ok?"

I nod because it's the only thing I can force myself to do. Trusting others isn't exactly my greatest strength. The lump in my throat is so big that I'm afraid nothing will come out but a croak if I try to speak.

I pull out my phone and send a quick text to Maggie, letting her know the turn of events and telling her to keep tabs on my location.

"Do you mind turning your phone off for the flight?"

I startle at Jack's voice and shove my phone into my pocket. "Sure. No problem."

The plane lifts off the runway, and my stomach flutters. Here we go. I'm flying into the eye of the storm in a plane named Betty White. What could possibly go wrong?

CHAPTER FIVE

Gwen

Rain pelts against the windshield in every direction, and it's a wonder Jack can see where he's going. I've flown through rain before on a commercial flight, but nothing could've prepared me for this monsoon of a rainstorm in a tiny puddle-jumper.

Every gust of wind jolts the plane, and I feel like I'm in a scene straight out of *Final Destination*. My racing pulse makes my Apple watch think I'm doing a cardio workout.

I swipe the workout prompt away and shove my sweaty hands underneath my legs. It's been at least fifteen minutes since I took my anxiety medication, and I still don't feel anything.

Biting my lip, I grab the bottle for further examination.

"Take one pill as needed for anxiety every 4 hours."

I contemplate for a moment and decide another one probably won't hurt. I mean, I probably need a higher dose because of the intensity of the situation, right?

I throw back the pill and swallow, shoving the bottle back in my purse.

"What are you taking now?" Jack's question startles me, and I jump. "Whoa, someone's on edge."

"It's just anxiety medication to take the edge off. No big deal." I assure him.

"Do you want to talk about it or something? Are you freaking out on me over there? This storm is nothing. Trust me. Planes aren't like cars. I've done this—"

"At least five times," I answer for him and force a smile. "While I appreciate your attention to detail, I'd much rather you focus it on flying than keeping tabs on me." I sit up a little straighter in my seat, "My doctor prescribed me those just in case of an emergency, and since I'm in a tin can thousands of feet above land with a five-time experienced pilot, I think I'd call this an emergency."

Jack sucks in a hiss. "Jeez, someone's touchy today. Relax, baby. This is nothing but a regular day on the job."

"Call me crazy, Jack, but I'm having a little trouble trusting you right now." I sink into the cracked leather seat, which pinches my legs every time I change positions. After a few more patches of turbulence, I pull my feet up and loop my arms around my legs, squeezing myself as tightly as I can manage.

If I can just breathe through this, the meds will kick in, and I'll be in a much better place to relax.

I sneak a glance at Jack, who's wearing aviator sunglasses despite the dark gray sky and rain.

"Can you even see where you're going with those glasses?" I try to hold back my words, I really do, but Jack looks too comfortable while I'm on the verge of a panic attack. I know I should find comfort in his calm demeanor—that's what a sane person would do—but instead, I'd like him to feel a little uneasy, too. Maybe then I could trust him.

"I don't really need to *see* where I'm going." He points to some circular meters on the dashboard. "I can tell where I am from these guys."

I perk up a little. Maybe he does know what he's doing? Maybe I was too quick to brush him off as a decent pilot because he doesn't seem to take anything seriously. "Oh, well, I'm glad to know the weather shouldn't affect our direction, then." I breathe a sigh of relief.

"Nope, I'm telling you, Gwen, I've got everything under control. I take pride in flying." He beats his fist against his chest, and I relax a little, breathing out of my nose really fast. It's not a laugh, but it's in the ballpark of amusement. The last thing I want to do is stroke his male ego, but I'm happy with this new bit of information.

I just need to see the bright side, right? That's what Maggie would tell me. I can almost hear her voice saying, "Gwen, you're such a pessimist. Don't you know you'll find whatever you're looking for?"

I nod as if answering the question and bite my lip, thinking of something to talk about to distract myself. Maybe we can start working on Jack's profile and get his backstory straight, so once we land in Costa Rica, I'm one step closer to finishing the job.

"So, you have some high-tech GPS telling you where to go or what?" It's the first question that comes to mind. Perhaps because my life dangles in his hands?

"Nope. Not this guy. I'm a bit of a flying purist." He grins and gestures to his setup again. "It's much harder to do it this way, but I like the old-fashioned way." He pulls his glasses down to his nose, peering over at me, and winks. "This is how my grandfather did it, and if it was good enough for him, then it's good enough for me."

I don't miss the exaggerated flex of his bicep, and a lump forms in my throat at his confession, the confidence I felt in him five seconds ago rapidly fleeting. I shake my head again to relieve the fear creeping back up.

"Your grandfather was a pilot?" I pause, considering this. "Can you tell me a little about him? Is that what inspired you to become a pilot?" I quickly realize I'll never be able to remember his answers, and I glance around for my suitcase. I know I've got a notebook somewhere in one of my bags, but Jack starts talking before I find anything.

"Yep, Pop-Pop was a military pilot in World War II. After the war, he bought a small charter plane, which he turned into a business. He'd fly local businessmen on day trips in their small, rural town. He loved being in the air." He smiles, but it's forced, and I don't miss the touch of sadness behind his eyes.

Not wanting to interrupt him, I sneak my phone from my back pocket and turn on the voice recorder. Sure, it may be crossing a line recording him without his permission, but I'm only interested in repairing his image, and my head's starting to spin from the meds. I don't want to risk forgetting anything.

A warm tingle flutters through my belly, and I melt deeper into my seat. Suddenly, the scratchy, torn seat feels so interesting. I rub my hands back and forth over the broken leather, and a giggle bubbles up from my belly. I cover my mouth in surprise and cut my eyes to Jack to see if he heard it, too.

"What are you doing over there?" His eyes scan me, and he tilts his head as if he's examining me.

"Nothing!" I blurt, suddenly feeling embarrassed for giggling. "Tell me the story of how you became Wombat Willy. Did you always dream of being a YouTuber?" I can't even get the words all the way out before I burst into another fit of giggles.

Jack tightens his grip on the steering wheel, or whatever you call it in a plane, as we hit another patch of turbulence. This time, my muscles feel much looser, and the bump sends me flying in the air for a moment before my seatbelt catches me and snaps me back down in my seat.

My eyes go wide, and I don't know what's come over me, but the adrenaline rush feels exhilarating. "Wee! I caught air that time!" I squeal.

He eyes me again, tightening his grip. If I didn't know better, I'd think Jack was starting to get a little nervous. The thought of Jack being scared, too, shakes up a fresh wave of worry, and I grab his knee, squeezing as a laugh escapes me, suddenly aware that we're connected on a whole new level. "You're scared, too, aren't you?" I let out an evil cackle, throwing my head back because I feel the laugh deep in my bones, and it feels so good to let it out. "I knew it."

"Exactly how much of that medicine did you take?"

"Oh, don't worry about me. Trust me. This is an improvement." I realize I haven't removed my hand from his knee, and when I look down at the connection, I can't not look at the bulge in his pants. My mouth waters at the memory of last night, and I glide my hand farther up his thigh.

"Gwen... what... what are you doing?" His voice comes out a few octaves higher than usual, and my chest swells with pride. I love that I make him nervous.

"Nothing. Your thighs are just so muscular. Can't a girl cop a feel when she's given a chance?" We hit another burst of turbulence, and I swear it feels like we're driving a Jeep through a forest, running over holes and tree limbs.

A clap of thunder steals my attention, and when I pull my gaze away from Jack's penis bulge, a bright bolt of lightning flashes before my eyes. "Jack, are we flying over the Bermuda Triangle right now?" I don't wait for him to answer. Instead, I flop back into my seat and grab my phone. "I've got to record this! What if I see a giant squid or something?"

"Gwen, what are you doing?" Jack snaps. "Please tell me your phone is on airplane mode."

"Of course, it isn't silly! How would I have service in case of an emergency?" I giggle at his joke. "Besides, I'm live-streaming this on my Instagram page. Say hi." I point my phone at him and turn the camera back to me. "In case you're just tuning in, we're in a tropical storm flying over the Bermuda Triangle. I'm going to zoom in." I push the phone to the foggy cold glass of the window. "Aw, it's blurry. That's sad."

"Gwen, I need you to give me the phone." Jack holds out his hand.

I clench my precious device to my chest in protection. "Jack," I steady my voice, "I cannot do that. This belongs to me. It's my property. Maybe you should work harder if you'd like to own nice things."

"For fuck's sake, Gwen, turn off the phone!" His voice comes out panicked, and a yucky feeling turns in my belly.

I flinch at his command and puff my chest out. "No means no." I cross my arms in defiance. "If you want this phone, you'll have to come through me." He reaches for it again, and I jerk away. The phone bounces off my seat, landing somewhere near my feet. I hold up my fists in a boxer's stance.

"What the actual fuck did you take?" He grips his long mane, pulling his neat ponytail down in a mess of waves.

"You kind of look like Aquaman. Has anyone ever told you that?"

CHAPTER SIX

JACK

I'm not going to lie; I'm really freaking out here. This thunderstorm is like nothing I've ever flown in. Even though I checked the weather, these winds are gnarly, and I don't know if I've ever seen so much lightning. I can hardly see where I'm going, purely relying on my Heading Indicator at this point. Now that I know Gwen's phone has been on, I can't help the panic rising in my chest. I glance at my fuel meter and hope the phone's magnet hasn't fucked us too badly.

I look at Gwen, who's now glued to the window like a child rubbing their face on every surface of a school bus. She's dragging her cheek up and down the glass, and is she humming? I don't know what she's done with her headset. She must've stripped it off when I wasn't looking.

"The cold feels so good on my face. It's sensational. Jack, have you tried rubbing your face on the glass? It's like a giant ice roller. I bet my face will look as chiseled and de-puffed as a supermodel when I'm done."

"Uh, no. No, I haven't tried that." I grit my teeth as I try to concentrate on keeping the plane steady, despite all of mother nature's attempts to take us down.

"You may not think you need to depuff, but I'm here to tell you that age creeps up on you if you don't stay on top of these things." She pulls away from the window, sitting a little straighter as if she's just thought of something. "Hey, Jack, where's the bathroom? I need to pee!" Then unbuckles her seatbelt before diving into the backseat.

"What are you doing?" I wipe my sweaty palms on my shorts as I try to keep calm. "I don't have a bathroom. This is a four-seater plane! I told you to go before we took off."

Something small and crinkly smacks me in the face, and I'm momentarily stunned when I look down and see a tampon in my lap. "What the—"

"Damn me for choosing tampons over pads. I knew I should've listened to Maggie and packed an assortment of menstrual products just in case." She's ruffling around in the luggage, and now I'm afraid she's looking for something to pee in.

"Do not take a piss in my plane!" I all but scream over the loud rush of wind and rain coming at us from both sides. I know I shouldn't be worried about that at a time like this, but I just got the upholstery cleaned last week.

"So, you don't have like a funnel or a diaper or anything?" She calls from the backseat, and I force myself to pause, taking a deep breath before I speak.

"Can you please come back up front and put on your seatbelt?" The words come out a little harsher than I hoped but polite enough considering the circumstances.

A bolt of lightning flashes, followed by a loud bang as the cabin lights flicker off for a moment. Although it's not uncommon for planes to be struck by lightning, I've never had it happen to me. I check all my instruments, and when I see everything seems to be working properly, I let myself relax. *It's just a storm. There's no need to panic.*

"Hi, ATC. This is Cessna N44429 requesting the status of this storm and that you have our location on the radar," I say in my headset.

No reply.

That's when I notice my compass pointing east when I know we should be flying south. I make a slight adjustment to test it, and my suspicions are confirmed. "Fuck," I hiss. "Gwen, get your ass up here and put on your seatbelt!"

I check the fuel level and see we've got about an hour of fuel left, which won't be enough if we've veered too far off course.

"Ohh, are you dirty talking now, daddy? You know I only like being told what to do when I'm on my back."

I shake my head, trying to rid my mind of the image my penis is sending to my brain. *Do not get a boner right now, Manning. This is neither the time nor place for that kind of thinking.*

My mouth goes dry as lust and fear mix in my cloudy brain. *Just stay calm and go through the motions, ignore her and focus on the task at hand,* I plead with myself.

"Just get your ass up here and listen while I try to figure this out." I bark, and to my surprise, she listens, doing a front roll over the seat and kicking me in the head in the process.

"Did you see the way I stuck the landing?" She giggles, clearly impressed with herself. Then in one swift motion, she leans over, grabbing my crotch. "I've been dreaming of this dick all night long. What do you say to a little airhead?" She throws her head back in laughter at her pun, and my balls actually shrivel in on themselves in fear. *Well, that's a first...*

I don't have time to argue, so I just nod my head. "Yeah, you really did great." I decide to play into the daddy-dom thing because it seems to be working. "You're such a good girl," I say as I grab the seatbelt and yank it across her, buckling and pulling it taut. "Now sit still, will you? I've got to figure out where we are."

She gasps, slapping her hand over her mouth. "You don't know where we are?" Her eyes are wide as saucers. "I've got to tell Maggie!"

Before I can say another word, she's on the floorboard, ruffling around in search of the contraband. "Hello! Maggie! Can you hear me? It's Gwen."

"For fuck's sake, that is the exact opposite of what I wanted you to do," I snap. "Hang up the phone right this instant!"

She covers the bottom of the phone. "Jack, you're being really annoying right now, and it feels selfish. I'll let you borrow my phone when I'm done–"

"Give me the phone this minute." I extend my hand, and she pretends to place it down but pulls it back at the last second. "Gwen, stop playing games and listen!"

"Gwen, stop playing games and listen," she mimics in a whiney voice.

That's it. I know if I want us to have any chance of actually making it to Costa Rica with enough fuel, I've got to take matters into my own hands. I wait until she's distracted and looking out the window, then lunge for it. "Give me the phone!"

"Make me!" she screams back.

I'm not expecting her to have the grip strength of five grown men, and before I can get out another word, she wraps her legs around me in a chokehold. Normally, I wouldn't mind having my face smashed forcefully between a woman's legs, but right now, thirty thousand feet in the air isn't the best time for this.

In our battle of wills, Gwen's foot kicks the yoke, sending the plane in a three-sixty rotation on its side. The force is enough to distract her, and I manage to grab the phone, sitting up in a rush. I follow the turn indicator and get us back to level after almost shitting myself. I breathe out a heavy sigh of relief as I will my heart rate back down to normal. "Are you ok?" I glance at the tiny pixie woman who must've switched bodies with Goldberg at some point.

"You bastard, you made me break a nail." Gwen pushes her middle finger against my nose. "Do you see this?"

The sound of the low fuel alarm blares while red and yellow lights blink on my dash. I swipe her hand away. "Can you please be normal for one fucking minute!" I pull my hair as I try to think of what to do. The plane's gone offline, and I don't have any connection to ATC for help, nor do I have the slightest idea of where we may be.

Squinting my eyes, I bring the plane below the cloud bank as I try to search for somewhere to land, but all I see is the ocean surrounding us on every side. Without fuel, it's a ticking time bomb. We either land the plane safely, or we fall to our deaths. No pressure at all.

"Look over there! Is that Costa Rica?" Gwen asks. Apparently, she's moved on from the wrestling match rather quickly and is back to her giant squid search from her window.

I squint my eyes and turn the plane so I can get a better view of what she sees, and through the dark gray clouds, I see the faintest outline of what looks like an island.

Hope swells in my chest, and I glance at the fuel meter, indicating we have about thirty minutes of fuel left. "Hold on tight. This is going to be a bumpy ride."

CHAPTER SEVEN

Gwen

The bright summer sun burns my retinas, and I feel like I've just been swallowed whole by a whale and vomited back up. Everything hurts as I sit up slowly and blink sand from my eyes, my body screaming in protest. My vision is blurred, and I do my best to wipe my eyes clean, but I only manage to rub more sand into them.

What the hell happened?

There's no use in trying to open my eyes, so I do my best crawling around in what feels like the Sahara desert. I crawl as far as I can in the magma-hot sand until I finally bump into a tree. It's a little cooler now, at least.

Crashing waves lull my racing heart and trigger a broken memory. A flashback of Jack's concerned face, the plane spinning, I hit my head... Did we crash? I vaguely remember the feeling of ice-cold water rushing up my body, and I clasp my hand over my mouth.

I reach up and feel a large lump on my head, which aches

like I've been run over by a truck, and my face stings from what I assume is a sand burn. Carefully, I blink my sand-encrusted eyes, but it's no use.

Did I actually survive a plane crash?

There's so much to process. I try to jog my memory, but it's only coming back in bits and pieces, like snapshots of a camera out of order. The images are all mixed up and–

"Look who finally decided to wake up." I hear Jack's voice in the distance, and my racing heart hiccups in relief.

I'm not alone. I close my eyes and take a deep breath. There, that's one question answered.

I sit up a little too hastily, sending a rush of blood to my aching head. "Jack?"

"Yep, that's me," he answers. "I hope you weren't expecting someone else."

I rub my eyes again, this time using the hem of my shirt, and manage to clean them enough that I can squint one eye open.

That's when I see a shirtless Jack with a t-shirt tied around his head, squatting down and sifting through a piece of luggage. With his sun-kissed golden skin and chiseled abs, he looks like a cover model for a survival magazine.

"Where..." My throat is so swollen my words come out more like a croak. I swallow and try again. "Where are we?"

"We're here," Jack answers before going back to digging through the suitcase.

I look around as if that's supposed to mean something before asking, "And where exactly is *here*?"

He scratches his beard and doesn't look up. "I'm still working on that part." I wait for him to elaborate, but he doesn't. He just keeps digging through the suitcase.

I narrow my eyes at the bag in question when the familiar bright red zipper catches my attention. Eyes wide in panic, I lunge for the bag, throwing my body on top of it. "What do you think you're doing digging through my stuff?" I'm breathless now, having leaped several feet to intervene, and my stomach aches from the impact.

"You can't just go rifling through a woman's suitcase!" I scold.

Jack rolls his eyes, "You really packed a lot of lingerie for this work trip." He gestures to a lacey pile of thongs and bralettes carefully laid out as if he's investigating a crime scene.

I roll off the bag onto the piping hot sand and snatch at the loose piles of negligées, shoving as much as I can against my chest. It really is a lot of underwear.

"Were you planning to seduce me? Or do you just shit your pants a lot?" he teases, and I can feel my blood boiling underneath my skin. Not that the scalding sun is doing me any favors.

"No, I don't shit my pants, you barbarian." I try to snatch the lone red lace thong, dropping several bralettes in the process. I'm so out of breath and confused about why my entire underwear collection is under scrutiny.

"How's your head?" he asks, moving on to the rest of my belongings.

I dive toward him, my face cushioned by lace and silk negligée, which is welcome padding compared to the harsh, scratchy sand, but it's no use. There, in the light of the midday sun, Jack holds up not one, not two, but three large vibrating dildos for God and everyone to see. "Well, well, well, will you look at that—"

"Will. You. Give. Me. That." I make a grab for the vibrators, but Jack's too quick. He holds them above his head, so they're out of my reach.

"Relax, sunshine. I'm not judging. Hell, I've seen the temptress side of you, and I'd expect nothing less," he teases.

"Do you mind telling me what the hell is going on here!" I

huff, blowing my short blonde hair out of my eyes. "Why are you going through my stuff?"

"It's Survival 101. I've got to see what we're working with, what we can use to make a fire. You know, gather all our resources."

"Resources?" I blink, trying to process it all. "Survival?" I have so many questions, but I'm hung up on those two words. I look around in every direction, searching for any sign of civilization, but empty beaches and trees are all I see.

As if Jack can see my wheels spinning—although maybe not all in the same direction—he offers me the answer to my question. "If you haven't gathered, we're not in Costa Rica." Turning his attention back to his task, he carefully lines the vibrators up in a neat line. Laying my makeup, curling iron, and toiletries beside them.

"Wh-what do you mean we're not in Costa Rica?" I stutter. "If we're not in Costa Rica," I gesture to the beach around me, "where are we?"

"Once again, I don't know. If I did, I would've told you the first time." He shakes his head in annoyance as he continues his task. "You can thank your cell phone usage on the flight for our current situation... You know, if you need someone to blame."

I suck in a gasp as red hot anger rushes to my face. "Excuse me? Did you just insinuate that somehow all of this is *my* doing?" I bark.

"No, princess, I didn't insinuate anything." He pins me with a stare. "This is one thousand percent your fault."

Finding words isn't usually a problem for me, but right now, I'm struggling. "How?" I scream. "How is any of this my fault? You're the one who crashed the damn plane, and don't you dare call me *princess*!" I hiss.

"And you're the one whose phone was on, throwing off my coordinates!" he retorts.

"If I wasn't allowed to use my phone, then why didn't you say that?"

"I did!"

"I've never been on a plane that didn't have WiFi." I cross my arms over my chest in a challenge. "So please explain to me how that makes sense!"

"I told you I'm an aviation purist. I like to do things the old-fashioned way. It's an art—"

"Oh my God! Are you really defending yourself right now?" I heave as my pulse pounds in my neck. "It's an art—" I mock.

"Are you happy with yourself? Do you feel better now?" He snorts and shakes his head before turning back to the luggage.

I jump in front of him, "No. No, I don't feel better. Have you tried calling for backup or something? How do we call for rescue?"

This earns me a laugh. "I don't know. Did you pack your Bat Signal? Because I left mine at home." He bumps my shoulder with his chest, then crouches back down to dig through my suitcase.

A wave of nausea rises in my chest. "I think I'm going to be sick." I run for the tree line just in time to heave what little I have in my stomach into the bushes.

"That's probably the concussion or the shock," he says, unmoving from his nest in the sand.

I wipe my mouth with the back of my hand, blinking back the tears that threaten to fall. I hate puking. I hate feeling weak. And right now, I'm two for two. I squeeze my eyes shut as I succumb to another wave of nausea.

"You ok back there?" he calls.

I moan in response. Steadying myself on shaking legs, I march back over to him and grab the largest of the vibrators, a giant hot pink number with the bunny ears for extra *stimulation,* and smack him on the head with it. The silicone phallus connects with his skin in a harsh thwack.

"What the fuck?" Jack leaps to his feet, but I hold my ground wielding the giant pink cock like a sword.

"Stop playing games with me. I'm not afraid to use this." I warn.

"You've made that clear, but I'm starting to wonder how hard you hit your head." He holds his hands up in surrender. "Why don't you put the cock down, and let's talk. There's no need for violence."

I eye him warily and slowly lower the dildo. "So, what are we going to do? If we're not in Costa Rica ... and you don't know where we are... can you use your radio or something and call for help?"

My brain takes the opportunity to present me with a detailed flashback of my thighs clenched around Jack's neck in a chokehold. *That's so not helpful right now...*

The flashback triggers another memory of me shoving my cell phone in my bra when Jack tried to snatch it from me on the plane.

I reach in my bra and pull out my beloved phone. "Ha!" I yell in victory. "I'll just call 911 or whatever, and we'll be out of here in no time!" I hold up the phone and examine it, but the screen is completely black.

The sound of Jack's laughter interrupts me, and I pull my attention back to him. "What's funny? Why are you laughing?"

"We crashed my plane in the ocean, your phone's water damaged. I don't have to look at it to know that." He sighs. "Besides, even if your phone wasn't submerged in water for over thirty minutes... it's not like you'd actually have a service out here in the middle of nowhere." He gestures to the island around us.

"What are you saying?" I purse my lips as my stomach plummets to my feet.

"I'm saying," He breathes in a long, controlled breath, "that if you want to survive, you're going to have to put down the giant dick and start listening to me."

"No. No. No." I shake my head, "This isn't happening. This cannot be happening to me right now." I flap my hands as the reality of the situation comes crashing down. Gasping for breath, I meet Jack's forest green eyes, which seem to crinkle at the ends. Does he think this is funny?

"You!" I scream as I lunge toward him in a frenzy, swinging the dildo with all my strength. "You did this! This is all your fault!"

"Whoa. Whoa. Hold your weapon!" He stands to his feet, towering over my small frame, and swipes the dildo from my sweaty grip. "I'm confiscating this. Have you completely lost your mind?"

I jump, trying to take back my weapon, but it's no use. Jack's got at least a foot of height on me, and unless I climb him like a tree trunk, there's no way I'm getting the vibrator back.

I cross my arms over my chest and let out a huff in defeat. I'm hot and exhausted, and I don't have the strength to keep fighting him, so I collapse on the sand, lying like a corpse.

"What are you doing now?"

"Obviously, we're as good as dead, so I'm laying here until the vultures come and put me out of my misery."

To my surprise, Jack laughs. "Dramatic much?"

I squint open one eye and see he's back to his original spot, hovering over all my stuff. *What is with this guy and my underwear?* Rolling over on my side, I examine him for a moment before I finally speak.

"So, we really crashed the plane? Like it's gone?" My voice is so quiet it almost comes out as a whisper.

"RIP Betty White." Jack makes the sign of the cross over his chest, and for the second time today, my stomach drops. "I was able to crash land in the ocean, but it wasn't pretty. The old girl got swallowed whole in no less than ten minutes, along with all of our stuff. Luckily, I was able to grab my survival bag with all my recording equipment and this." He holds up something resembling a gun, but the barrel is bigger.

"What's that?"

"A flare gun." He shoves it back in his backpack. "There's only one shot, so we can't waste it."

He pushes his hand through his long hair and points to the pile of things in front of him.

"Besides that, it looks like we're working with–" He begins counting off as if committing it to memory. "Twenty-seven thongs, five bras, seven bikinis, four tampons, a curling iron, three vibrators, a tube of lipstick, and one toothbrush." He sighs, pondering the obscure pile before him.

"Well, it's not my fault that you only managed to grab *this* bag!" I snap. "If you want to be so judgmental, you should pack your own survival bag." I huff. "If you wouldn't have crashed the plane–"

"If you wouldn't have had your cell phone on—or been trying to molest me—I wouldn't be trying to figure out a way to survive using your elaborate collection of lingerie and dildos! I wouldn't have had to decide what bag to grab, and I wouldn't have had to give you mouth to mouth on the beach after you almost drowned!" he yells back.

I cross my arms over my chest and back away from him. This can't be happening right now. I'm supposed to be sipping Mai Tais on a beach in Costa Rica, not washed up with a wannabe Bear Grylls who seems to think there's a solution in my underwear bag.

Without another thought, I take off in a sprint along the

beach, running as fast as I can in search of anything that would indicate human life.

"Now what are you doing? Come back before you hurt yourself... again!" Jack chases behind me, and it doesn't take long for him to catch up to my head start. He's running next to me now, and it's almost comical. If someone didn't know better, it would look like we're a couple taking our exercise regime very seriously on vacation.

But nothing could be further from the truth.

CHAPTER EIGHT

JACK

I collapse from exhaustion underneath the shade of a palm tree near the beach. I've just spent the last twenty minutes chasing Gwen like an off-duty parole officer, which isn't the best use of my time. Apparently, she needed to see for herself just how alone we actually are on this island rather than taking my word for it, but what I do know is that I'm the survival expert.

She eventually got tired and gave up on her one-woman hunt, and now we're back to where we started, sitting with our backs propped against opposite sides of a palm tree because neither one of us can manage to look at the other right now.

I've got the contents of both of our bags splayed out in front of me as I try to catalog everything in my mind. Unlike Gwen, I've come to accept our situation, and instead of denying it's happened, I'm trying to formulate the best plan to keep us safe until I can figure out a solution.

I close my eyes and try to focus on the task at hand. It's so easy to get caught up in fear of the unknown, but smart survivalists know that the faster you adapt to your environment, the more likely you'll have to survive.

I shake my head at the irony of the situation. Sure, I've intentionally set out to emulate similar situations for my viewers, surviving off the land and using only the things I'd normally keep in my backpack, but I've always known there would be an end. My life was never really in danger, not to mention I've always done those extreme-survival excursions alone.

Gwen's hushed sniffling brings me back to the moment, and I feel like I've been punched in the gut with a wrecking ball. Not only do I need to keep myself alive long enough to be rescued, but now I've got another person to worry about. And it's not as if she's exactly easy to work with.

I grab a nearby twig and begin to draw a map in the sand of Florida, Costa Rica, and the nearby islands, adding every detail I can muster from memory. I mark an X and draw a large circle around it that takes up most of the ocean space on the map, indicating the approximate vicinity where I think we landed. The problem is, I don't know when the compass was compromised, so it's hard to predict just how off course we are.

I do the quick mental math, trying to predict the search radius as a wave of sinking dread sends another blow to my stomach. The odds aren't looking good for us, but I cling to the hope that maybe we'll get lucky. I need to start thinking of an escape plan.

One thing at a time, Jack.

I can't focus on the probability of being rescued right now because the most important thing is surviving, so we actually have a chance. I shake the heavy intrusive thoughts away and try to spin my fear into a more productive emotion.

I can't control the search radius or whether they'll find us, but I can control my attitude and how comfortable we are until they do. I sit up in a rush with my newfound enthusiasm and grab my recording equipment, garnering Gwen's attention.

"Jack? What's that? What are you–"

I ignore her as I hit record.

"What's up, Dubbies. Wombat Willy here coming at you from a real-life plane wreck. We've got a survival challenge as you've never seen before! Hell, I don't even know if we'll make it out of here alive for you to actually watch this, but hey, my fans are always the first to know about my quests."

"Absolutely not!" Gwen whisper-hisses from the other side of the tree. "I do not consent to this. As your PR representative, I forbid this. Now turn off the camera right this second."

I can't help but chuckle at her use of the word forbid, and rather than ignoring her further, I pull her into the frame in a side hug. "This here's Gazelle Gwen, and she'll be tagging along for this adventure. Well, mostly because we're stuck here together." She tries to pry herself free, but I don't budge, pinning her against my side as she struggles to push me away. "You'll have to forgive Gwen here. She's still getting used to the idea of roughing it out here all alone. She's a bit of a city girl," I whisper. "But don't worry, by the end of this series, I'll have her building fires, shelters, and living off the land like a pro."

"Will you let me go!" she huffs, and I pull her face next to my own.

"Well, as you can see, I've got my work cut out for me, so I'll check back in tonight. Adios!"

Her boney finger stabs me in the eye, and I release her, then click off the camera. "Ouch! What the–"

"I cannot believe you right now!" She pushes herself up to stand, placing her hands on her hips. "Is this some kind of joke to you, Jack? Do you really think making content is the best use of your time? Why am I the only person on this island—with a population of two—who's freaking out right now?"

I purse my lips in a flat line and shrug. "I'm the survival expert, and I've just landed on a deserted island with all my recording equipment. I'm making lemonade."

"Lemonade! You call this–" she gestures in a circle around us, "lemonade?"

"The way I see it is, we're already out here stranded. That's not going to change ... so we may as well make the most of our time and create some epic content." I shrug. "Then, when we're rescued, we'll at least have something to show for it. Just think of the content we can make. Who wouldn't want to watch two people surviving off the land when the stakes are so high? I mean, that's literally what I'm doing in my videos, trying to mimic a real-life survival situation. This would be the behind-the-scenes, gritty details documenting it all. My viewers are going to eat this shit up like root beer flavored Kool-Aid."

Gwen's silent for a moment as she stares at me, blinking. "So, like actual root beer, then? How is root beer flavored Kool-Aid any different than real fucking root beer, Jack!"

"Obviously, Kool-Aid isn't carbonated."

"I can't do this." She scowls and tries to storm off, but I catch her hand and stop her.

"Think about it, Gwen. You're here to fix my reputation, right? What better way to do that than give the people something so juicy they can't turn away? There's no way my sponsors will pull out when I've got this kind of content."

She pinches the bridge of her nose. "Jack, it won't fucking matter if you have the best content in the history of YouTube if we die here alone and no one finds us!"

"At least we'll have documentation of our last moments alive. I don't see the problem."

"Ugh!" she screams, turning her head up to the sky.

"I'm going to take that as a yes." I smile and pull her to my side. "Okay, now that you're on board, we should probably find somewhere to set up camp for the night." I glance at my watch, realizing we're going to be cutting it close if we want to get everything done before night falls.

I pull out a small machete from my backpack and lead us toward the dense tropical forest. "Come on. We've got a lot of work to do."

CHAPTER NINE

JACK

"There we go." I blow the burning red ember in the palm of my hands. We spent most of the afternoon carrying bamboo branches and palm leaves to the temporary lean-to shelter I've propped up by the rocky side of the beach. Ideally, I'd like to set up camp near freshwater, but since we haven't had time to scout the island, I wanted to make sure we at least had somewhere dry to sleep tonight. The tide's starting to rise, and the sky is painted in the most beautiful orange and pink sunset I've ever seen. I inhale a deep breath and savor the clean salty air wafting in from the sea, and even though I have no clue where we are or how I'm going to get us out of here, I'm doing my best to enjoy the gift of the moment.

It's not that I'm not worried. Hell, it's taking everything in me to keep my mind on the task at hand. It's just that I don't see any use in both of us being miserable. Especially since Gwen seems so determined to carry that burden like a badge of honor. She's wound up so tightly it's not a matter of if she snaps but rather a matter of when. Meanwhile, I'll do my best to keep things light, and maybe, just maybe, I can help her to see there's another way to live than taking things so seriously all the time.

The ember sparks to life, and I gesture for Gwen to zoom in on the shot of me transferring it to the larger pile of dry sticks and leaves. "Ugh, we get it. Tarzan make fire." She rolls her eyes.

"That's right, babe. Tarzan make fire and shelter." I gesture toward our camp. It's not much, just big enough for each of us to lay side by side and still be covered.

"It's freaking hot out here, Jack ... er, Willy?" I nod when she corrects herself for the footage. "It's freaking hot out here, Willy. Why the hell are you so concerned with building a fire? I'm glistening with sweat, and it's muggier than Satan's armpit."

"Why am I building a fire?" I mockingly ask as I crank my neck toward the camera. "Hey Dubbies, you know, don't you?" I look back to Gwen. "Tarzan build fire near bed to make bugs leave Tarzan and Jane alone while sleeping." I wink.

"Ok, enough with the Tarzan talk. I am definitely not Jane in this scenario!" She shoves the camera to me and crawls into our bedroom. I focus on the blaze, explaining the process of building a fire and the best items to use in a survival situation, and then switch the camera off.

"That was good first-night footage. I think the fans are going to eat this up! Especially your privileged pretty girl attitude. We're like one of those couples in a romance novel who are so opposite they can't stand each other, and then they eventually combust with sexual tension and have hot angry sex." I waggle my eyebrows at her seductively—well, as seductive as a man with a headlamp strapped to his forehead can be.

"First off," Gwen holds up her finger, "there's nothing wrong with being *indoorsy*. Secondly," she gestures between us, "this is nothing like a romance novel because *this* cannot happen! Like I could lose my job and my entire reputation in the industry."

I nod my head, doing my best to suppress a smirk.

"What's that look? Jack, I mean it! This is forbidden! It's Sandra's number one rule at Éclat. And once you cross her, it's basically career suicide. She's got contacts all over. I'd never get hired with that kind of stain." Her voice cracks in a rare display of emotion, and it's nice seeing such a vulnerable side of her, even if it's not what I want to hear. "Besides, how do you know so much about romance novels?"

Her question surprises me. I can see we teetered a too personal line, and she wants to deflect the attention onto me. That's ok. I'll bite this time.

Poking the fire that's now blazing thanks to my expert fire-building skills, I shrug. "I grew up with three older sisters. When I was fifteen and started to really hit my stride with the ladies, I got curious. I opened one of their racy romance novels one day, and what do you know? It was like a man's guidebook into the female psyche. Who knew that all this time that women were actually writing out their deepest fantasies and desires, and us guys were too dumb to actually pay attention?" I elbow her gently in the rib. "I took notes and devoured as many romance novels as I could get my hands on. But I'm sure you're not surprised by that if you have any memory of the janitor's closet." I wink.

She hits me in the chest. "You're such a dick. You're never going to let that mistake go, are you?"

"Oh, that was no mistake." I shimmy myself up into the narrow enclosure. "That was just the preview, the prologue if you will. Mark my word, Gwen, by the end of this *experiment*, you'll be begging to suck on this lollipop." Her eyes go wide. "Oh, wait, you already did that." I grin, pulling my hands up behind my head as a pillow.

Our bodies are packed so tightly together that there's no way for us not to be touching. I'll admit, I made it small on purpose, but I wasn't expecting the complete lack of breeze. Gwen's right; it is muggy as hell in here. I lean up, take off my shirt, and pull down my shorts, leaving me in only my black boxer briefs.

"Wha—what do you think you're doing?" Gwen stutters.

"You're right. It's hot as fuck." I lay back down, "And since you've made it perfectly clear that you have no desire to ride this bucking-bronco again any time soon, I may as well make myself comfortable."

She turns on her side, pushing her ass into my leg. "You're absolutely ridiculous. And you know what? You're right. I wouldn't touch you if my life depended on it!"

"I guess we'll see about that," I whisper.

"Go fuck yourself," she growls.

"Now, you say that, but I have a feeling that would be crossing a boundary—"

"Jack, if you don't let me get some sleep, I swear to God, I'll rip off your favorite body part and wear it around my neck as a reminder to not fuck with me!"

I can feel the venom in her words, but I can't help myself. "Suit yourself. You want to wear my calves around your neck. Who am I to judge?"

I'll admit, I've done my fair share of extreme camping. The fans love when I pick a random location and survive with just a few items for a weekend, but last night sucked. Between the throbbing of my cock, which didn't get the memo that Gwen is off-limits, and Gwen's ass sticking out so far she took up most of the tent, I was forced to big-spoon her. Which only made my cock angrier that we had to be on our best behavior. I dozed a few times, but between fantasizing about this feisty woman and trying to figure out my game plan moving forward, my mind wouldn't relent and let me relax—and I'm the king of relaxing. For the first time in my life, I feel a prickle of fear poking at me. It's fucking annoying.

The camp fire's long burned out, with only a large pile of ash in its place, and I can barely see the sun peeking over the horizon. With a frustrated sigh, I peel my clammy body off of Gwen, who seemed to have slept like a baby. Maybe it was an aftereffect of the shock, or maybe she just felt cozy in my embrace, but I don't miss the trail of drool seeping from the corner of her mouth or how she screws up her face when I dislodge myself from her. If I didn't know better, I'd say she actually enjoyed my snuggles.

I decide to keep this information to myself, knowing if I tease her, she'll shut it down for the rest of our time on this island—however long that may be.

On my way out of the tent, I grab my camera and my noodle fishing pole from my bag. Luckily, I always keep this little guy in my backpack in case of an emergency, so I should be able to catch us some fish for breakfast. I only have a few baits on me, so I'll have to make due until I collect some small fish and worms for a longer-term solution.

I walk several hundred feet from the campsite until I find a rocky cliff. It's the best option right now, so I'll take it. I set up my chest camera, bait my hook, and make the first cast of the day. "Good morning! It's our first cast of the day, and I slept like absolute dog shit last night. You know what I always say, though, 'An early cast gets you an early win.' It can only go up from here, right?"

The morning breeze feels amazing on my bare chest, though it's not exactly helping my cast. I spot a nearby tide pool with several small fish and set my aim just to the left, letting the breeze push me right on target. A few more casts and some on-air pep talks later, I get my first bite.

"Woohoo! Did you see that? Patience is the key here." I reel in the small fish and hold her in front of my camera. "Would you look at that? It's a female!" I point to her protruding abdomen. "Ok, Dubbies, usually I'd throw this one back since she's with child, but we've got ourselves a survival situation on our hands, and I'm not going to turn down the extra protein. I hope you all understand."

After making a line in the water to keep my catch fresh, I make another cast. "Here's to surviving paradise with the hottest woman in the whole world. Jeez, how did I get so lucky?"

Two hours later, I carry my catch of three back to the campsite. I scan the ground as I walk, looking for any debris that washed ashore last night that I can use. I find an empty plastic water bottle, two left-footed flip-flops, and an old coconut. Maybe if I'm lucky, I can get at least enough coconut water for Gwen until I find a fresh source. "Pro-tip," I say to the camera, "never underestimate the power of trash in a survival situation." I hold up my findings. "These things may look like ordinary beach trash, but they could be lifesavers in the right circumstances. Don't worry, Dubbies, stay tuned and find out." I switch off the camera as I make my way to the campsite to wake my sleeping beauty.

"Oh, Gwenny-Poo, rise and shine!" I pull the straw curtain back and find her sprawled like a starfish. She jerks up, scanning her surroundings as if trying to figure out where she is. "I've got breakfast fit for a queen." I extend my hand and help her climb out of the cramped space. "I hope you like caviar."

"Jack, you can't be serious. I'm not eating that. It still has eyeballs!"

We're sitting over our new campfire; this one is much smaller since I only needed to cook the fish. I've created a makeshift grate from wet bamboo shoots to use as a grill, and I've been slow cooking the fish above the small flame, hoping the smoke will mask some of the fishy taste.

"Eyeballs are a great source of protein, and you'll need all the strength you can get because, after breakfast, we'll be scouring the island for fresh water. Who knows how long we'll be in there." I gesture to the densely covered row of trees behind us.

"I'm not going in there. Jack. It's probably crawling with snakes and spiders and who knows what else." She huffs. "You can find me laying out over here on the beach, getting some sun in the safety of the open air."

I ignore her, passing her a whole smoked fish on a skewer. "Eat up, baby. We've got work to do, and you're going to need the strength."

"Do I have to? Don't you have some MREs or something dehydrated like rice and beans in your magical backpack of wonders?"

I throw my head back and laugh at her backpack reference. "You know, I forgot to bring the beans and rice this time, but I promise next time we're stranded on a deserted island together, I'll bring an array of dehydrated food. Pizza, tacos, red wine–"

"Ugh, fine." She snatches the fish from me and takes the tiniest bite. Her eyebrows rise in surprise, and I can't help the grin that covers my face. I could record this for the show, but I think I'll keep this moment to myself.

"It's not too bad, right?" I wink, then suck an eyeball from the socket with an exaggerated slurp and pass the fish eggs over on a flat rock I'm using as a serving dish. "Caviar for the lady?"

Gwen throws the fish down and stands up. "That's it. I'm done. You lost me at sucking eyeballs." She pulls her shirt over her head as she walks toward the ocean.

My mouth goes dry at the view of her gorgeous exposed back. "Um, Gwen. What do you think you're doing!?" My voice comes out a few octaves higher than usual.

She turns to face me, covering her bare breasts with the palm of her hand and forearm. "I smell like jet fuel and sweat. I'm taking a sea bath before I do anything else." She drops her bottoms, exposing her round ass, and my mouth waters in response. "I don't suppose you have any soap?" she calls as she sinks into the clear blue water.

I shake my head, unable to form words from the unexpected sight of the naked woman in front of me.

"I guess I'll just have to exfoliate with the sand, then." She plugs her nose and disappears under the water.

Fuck me. There's no way in hell I'll be able to keep this erection in check for the rest of the day after that surprising show.

"I've got to go check on something. Be right back!" I yell before she notices just how much I enjoyed what I saw.

CHAPTER TEN

Gwen

I've scrubbed every inch of myself with the gritty, rough sand. My angry skin feels as clean as it can get considering the circumstances. I'm not going to lie and say I hate how the salt water gives my shoulder-length hair enough texture to stay out of my face, but I cringe thinking of the irreparable damage I may have just done to my platinum blonde locks. My hairdresser will kill me when she sees the mess I've made of her masterpiece— that is *if* she ever sees it again.

I know Jack is supposed to be some survival guru and all of that, but I can't say I've got complete trust in his abilities after the flight ... and the crash landing. I spent the whole night racking my brain for an idea of how to get us out of here without having to rely solely on the seemingly carefree survivalist I'm trapped here with. I don't know what it is about Jack that annoys me so much. He's the opposite of me in every single way, but it's not just his carefree attitude.

Growing up, I was expected to be absolutely perfect in

every way. It was drilled into me from as early as I can remember that love and attention came with a cost, and my perfection was the currency.

Seeing Jack so content with all this feels like he's squeezing a fresh lime wedge right in my deepest childhood wound. How can he be so... happy? It's unnatural is what it is.

I know it may be bratty of me, but a small part of me wants to torture him... just enough to see him crack. It's only fair that if I'm freaking out, he should at least feel a little stressed, too. Right?

Today the plan is to find fresh water, and since I just washed my only real clothes in the ocean, it looks like I'll be prancing around this island in my silk nightie ... like an idiot. I roll my eyes as I pull on a thin pink nightgown that barely covers my ass and pair it with some boy shorts. It's the best I can do with what I have.

I could kick myself for packing so systematically. If I live to survive this, I'll never organize similar things in one bag ever again. I can't help but think that Elliot would never have had this problem. She'd probably have an entire wardrobe pieced together that included every season with arts and crafts to go with it.

My heart aches at the thought of my friends. Do they know by now that we didn't make it to Costa Rica? Are they looking for us?

A small spark of hope ignites in my chest when I remember the Instagram live video I tried to record during the crash. I squint my eyes, trying to recall the memory. Did it actually go through? My account is private, but maybe someone watched it in real time? If so, maybe someone saw our last moments before we lost signal?

Maybe we have a chance of getting out of here alive?

It's the only hope I have, considering my other option is to depend solely on Jack.

I scoff at the thought.

Maggie would say the universe is using this as an opportunity to teach me a lesson, but I think it's just another case of my bad luck at play.

Either that or Pantone put some kind of curse on me?

I'm considering them both solid explanations.

"Are you ready to leave?" I slide on my leather platform sandals that are clearly not designed for hiking, brewing a fresh wave of annoyance at my wardrobe's lack of functionality.

Jack's packing his backpack, removing certain items to eliminate weight, and checking for anything we may need. He glances over his shoulder and freezes. "What is that?" He points to my outfit. "What the hell do you think you're wearing? You look ridiculous."

"Thanks for the vote of confidence." I sneer as I pull the nightgown away from my body and look at it. "In case you've forgotten, my wardrobe is quite limited at the moment, considering it's the only bag I have." I pin him with a stare because even though I know he didn't realize what bag he grabbed, I fully blame him for my lack of proper clothing.

"I ... I can't record you looking like—" he gestures to all of me and bites the knuckle of his finger, "—*that*."

"Well, I don't know what to tell you other than try not to record me. This is the most decent option I could find. I'd rather not give the bugs anymore real estate to feast upon than necessary." I roll my eyes and give him a shove as I pass him and head toward the tree lines.

He huffs his annoyance and pulls his backpack up a little higher. "Fuck me. This is going to be a long day. Follow me. We have some climbing ahead of us. I don't want you out of my sight, and for the love of God, please watch your step in those shoes."

"Yes, sir." I mock salute.

Then as if on cue, Jack turns on his body cam and begins talking to his invisible audience.

"Good morning, Dubbies. We've just feasted on a delicious spread of grilled fish. I even got Gwen to try discount caviar! We're headed to find a fresh source of water. Water is the most important thing in a survival situation and should be your top priority."

He stops at the base of the hill, pointing out several edible plants before snagging some and putting them in his backpack. He goes on to explain the best ways to track fresh water in the area. "Now this," he holds up a plant, "will make a delicious tea before bed. I have a feeling Gwenny-Poo won't sleep quite so soundly tonight, so it'll be a real treat."

I roll my eyes at the annoying nickname. Gwenny-Poo, the office girls won't ever let me live that down—much less Elliot and Maggie. I'll have to do my own rebranding just to salvage my image when we get home. But I'm up for the challenge. I can see my name on that corner office door as clear as day. I've just got to suck it up, bear this grueling heat, and try my best not to strangle the only person actually qualified to get us out of here.

Piece of cake.

Two hours later, we're still walking, hiking really, what seems like straight up the side of a mountain. I've got a splitting pain in my side, and my mouth is as dry as the Sahara Desert. "How much longer are we going to do this exactly?" I groan.

Jack swipes his giant machete knife, knocking down all the greenery in our path, and I'm not going to lie and say he doesn't look sexy as hell, all sweaty and dirty. The whole Tarzan thing is really working for him.

"Should be getting close. I can smell the water in the air."

"You can *smell the water?*" I mock him.

"Indeed, I'm well attuned to my senses." He winks, and my stomach does a flip flop. *Traitor.*

"Your cheeks are looking a little flushed." He pulls off his hat and slaps it on top of my head. "We need to keep that fair skin of yours from getting burned until we can find some coconuts to use as sunscreen." He turns back around and makes another swipe with the machete.

"So, what made you decide to change your identity and become a wild man teaching the masses about nature? Did you watch a lot of Crocodile Dundee growing up or what?

He smirks. "Something like that. I actually started off doing the whole nine-to-five grind, but after a couple of years of living the same damn day over and over again, I just felt this calling for adventure." He smiles over his shoulder. "Come up here and stay next to me. I don't like not being able to see you." He pulls me by the hand, and I obey.

"So, you just, what, bought a plane ticket and set out to find yourself?" I laugh. "That's some *Eat Pray Love* shit if I've ever heard it."

"Well, it didn't happen exactly like that." He nudges my shoulder. "I took a vacation to Tahiti and fell in love with the laid-back lifestyle. At first, all I wanted was to move to a foreign country and live a simple life. Then I started a vlog that rapidly gained popularity. Then it turned into a Youtube channel. Benjamin's agency actually helped me come up with my alter ego, and I got my agent from Elliot's company, Clutch. It's all gravy from there."

"Uh huh," I say as he pulls my elbow, guiding me over a fallen tree limb, ever the gentleman. "And you're happy with this? Living out of a suitcase, never knowing how much income you'll have in a month, being dependent on sponsors to fund you?"

"It works for me at the moment. I'm single, unattached. There's no reason for me to be tied down to anything or anyone. The world is my oyster, and I never feel more at home than I do in the wilderness with the dirt beneath my feet."

My strap falls down my shoulder, and he brushes a gentle hand to straighten it. Our breathing is heavy, and we stop, gazing into each other's eyes. Jack Manning's eyes are the deepest green I've ever seen, with a gold rim around the middle. They look as if he was made from the forest, like it's his natural habitat. He's a wild man oozing testosterone and freedom. I shake my head and pull the cap down lower over my face. The last thing I need is for him to see just how much I'm affected by him. I don't know if we'd have enough room on this island for the two of us, *plus* his giant ego.

"And what about you?" he continues the conversation. "When you were a little girl, growing up in..." He pauses.

"Atlanta," I answer.

"Atlanta. Did you always want to move to the big city and work yourself to the bone day in and day out?"

I fall silent, thinking about the question. I know Jack has no idea what he's talking about, nor do I want to offer more information than necessary. "When I was a little girl," I swallow the lump in my throat, "I wanted to grow up to be the most powerful, successful woman I could be. I wanted to be so independent that I'd never have to depend on anyone for help ever again." I cough to mask the emotion from my voice. "So, yes. I guess you can say that I did."

"Well, then, how's that working out for you?"

I stop and look into his forest eyes, sparking with whimsy and wonder. "What do you mean? I'm here to help you, aren't I? I suppose I'm doing something right."

"No, I mean, are you happy?" He lifts my chin so he can see my eyes under the bill of the hat. "When you lay down to sleep at night, are you fulfilled? Are you living your life by your own rules or for someone else?"

Biting my lip, I fight the tears that threaten. My throat's gone so tight I can barely speak, so I do the only thing I can think of to do. I shove him away. "Yeah, I guess I am. There's never anything a good fuck can't fix. Let's go, Mister Rogers, I'm thirsty, and I didn't sign up for a therapy session."

He gestures for me to go ahead. "By all means, lead the way."

"Ok, but give me the machete." I grin. If he wants to prove a point, then two can play at that game.

Reluctantly, he hands me the knife, with the blade facing away from me. "Do you know how to use this thing, or are you going to chop a finger off? Because I must warn you, I'm shit when it comes to stitches."

I swipe the branches away, mimicking his gestures, and they fall away at our feet. When I glance back, I see his mouth agape, eyes as wide as saucers.

"Hold on a second. I need to adjust my boner." He grunts. "Dear Lord, where'd you learn to use a knife like that? Do you frequently spend your free time swinging machetes, or have I misjudged you?"

"Something like that." I wink, using his own words against him. "Now, come on. Let's just get this over with."

———

Before I know it, we're standing in front of the most beautiful waterfall I've ever seen. The cool mist hits my warm skin, and it feels so heavenly. We're standing on a rocky peninsula about one hundred feet above the clear blue water. Jack and I are carrying everything we own on our backs since he hoped to make a new campsite near the fresh water. The peninsula is steep, and loose rocks and weeds lead down on each side. I look at my swollen ankles, covered with scratches from all the brush on the hike. "So, how exactly are we going to get down there?"

Before I can protest, Jack turns on the chest cam and makes some kind of wild animal call. It echoes from the trees, and every hair on my body stands on end.

"We jump!" I feel a firm hand on my back, but I shuffle to the side just in time as Jack launches himself off the waterfall, falling at least twenty feet into a pool of clear fresh water.

One gigantic splash later, I see his head pop up among a heap of bubbles, and I exhale a sigh of relief.

"Jump in. The water feels amazing!" he calls from the pool below, and I wince. Yeah, that's not happening.

"I think I'll just look for a trail or something," I call to him. "I, uh, I don't want to get this silk wet. It'd be ruined."

He lets his head fall back dramatically and rolls his eyes. "Ok, princess, have it your way! But I'll have you know that this," he splashes around, "is way more fun than climbing down."

"I guess I'll just have to take your word, then." I retort as I look around for a way to get down.

It takes me much longer than I care to admit, but I eventually find a route that isn't too steep leading to the fresh-water pool below. I'm careful to cover the giant mud stain on my ass that will surely ruin this expensive silk nightgown because there goes that excuse.

Jack shoves the water containers in my arms, "Here ya go. Help me carry these back to camp."

"Gee, carrying heavy water bottles on a hot, humid day? You really know how to treat a lady, Jack."

"Trust me, babe. You'll thank me tonight when you have clean drinking water within arm's reach." He steadies my shoulders, letting his eyes wander down my backside. "It's a good thing you didn't ruin your nightgown from jumping in the water," he teases.

I shrug my shoulders. "I may have slipped on my way down the waterfall, but at least I don't smell like fish pee and mildew." I plug my nose and turn on my heel, leaving him to follow as we trek back to the campsite in awkward silence.

CHAPTER ELEVEN

Jack

I only found a few empty water bottles and one jug on the beach this morning, so we'll have to replenish our water supply a little more frequently than I'd like. Luckily, I've got my small water pot stowed in my backpack. After setting up my camera on the tripod, I call Gwen over for a lesson in water safety.

"Hey Dubbies, so we've got ourselves a bit of a predicament here with the water situation. We need to find storage, so we don't work ourselves to death trying to stay hydrated, but until I find a solution, let's have a fire-making lesson."

Gwen rolls her eyes in annoyance and scoots out of the shot, but I pull her back. "Not so fast there. I'm going to show you an alternate way to make a fire. All you need is–" I reach in my shorts pocket and pull out the ziplock bag I found on the shore this morning and hold it in front of the camera, "–a plastic baggie, some water, and a pile of dried moss and leaves." I get up to fill the bag with water and rush back before Gwen can protest. I pass her the filled water bag and point to my leaf pile. "Gwenny Gazelle is going to show you just how easy it is to make fire on a sunny day like we're having here."

I hand her the bag, and her eyebrows pull together in confusion. "What the fuck am I supposed to do with this trash?" she half-whispers.

I point to the sun and line the bag up, creating an effect like a magnifying glass. "Hold the bag right here, and don't move." I encompass her hand with my own and steady her.

"So, how long am I supposed to sit here holding a bag of water like an idiot?" she snaps.

"Just trust the process." I zoom the camera in on her hands, showing how the light is concentrated into a small dot on the leaves, and beads of sweat start to fall down my face. Jesus, it's hot out here today. I couldn't ask for better weather to demonstrate this technique, but my skin is begging to take another dip in the cool pond next to us.

I cut the camera off to save some battery life since I really need to start rationing my stash. I want to make sure to get a little bit of everything during this experience, and since I don't know exactly how long it's going to take me to figure out an escape plan ... it could be a lot longer than I expect.

"Oh my God, Jack! Look!"

I turn the camera back on and zoom in on the tendril of smoke rising from the leaves. "That's it, babe. You've got it. Let me just–" I grab Gwen's hands in mine and cup them over the tiny ember. "Now blow."

Her eyes go wide at my accidental innuendo, and I can't help but crack a smile.

"I don't take orders from anyone," she mocks.

I pin her with a stare and look toward the camera, reminding her that we're filming. "Ugh, fine." She rolls her eyes. "But don't get used to this. I don't like being told what to do."

"When you're in my domain, you better damn well listen to what you're told. Now, blow," I command.

The air between us is thick with tension, and I know I'm not the only one feeling it because I can see Gwen's nipples harden under that fuck-me nightgown. I know I'll need a few more trips behind the bushes to alleviate these blue balls that I'm afraid may calcify if I don't have sex soon.

Gwen's eyes sparkle with mischief, and she leans over the ember, sticking her ass in the air in a very suggestive manner. She presses her sexy full lips together and blows ever so gently on the ember.

My balls clench in defiance, and I watch as the tiny ember sparks to life. I don't miss the genuine smile that breaks across her face before she quickly reigns her natural RBF back in.

I tuck some more dried leaves around the growing flame and sit back as the fire comes to life.

Gwen's breathing is heavy, and I adjust the camera, framing only her face in the shot. I'll be damned if I'm sharing this perfect view with my millions of followers. "Well, look at that. She can follow orders after all." I laugh. "How does it feel to make your very first fire, Gwenny Poo?"

She rolls her eyes, "And what makes you believe I don't know how to do any of this stuff? Maybe I was just playing along to give your male ego a boost ... You know, to keep up morale around here?"

"There you go, Dubbies, an easy fire anyone can make. See you soon." I click off the camera and tuck it back in my bag, grabbing the pot to start boiling the water so we can drink it safely.

"What's that for? Are you making fish soup now? Because I draw the line at fish soup!"

"To purify the water, obviously." I walk over to the pond and fill the pot, placing it over my new bamboo grate.

"What do you mean, purify the water?" Gwen's eyes me in confusion. "It's crystal clear. I can see the bottom twenty feet down." She laughs.

"Babe, please tell me you didn't drink the water already?" My face is stern, and my heart begins to race with worry.

"Of course, I drank the water, Jack!" She snaps, "We hiked like five miles up the side of a mountain, and it's a million degrees outside and humid as shit. What's the big deal?"

I clench my teeth and grimace. "The big deal is that you've probably ingested some form of parasites, and you're likely going to be shitting your pants pretty soon," I say bluntly. "I mean, that would be the best case scenario."

"You're joking." She looks around as if I've got a hidden camera and I'm pulling some crazy prank on her, which is ridiculous because, as far as I can tell, we are literally the only ones on this island.

"Nope." I push myself to a stand, brushing loose wet sand from my shorts. "Can you just stay here and watch the water while I search for some papaya and coconuts?"

"You're serious?" she asks again.

"Yes. Serious as a heart attack. Let that water boil for two minutes before you remove it from the heat and transfer it into those bottles. I'll be back as fast as I can."

"You've got to be shitting me!" she screams and falls back onto the ground, covering her eyes with her arm.

"Sorry, babe, but the only one that'll be shitting soon is you." I grab my backpack and toss her a small package of tissues. "Enjoy the plushy softness while it lasts because, once this is gone, you'll have to use leaves, which unfortunately are not so pleasant." I walk to the tree line and turn back before I forget. "Oh, and make sure you shit far enough away from camp, so you don't attract predators to us tonight."

"Fuck my life!" she screams into her hands, and I walk away

silently laughing. Although I do feel bad. That's survival 101…
Clearly, Gwen didn't do her homework and stalk my channel
before coming out here, and now she's going to pay for it.

———

It's been nearly two hours, and I've managed to find a few fallen
coconuts and, surprisingly, several papayas that I had to climb
twenty feet to get. They're not all the way ripe, but for our
purposes, they'll do just fine.

As I approach the campsite, I hear the groans of a woman
pleading for her life, which can only mean one thing; the
diarrhea kicked in.

I smirk because this is actually funny as hell, and she better
know I'm making a lesson of it to my audience. "Hey, Gwenny,
everything coming out all right?" I call in her direction.

"Fuck you, wild man!"

I laugh and get to work, cutting open the papaya with my
small pocket knife and scooping out the seeds into the shell of
an old coconut. She's not going to like this, and it'll likely make
it worse before it's better, but I'll feel better knowing we can nip
this in the bud, and she won't have any lingering effects for the
rest of our time here.

I see the leaves moving around before her pale face appears
above the branches, happy to see that she at least listened to me
and went away from the campsite. "Come over here. I've got a
little something that'll help take the edge off."

She waddles over and plops down on the ground next to me,
her eyes bloodshot and her body shaking like a leaf. Diarrhea
isn't good under any circumstances, but when you're
dehydrated with a minimal amount of food and her being as tiny
as she is, I'm actually growing more concerned.

"Kill me now," she cries. "Jack, I think I just shit out

everything in my body. Surely there's nothing left, and yet—"
She throws her head in my lap, and I'm surprised by her
vulnerability. She must really be hurting.

"Hey, babe, I know you don't feel like it, but I need you to
eat these papaya seeds. They're going to taste bitter as fuck, but
you need to chew them all the way. It's going to kill whatever
bugs you have living in there." I rub her belly and pass her the
coconut shell.

It only takes a little fighting before she relents and does as
she's told. Swearing and spitting between each mouthful. "But...
can't I just swallow it whole." She winces. "It's so nasty."

"I know it's bitter, but chewing the seeds will give the best
anti-parasitic properties."

I pass her the water bottle of *purified water* and encourage
her to drink as much as she can. When she's done, I start peeling
the coconuts, so she can eat the meat. I'll drink the water since it
can also cause diarrhea if not eaten with the right amount of
coconut meat. I'm not taking any chances.

"You know I hate coconut, right?" She gingerly takes a bird-
sized bite.

"Come on. You'll have to do better than that." I cut a
decent-sized piece with my pocket knife and pass it to her. "I'll
make a note, no coconut cake at the wedding."

"Who's wedding?" she says through a grimace as she gnaws
the ripe coconut.

"Ours." I wink.

"And on that note, I need to make another visit to my special
bush." She hops up and scurries away, grunting and griping
under her breath the whole time.

I bite my lip, holding in the retort about wanting to visit her
special bush later because, at this point, I know she's basically a
rabid animal with zero fucks to give. And we're deserted in the
middle of nowhere. She could literally get away with murder.

I have no reference of time other than it's been about three hours since sunset. I've built us another shelter against an old palm tree. I think I'll expand it a bit tomorrow, and I've got to do something to help waterproof it.

Gwen's stomach has finally calmed down, and after forcing her to drink three pots of clean water, she's finally found a comfortable position and seems to be resting a little. I relax my muscles and snuggle into her warm, soft body. She's so exhausted that she'll probably sleep like a log, and my curiosity gets the best of me. I know this will probably be my only chance to sneak in a snuggle, so I suck in my breath and just go for it, wrapping my arm around her tiny frame, pulling her as close to me as I can get.

My oxytocin receptors fire off like the Fourth of July as warmth flows from my stomach to every nerve in my body. Gwen's body fits next to mine perfectly, her head just below my chin, so she's all tucked in and safe. For the first time since we landed on this island, I let myself relax.

I'd never admit to her that I have zero ideas for getting us out of here, but I do know I'll think of something. I always do. Only this time, having to keep Gwen safe makes this whole experience actually scary. I feel so much pressure to keep my emotions at bay. I want to appear calm and confident because the last thing I want is for her to feel like she has to worry any more than necessary.

The muscles in my back ache from the constant chopping of wood and overall manual labor, and I'm exhausted to the bone from having to be on high alert twenty-four-seven.

I inhale the scent of her hair, happy that the shampoo scent has dissipated since she hasn't washed it recently, letting me smell the real her. I can't hide my growing boner from the contact, but I'm not trying to take advantage of her. I just want a cuddle while my little feral kitten is too exhausted to fight me. Tomorrow, she can go back to biting my head off if she wants to, but I'll savor this moment while I can.

Closing my eyes, I drift into a soft, peaceful sleep.

Drip. Drip. Drip. Cold raindrops land between my eyebrows in succession, and I shiver as a gust of wind blows through the poorly structured shelter. I curl into Gwen, my source of warmth, and try to fall back asleep before another gust of wind sends a stream of ice-cold rain down my back. It's like an ice bath after a full-body workout, and it certainly gets my attention.

"Shit." I shoot up, rubbing Gwen's arm to wake her. "Hey, wake up. We need to find a new spot to sleep to wait out this storm." I turn on my small solar-powered lantern, shining a warm light on her.

She sits up with sleepy eyes and the cutest bedhead I've ever seen, and I have to stifle my laugh. We don't have time for teasing right now, and the last thing I need is for us to be drenched and cold all night long. We need sleep, so we can conjure up an escape plan tomorrow.

She blinks, rubbing the sleep from her eyes. "Huh?"

"Wait right here. I'm going to take the lantern and find us a dry spot. I'll come back to get you in just a minute."

"Ok." She goes to lay back down, but a crack of lightning lights up the tree-covered sky above us. "Fuck that. I'm not staying here to get struck by lightning under this flammable shelter. I'm coming with you!"

"Then you better stay close. Don't let go of my hand. The storms out here can get nasty really quick, so we need to make our way to higher ground. We're going to have to climb." I glance down at her bare feet as the crack of thunder rumbles through my chest. I scoop her up, throwing her on my back. "Here, hold the lantern and hold on tight." I pull her arms around my shoulders, shoving the lantern in one of her hands. "We don't have much time before it really starts coming down."

I grab my backpack with my recording equipment and pull it around my chest before ducking as I climb out from under the collapsing shelter, heading north away from the small pond, up the rocky hillside.

"Fucking shit, this rain is cold!" Gwen cries.

I hike her up higher as the rain loosens my grip on her legs. "This is nothing, only a fraction of how bad these spring storms will get."

I climb the steep hill, trying my best to balance with the unequal weight distribution, using small saplings and weeds as a grip to help me climb. Once I'm up the worst part, I take the lantern from Gwen and look for any signs of a cavernous overhang. The range on this lantern is absolute shit, and I'm spending more time walking around than I'd like to be.

Gwen's shivering like a leaf, and I grit my teeth, trying to keep myself focused on finding a solution rather than worrying about her pain. Every second that ticks by while the cold rain pelts against her has my blood boiling with rage. Rage that I didn't build a sturdy enough shelter. Rage that I should've prepared better ahead of time.

When I finally see a glimpse of what I think is a cave, I launch toward it and am relieved to find a good overhang of at least four feet. It's small, and it'll be a tight fit, but tonight, this is all we need.

I sit Gwen down next to my backpack, happy to be out of harm's way, as we watch the lightning show in awe. She leans against the hard rock, tossing and squirming to get comfortable before I pull her into my lap. "I promise not to take advantage of you. Just get some sleep, ok? We've got a big day tomorrow."

I'm surprised at her lack of fight, making me wonder what's got her so quiet. She curls her body against me, laying over my lap, and I caress her silky blonde hair. I can feel her quivering against me, and even though I know it's cold, I know she's terrified, too. And I can't blame her.

"Get some rest. I'll be right here. I've got you." I tuck her hair behind her ear and rub my palm up and down the length of her arm, like my mom used to do when I was a kid and couldn't sleep.

Something about this woman drives me wild, and I have this carnal sense of protection over her. It's not something I've earned or even deserve, but she scared me today. I can't protect her from everything out here, which scares the shit out of me. This storm is just another reminder of the dangers to come. Tomorrow's top priority is figuring out a plan to get us the fuck out of here. There's no content worth the risk of staying here any longer than necessary.

I close my eyes and do my best to relax, knowing I'll need all the rest I can if I want my brain to actually function tomorrow. But each crack of thunder and streak of lightning has my nerves standing on edge. It's going to be a long night.

CHAPTER TWELVE

Gwen

I wake from a restless night as the sun shines its morning glow on my face, a welcome change from last night's storm. Glancing up, I see a sleeping Jack propped against the side of a rock. Somehow, he conjured me into crawling onto his lap like a frail kitten in the middle of the rainstorm. I shudder at my weakness, though his bulging leg muscles and strong biceps did make for a more comfortable night's sleep than I've had in quite some time —though I'll never tell him that.

I watch the sunrise, trying my best not to move and wake Jack. Not only does he need the extra rest, but selfishly, I want to savor this moment for myself. I can't remember the last time I saw the sunrise and wasn't rushing through traffic to make a flight or running down the busy downtown streets in stilettos to fix another celebrity fuck-up.

My life has been a constant rush repairing one public image to the next. Sure the money's great, and I have a nice condo downtown, but on the rare occasion I'm not working, I'm either thinking about a client or planning my next move to gain one. It's only now, lying in Jack's lap after sleeping in a thunderstorm on an island in the middle of nowhere, that I realize what my busy life has become. I've spent every day chasing a dream that's getting blurrier and blurrier with each day I spend on this island.

I let out a stale breath, horrified that I allowed Jack this close to me without brushing my teeth for over twenty-four hours. Dear Lord, what must I smell like? I have no mirror or way of checking my teeth. I probably had day-old fish eggs—that Jack insisted I try—wedged between my two front teeth while that fucker recorded me making fire for all the world to see.

I clench my fist, suddenly reminded of why I don't need to let my guard down, and try my best to free myself from his death grip.

I lift a heavy arm from my torso, laying it down gently on the rock next to him, and roll down the length of his extended legs. When I'm finally free from his hold, I stand up and stretch my aching back from sleeping on the ground for two nights in a row—it's going to take me at least three sessions with my masseuse to get these knots out—and begin scrambling through the backpack.

I'm looking for anything that remotely resembles toothpaste or a breath mint.

Searching the bag, I pull out the large camera equipment, random trash bags, petroleum jelly, some weird rock thing, as well as an assortment of beach trash he must've picked up along the way.

Who knew Jack Manning was a trash hoarder? I guess everyone has their thing, though.

When my search comes up empty, I take off to find a plant or something.

I remember Maggie used to have all these herbs and shit

outside her apartment, and I think I remember what mint looks like.

I glance behind me, making sure Jack is still sleeping before I tiptoe through the dense shrubs, searching for anything to take the edge off my dragon breath.

After a thorough search, I finally find something resembling the mint plant. And who says I don't know anything about botany? Maggie would be so proud of her protégé, forced or not. I shriek with excitement and grab the stem of a large leaf. Just as I begin to pull it free, I feel his large presence before I see him. It's either that or I'm being hunted by a wild animal. Which, in that case, I'm done for. I don't stand a chance fighting actual predators in the wild. I'd be a goner within seconds.

Jack clears his throat, interrupting my lucid daydream. "And just what are you planning on doing with poison ivy before the sun's even completely risen?"

I drop the leaf and back away, remembering when I tried to run away in grade school and came home covered in welts from poison ivy. My mother had to cover me in calamine lotion three times a day for two weeks to keep me from clawing my skin off.

"I... um... I thought it was mint. I need to brush my teeth, and I didn't want to wake you."

He breathes a frustrated sigh, placing his hands on his hips. "Gwen, this isn't a fucking joke, ok? When I ask you to stay with me, I mean it. Anything could be out here, and you're just a—"

A stick breaks in the distance, and Jack goes quiet, stretching his arm out to me, gesturing for me to come close to him.

I roll my eyes and stand beside him, though it physically pains me to listen. I suppose I owe him a tiny bit of respect after the whole dirty water escapade.

"So, about that toothpaste—" I whisper.

"Shhhh!" Jack pushes me behind him, so he's standing in

front of the supposed threat. "There's something out there, and if you could keep your damn mouth shut and let me figure this out, I will find you some fucking toothpaste!" he whispers.

He's crouching now, straining to see what made the noise in the dense rainforest, and fuck, if it's not hot watching him in his element. I fan myself behind him as heat shoots through my core. How am I supposed to react to a potential threat when all the blood in my body is swirling between my legs?

Another snap of a twig may as well sound like a whole tree falling in the early morning stillness, and I jump on Jack's back. "Oh shit, ok, so there is something there."

"Gwen, shit." He struggles to pry my elbow from his throat, but I only suction myself tighter to his back, clenching my thighs around his waist. "Would you just get down for just a minute? I think I see something."

I follow his finger and see a large Toucan bird sitting on a heavily covered tree branch nearby. It's beautiful, like it's right out of a movie, never something I thought I'd see in the wild.

"Oh my gosh!" I squeal! "Jack, it's the Fruit Loop bird. Oh, wow, look how big its beak is!"

I slowly release my grip on him, letting my bare feet touch the soft grassy earth below, and tiptoe toward him to get a better look.

I gasp in wonder and walk even closer, ignoring Jack's attempt to pull me away. "Tookie tookie!" I call, cupping my hands over my mouth, not sure why, but I saw it in a movie once, and well, what else are you supposed to say to a wild bird.

To my surprise, it flaps its wings dramatically and spins around in a circle.

"Jack, I think he likes me!" I skip forward to get a closer look and repeat my call.

Again, the bird gives me a show, fluffing up his feathers and stomping his feet. I feel like I've shed some piece of myself by immersing in something bigger than I ever imagined. I kind of get it now.

Eyes wide and heart racing, I glance back at Jack, who's wearing a proud grin on his face. He's got his camera pointed at the colorful bird and me, and I can barely hear him teaching his audience about the rare encounter.

I'm encouraged by the attention and make sure to adjust my sleep dress for as much modesty as possible. I walk toward it, extending my hand out as an offering. The bird seems just as fascinated by me as I am by it. When I'm finally an arm's length away, I stretch my fingers, channeling my inner Snow White and singsong, "Here, birdie birdie birdie."

To my absolute delight, he fluffs up his feathers and clamps a scaly foot around my finger. I'm surprised by the weight of him, and my hand falters just a little—then he lunges at me.

Black and yellow feathers flap angrily against my face, and I try to shield myself the best I can with my arms, but then it begins dive bombing me. "Jack! Help me! I think it's trying to kill me!"

I hear Jack laughing in the distance, and I don't have to look to know he's recording every second of the attack.

"Mother fucking devil bird!" I scream as I swing blindly at the flying tyrant, never making contact. Another ambush to my face makes me fall back onto my butt, and pain radiates up my body. The bird, satisfied with its K.O, rushes toward the tree line, and I moan, half humiliated and half furious that Jack caught the whole thing on camera. I can sufficiently die of embarrassment now.

"Ouch!" I whine. "What did I ever do to you, you damn bird!"

As I start to get up, Jack sternly whispers, "Don't move."

I immediately lay back down, as if Jack's somehow used a Jedi mind trick to control my body. I've never heard this tone from him, and chills pebble along my skin. I find him staring at me, his eyes wide and dark like he's on high alert. His face has gone pale, and he's standing only a few feet away from me, but it may as well be miles as far as I'm concerned.

My body stiffens, and I freeze as my fight or flight response takes over. "What is it?" I hiss. Urging him to tell me as I try to look for whatever has Jack looking like he's just seen a ghost.

"There's a highly venomous snake right by your—"

Before he can finish his sentence, I feel something slither around my thigh. "Oh my God," I whimper. "Jack, please get it off."

My heart is pounding so hard, and all I want to do is get up and run as fast as I can, get as far away from the threat as possible, but I've seen Jurassic Park, and I've never identified with such pure paralyzing fear until now.

"Gwen, I need you to hold very still. Do not move an inch, do you understand me?" Jack lowers himself to a squat ever so slowly but doesn't make a move to get any closer.

"Yeah, I can do that, but... it's... it's—" I squeeze my eyes shut, stifling a cry, as the snake's smooth, heavy body slowly inches its way up toward my torso, its head creeping up the bottom of my nightgown.

Jack inches a little closer, now that the animal's head is fully covered by the hem of my nightgown. "You're doing great," he assures me in a low, calm voice.

I plead with him with my eyes as a hot tear rolls down my cheek.

"I'm going to come closer now, but I need you to be brave, okay, baby? Hold perfectly still."

I nod ever so slightly and squeeze my eyes closed as I breathe slow, shallow breaths, trying my best to hold as still as possible.

"That's it. You're doing great," he assures me. "On the count of three, I'm going to lift your shirt and grab it, okay?"

"Okay," I say through a silent sob and let my head fall back on the cool, hard earth. I haven't given much thought to how I would die, but lying here completely helpless while an actual predator creeps up my body isn't how I'd ever imagined it happening.

A wave of memories flashes through my mind as my brain forces a replay of some of my core memories. My angry father, screaming at me when he found out I didn't apply to law school; the equally terrified yet delightful feeling of walking through my college campus for the first time; the awkwardly disappointing loss of my virginity at my senior prom; but mostly the long lonely nights spent at home combing over work that bleeds into the late night hours.

I want to shake the memories away, to get up and run as fast and as far as I can so that I never have to face them again.

"I'm going to lift your shirt now, okay?" Jack's calm voice frees me from the tortuous playback reel, and I suck in a sharp breath, clenching my hands so hard that my fingernails pierce my palms.

I feel him move beside me as he slowly lifts the hem of my night dress. "One. Two—"

He clamps down on the snake's heavy body before he says three and jerks it off me. A flash of cold air coats my skin where the snake's body used to be, and I cry out in relief. Shivers run up and down my body as I begin to shake, the fear finally running its course.

I turn on my side, pulling my legs up to my chest as the guttural cries rip through me.

I'm safe. I'm safe. I'm safe.

I hear a loud hiss, then a slice... rendering complete and utter silence. The jungle goes quiet, leaving only the soundtrack of my panicked sobs.

CHAPTER THIRTEEN

JACK

"Come here. I've got you. Shhh. It's okay." My body shakes with relief as I fight back the tears and scoop Gwen into my arms. She's trembling as shock floods her system. I do my best to stifle my own emotions as I carry her to our campsite, taking my time to watch my every step. I don't mind the slower pace if it means I can make her feel safe.

When we finally return to camp, Gwen's whimpers have started to calm. I sit her down gently on a rock as I start making a fire for breakfast.

I boil a pot of water first, adding some herbs to give it a little flavor. Once the water's cooled, I divide the tea into two water bottles. "Here, drink this. It'll calm your nerves."

To my surprise, she doesn't object... Yeah she's definitely still in shock.

"Jack?" she finally speaks. "What kind of snake was that?"

I take a long sip of the hot liquid before I speak. "It was a Fer De Lance." I swallow a gulp.

"You said it was extremely venomous, right?"

I nod.

"What ... what would've happened if it bit me?" Her voice trails up at the end, and it's like a punch to my gut. I don't want to think about it ever again. As it is, I know the fear I felt this morning will haunt me in my dreams for the rest of my life, but I owe her the truth.

"You would've died within an hour. There wouldn't have been anything I could do to save you."

Gwen's red-rimmed eyes widen as a fresh wave of tears falls down her face. Seeing her scared is like a punch to the gut, and I can't help but blame myself for causing it.

"Shhh. Don't cry." I pull her to my side, wrapping my arms around her and doing my best to offer her comfort. "You're safe now. I've got you."

"Th-th-thank you," she says through a sob. "Thank you for saving my life."

I don't know if I want to scream with relief or fall apart alongside her; the feeling of complete and utter relief battles against the reality of what could've been, both fighting for their rightful place in my head. I squeeze her tighter, thanking all my lucky stars that she's safe.

"Listen to me, Gwen." I lift her chin, so she's looking at me when I speak. "I am so proud of you for keeping it together back there." I fight back the tears as my throat tightens. I don't want her to know just how scared I was because I need her to know that I'm strong enough to keep us both safe, but fuck, if it's not the hardest thing I've ever had to do.

"Thank you for listening to me, but from now on, you've got to stay near me because there are too many threats on this island, and I can't protect you if you wander off alone." I suck in a long calming breath before I continue. "I need you to promise me that you'll stop being so stubborn. You're too important to me, and I don't know what I'd do if something happened to you."

Her lips quiver, and she buries her face in my chest. "I'm sorry, Jack. I didn't know," she sobs. "I didn't know."

"I know you didn't, and it kills me to see you this upset." I hand her the bottle of tea. "Please drink this, and let's focus on the good news, okay?"

She takes the warm bottle of liquid from me, drinking over half of it. "Wh-what's the good news?"

"That'a girl." I smile as I hold up the beheaded snake. "We've got breakfast."

A sad smile pulls at her lips as she wipes the tears from her eyes. "Does it really taste like chicken?" she smirks.

"Yeah," I laugh, "It tastes like chicken and sweet, sweet revenge."

This earns me Gwen's very first authentic laugh. She throws her head back and cackles, and the sound is music to my ears.

If I could bottle up Gwen's laughter, I'd wear it around my neck and never take it off.

This woman's slowly wrapping me around her finger so tightly that I'd do just about anything to make her smile.

***

After we feast on our revenge breakfast, which just so happens to be the best damn meal of my life, we take a long walk on the beach.

I know I need to be working through a plan to get us out of here, and I have some ideas brewing around in my head, but after the near-death experience this morning, I just want to relax and have a little fun. We're walking along the shore when I get an idea.

"How about we have a sandcastle contest?" I suggest.

Gwen's lazy steps come to a stop as she turns to look at me. "You want to make sandcastles?" She laughs. "Do you really think that's the best use of our time?"

I shrug, "Why not? I'm confident I can catch a fish before dinner, and we've still got some leftover papaya. Let's have a little fun today, and tomorrow, we can work on a plan to get us out of here."

She studies me before asking, "Do you need content or something?"

"No." I place my hands on her shoulders, looking her in the eyes. "I just want to play. You know, have a little fun?"

She shakes her head like she doesn't understand.

"Fun. You know, something you do just because you want to ... not for any other reason?" I press.

A small smile pulls at her lips, and she nods. "Ok, Jack. Show me how to have fun."

"It would be my greatest honor to teach you how to play." I offer her my hand. "Come on. We'll need some supplies before we can get started."

We spend the next hour gathering random sea trash, more water bottles, a couple of mismatched flip-flops, and seashells of all sizes. When I feel like we've got enough supplies, we pile them in a heap between us.

"So, the rules go like this, you can use anything in this pile to make your sand castle, and we have one hour to build the most unique structure possible. The person who utilizes the most trash in their design wins."

She lifts a brow and crosses her arms over her chest, "Then can I technically just make a pile of trash and call it good?"

"Absolutely not. That's cheating. Your sandcastle has to be made up of ..." I tap my lip as I think, "eighty percent sand."

"That's rather technical, don't you think? Who's going to be the judge?" She looks around mockingly.

"You're right." I twist my lips to the side as I try to think of a solution. "Whoever makes the tallest sandcastle—using twenty percent trash—wins."

She shakes her head and laughs. "This is the most ridiculous game I've ever played ... I hope you're ready to lose!" Then she takes off in a sprint toward the water to collect her first batch of wet sand.

My smile stretches so far across my face that it hurts, and fuck, if it's not the best feeling in the world.

"Hey, wait up! That's cheating! I didn't say go!"

"You're just jealous that you didn't think to use the condom to add stability." I shrug.

"No, I'm not!" she argues. "I can't believe you actually touched a used condom in the first place!"

"How else was I supposed to ensure my tower wouldn't fall? The condom stuffed full of wet sand was the perfect structure. Besides, you can't deny that tying that knot around the tip as a flag gave my castle a prestigious quality that your basic sand castle just didn't possess."

I shrug., continuing my defense, "Not only was my sand castle taller, stronger, and more practical in the face of danger, but it was creative." I tap my temple. "Just admit it. I'm a better sand castle architect. Those are just the facts."

"You certainly have had more experience playing in the sand than me," she scoffs. "But I'll have you know that my tower was beautiful ... more of a feminine energy if you will."

"Let's call a spade a spade. Your tower looked like two boobs —complete with delicately crafted areolas—"

"And your's was a giant dick!" she interrupts.

"A strong and quite endowed sand dick." I correct her. "Which fit the criteria for winning." I wink.

"Yeah, yeah. Maybe so, but I still think mine was more beautiful. I used flower petals as the areolas. That's thinking out of the box!"

"How about we call it a tie?" I concede, offering her my hand.

"I don't want your pity, Jack." She turns to walk away, and I scoop her up, tossing her over my shoulders as I run into the ocean, letting the cool waves crash over us.

She squeals and kicks and clings to me tightly, and I don't let her go, not for a minute, soaking up this rare moment of peace between us.

"Come on," I say after I feel thoroughly refreshed. "Let's get cleaned up for dinner. I think we should celebrate our small victory."

"What victory is it you're referring to exactly?" she presses.

"We've gone almost an entire day without fighting." I smirk as I carry her out of the water and gently place her down. "And that calls for a special treat. I'm going to see what I can catch for dinner. Why don't you go get cleaned up?"

She studies me for a moment, then finally speaks, "Don't get used to it. I was off my game today. I can't make any promises about tomorrow."

"I'd expect nothing less."

A few hours later, we're sitting around the campfire with our bellies full of fresh fish and oysters, still laughing and arguing over who technically won the sand castle contest.

My heart flutters in my chest every time Gwen giggles, and

if I had to relive this day over again, I'd do it a thousand times, except for the near-death experience this morning, of course.

I take Gwen's empty plate—technically, it's just a flat rock. "Allow me to do the dishes. Are you ready for your surprise now?"

She clasps her hands together in delight. "As long as it's not another disgusting fish eyeball... or eggs."

"Don't worry. It's not." I stand to leave. "I'll be right back."

I take off toward the tent, and once inside, I dig through my survival bag, grabbing the rum and two coconuts I've been saving before I make my way back to the fire.

From a distance, I watch her bent over the fire, poking it with a stick. She looks natural; her shoulders are softer than I've seen them, and her eyebrows aren't all scrunched up—like how she usually looks around me. It's nice. She looks like she's at peace.

"Close your eyes," I call as I climb the last rock on my way back to her. I have the coconuts pinned underneath each arm as my hands cradle a full bottle of rum.

She looks up through hooded eyes, and my heart feels like it could explode.

"Where did you get that?" she gasps.

"It's actually something I keep for emergencies, to clean wounds. You'd be surprised at how frequently it comes in handy."

"Are you sure we should drink it, then?" Her eyes pull together in worry.

"Ah, it's eighty proof. It won't hurt for us to have just a little. Besides, all work and no play makes Jack a dull boy."

"Really, you're quoting *The Shining* now?"

I dig my knife into the coconut to create a small hole and pass it to her. "Drink this one first, so I know you're hydrated.

We've got to be extra careful since we've been in the sun all day."

Her eyes go wide at my command, and surprisingly, she obeys, turning the coconut up and letting the water drip into her soft, pretty mouth.

That mouth I remember all too well. *Fuck, get it together, man. This is definitely not the time to think about her like that.* Though I'd be lying if I said the memory of that night didn't cross my mind every time she bends over in that ridiculous dress-thing or when she wipes the sweat from her brow with the back of her hand.

I snap out of my daydream when she passes the coconut back to me. I shake it, satisfied that she drank most of the liquid inside.

"I know I may have already mentioned it... but I really hate coconut."

I laugh. "Well, babe, I hate to break it to you, but the coconuts are survival 101. Frankly, we're lucky they're so plentiful around here." I break the coconut in half over a rock and slice the meat to loosen it before pouring a generous amount of rum over the top. "Sorry, I don't have a straw and a little umbrella."

Gwen rolls her eyes and takes the peace offering. "Cheers" She clanks her coconut to mine, and we both throw back the liquor without even wincing.

"I think I'll have another," she says before I'm even finished.

I crack my knuckles and wink. "Another Jack Manning special coming right up, m'lady."

CHAPTER FOURTEEN

Gwen

The cool, salty breeze blows my hair back from my face, and my body hums in response. From the crackling fire and the sound of the ocean's steady waves crashing along the shore, and of course, the three coconut rums, I can't help but feel relaxed.

Jack and I have moved to the side of the fire, where there's a break in the trees above us. We're lying on our backs, giggling as we recall the events of the last couple of days.

"I swear to god, if I knew Betty White was going to crash anyway, I would've let you suck me off as we went down. I can't think of a better send-off than that!"

I elbow him in the side. "You're so confident that I would've followed through, are you?" I chomp my teeth, "I think medicated Gwen could be pretty feisty. I don't know if you and your dick would've made it out alive."

Jack flinches as he ponders this and lays his head back down in his hands. "Yeah, maybe you're right. Besides, I don't know what that crooked can-opener tooth in the front is capable of. My dick could've been mangled beyond repair." He laughs.

I gasp, covering my mouth. "You asshole! How dare you bring my crooked tooth into this! I'll have you know, I've only had rave reviews from my oral skills, crooked tooth and all." I rub my tongue over the rogue bottom tooth. Besides that, my smile is damn near perfect.

"I'm just teasing." He nudges me. "I think your snaggle tooth is hot as fuck."

I blush, feeling a warm tingle work its way from the top of my neck to my toes. I rub my tongue over my tooth and smile. "It used to be straight. I had the most expensive orthodontic plan money could buy." I pause, considering how open I feel like being tonight. But there's something about how he's looking at me that makes me want to share all my secrets with him like he's got some kind of spell on me that's slowly pulling down my layers.

"I feel like there's more to this story..." he presses.

I roll my eyes and give in. "Of course, my parents insisted on braces as soon as I was old enough to have them. How could you have a perfect daughter without a perfect smile to go along with it. After I moved out and distanced myself, I decided to quit wearing my retainer. It was my very first tiny act of rebellion, so even though my smile is flawed, I kind of love it just the way it is." I beam.

"I knew you were a rebel with a cause. Watch out, world, or she might hit you with a retainer strike," he teases, then lightly boops me on the nose. It's a playful gesture that would've enraged me a few weeks ago, but somehow, Jack makes it endearing.

"You have no idea the kind of grudge I'm capable of holding, Jack Manning. You better watch yourself, or you may find a detached ponytail laying next to your head in the morning." I giggle.

"You wouldn't!"

"Oh, I would."

"So, what must life as a stubborn rich girl from Atlanta have been like to make you resort to such harsh retaliation?" Jack says through a cheeky smile.

"Technically Buckhead Village, it's a suburb outside Atlanta." I correct him. "And growing up wealthy isn't all it's cracked up to be." I offer him a forced smile. "I know. I know. Poor little Gwen, it must've been so hard growing up having everything your heart desired."

"I didn't say that. Don't put words in my mouth." He pushes a strand of hair behind my ear, letting his fingers linger on my cheek before pulling away. "Having money doesn't always mean happiness. Believe me, I see that every day, dealing with all of these rich kid pricks."

I look down at my hands and nod. "Yeah, my dad's this self-made rags-to-riches businessman, so he expected a lot from me." I sigh. "It seemed like nothing I ever did was good enough. Mix that with my mother's hyper-critical opinion of my appearance ... and you get this." I open my arms wide. "A workaholic perfectionist who doesn't know how to relax." I scoff. "You must be exhausted being around me this long. I don't know how you haven't tried to ditch me yet."

Jack's eye bore into me like he's examining my innermost thoughts under a microscope, and though I try to force a smile to play off my embarrassing moment of vulnerability, he doesn't match my smile. "I don't think I could ever tire of someone who cares so much about what they love. Maybe you see it as neurotic, but I see someone who's dependable, hardworking, and tough."

I suck in a breath, his kind words are like a balm on my

lacerated heart, and he slides over, putting our mouths so close I can almost taste him. "I can't help but notice you're speaking of them in past tense…"

"Well, when it was time to decide what I wanted for my future… I guess we didn't share the same vision. I started out on the path to law school like my parents always dreamed of, but I was miserable and hated everything about that life. So after my first semester, I transferred schools to pursue a communications degree… and then they cut me off." I shrug like it's no big deal.

I don't know what's got me so loose-lipped tonight, if it's the long day in the sun or the rum or just a combination of the two, but I feel safe here with Jack, so my secrets just seem to be seeping out.

"I'm so sorry you had to go through that." His fingers trace along my forearm, and my heart races from the contact. It's a comforting gesture laced with something I can't put my finger on. When our eyes meet, his look is serious and protective.

"It's fine. I'm happier now that I'm not constantly vying for their approval. It's freeing to finally let myself decide who I want to be rather than my parents." I roll onto my back, so I'm looking up at the night sky.

Of course, Jack wouldn't know anything about suffering or pain. From what I see, I bet he has two loving parents who poured all they had into him, supported him, and encouraged him to grow up to be whatever he wanted. You can just tell when people come from loving homes, and Jack's lack of worry about anything in the world tells me he's always felt safe to be himself fully. It's what annoyed me most after getting to know him. His joy about his career and life is like a searing hot fire poker burning me every time I get close.

"So, how about you? Do you have parents waiting on your safe return back in—"

"Tennessee," he answers. "Yeah, although I don't visit them

as much as I probably should." A warm smile spreads across his face, "I've got four sisters, too. And three nieces and two nephews."

"Wow. And you're close to *all* of them?" I ask, a bit surprised. I can't imagine having a family that large.

"Oh, yeah. My parents are the coolest people. My mom's a high school history teacher, and my dad just retired from the fire department last year."

"The All-American family," I add.

"I guess you can say that. I grew up with two loving parents. I've always been close with my sisters. Growing up and seeing them all go through puberty and rage with hormones taught me more than I cared to know about women." He grins. "It's why I'm such a ladies' man. I understand the way it all works." He gestures over my body, and I laugh out loud. The arrogance of this man. He truly believes he's got some kind of superpower that other men will never know.

"Ok, Casanova. You can stop your bragging," I mock him, looking around. "I don't think there's anyone around to overhear the bullshit. You're safe to drop the act."

"It's not an act, just the truth. Anyway, I know I've had a leg up on most people, and I think that's why I had the confidence to break away from the traditional workforce so young." He shrugs. "I've always been lucky knowing that my family would support me no matter what. It's unfair, but it's why I do what I do. I want to inspire people, show them there's another way to make a living, but mostly to show them just how awesome this world actually is... if only they'd slow down long enough to see it." He smiles, pulling his hands behind his head as he looks up at the stars.

A strange mix of jealousy and endearment crash together in my chest, and I don't know what to make of it. Lying underneath the stars with Jack Manning, sharing pieces of myself that I've never spoken of to anyone, isn't something I ever expected, but it's somehow exactly what my calloused heart needed. I wipe the lone tear that falls from the corner of my eye, hoping Jack doesn't notice as the crackling of the campfire fill in the space between all the words left unsaid.

Maybe in another life, I could be so lucky to be born into a family where I didn't have to earn love, but the more time I spend with Jack, the more I realize maybe things don't always have to be such a struggle. Maybe it really is okay to let myself rest every once in a while?

"Why don't we sleep out here under the stars tonight?' Jack's soothing voice breaks me from my thoughts. It's as if he knows I've shared more than I feel comfortable with and need some time to recover from my vulnerability hangover.

"That sounds nice." I turn on my side and pull my knees up to my chest, sinking into the sandy earth. It's a far cry from a five-star hotel, but somehow, I find comfort grounded in the earth blanketed by a sheet of stars and moonlight.

I let myself relax into the warm sand, and for the first time in a long time, I don't dream of work but rather sandcastles, waves, and forest green eyes that seem to watch over me as I sleep.

CHAPTER FIFTEEN

Gwen

I squint open my eyes as the morning sun peeks over the horizon. It's still dark out, but there's a pink and purple hue to the sky that you just don't see in Chicago ... or maybe I've just never made time to see it?

Regardless, it's a beautiful day. Perhaps it's the sunrise or the brisk ocean breeze, but this morning, I feel hopeful. I roll on my side, straight into Jack's enormous chest. If it wasn't for my screaming bladder, I think I'd curl into him, stealing whatever comfort I could get away with. Besides, who could blame me if I were sleeping?

The thought of Sandra's onboarding process flashes through my mind. A whole day devoted to HR protocols and case studies about employee/client relations. We even had an acting segment where we had to resist the charms of some extremely attractive male strippers while Sandra watched behind double-sided glass. You'd be surprised about how many we lost that day.

It's never been an issue. Until now.

It's almost comical, really, that I was so concerned about losing my job over fraternizing with a client when I'm literally stranded on a deserted island with him. Even if we manage to make it out of here alive, somehow, the idea of losing my job isn't as scary as it was before. I don't know if it was my near-death experience yesterday or last night's confession, but I feel like all the annoyance I felt for Jack is quickly being replaced with something else... Curiosity, maybe?

Everything about the man's everything's-going-to-be-ok demeanor infuriates me, but at the same time, I've never met someone who makes me feel so safe and whole. I feel like I can breathe when I'm around Jack, but maybe it's just the whole deserted paradise island thing? Or maybe someone's finally getting through to my tiny little Grinch heart?

My bladder spasms again, bringing me back to the urgency of the situation. I have to hold in my whimper of frustration. I don't think I've ever been quite so comfortable, but unless I want to piss myself, which I don't think Jack would be too happy about, I need to find a bush... fast.

I roll over a few times until I'm far enough away to stand without jarring Jack awake. I see his backpack from the corner of my eye and remember the small package of tissue. I know it's probably a waste, using the last of the rations for a number one emergency, but this day feels like something that should be celebrated. I think it over and decide to treat myself. I mean, who knows what tomorrow will hold anyway? Jack could accidentally fall in the ocean or something and get the tissues wet. Then I'd wish I'd splurged.

I carefully unzip the backpack, squatting just a few feet away from Jack. I don't want to wake him. Between building new shelters, fishing, and making fires, it seems all he does is physical labor. I guess that's where all his muscles are made. Jack Manning is sculpted by the land, not the gym, and somehow, I find that incredibly attractive.

I stick my hand into the deep, dark backpack, feeling around until I find the nearly empty bag of tissues. It's wrapped around something firm, and when I pull it out to examine it, I'm holding the barrel of the flare gun. *Our only hope of survival*, I hear Jack's words.

Just as I start to place the flare gun back in the bag, something moves across the sky, catching my eye.

No. It can't be. I hesitate for a moment, remembering how my wandering off almost got me killed the day before. I glance over at Jack and bite my lip, he'll be furious with me, but this may be our only chance of being rescued.

I grab the flare gun and take off in a sprint toward the beach. My adrenaline kicks in, giving me a temporary distraction from the urge to pee my pants, and I watch each step as carefully as possible, making sure to look for any signs of snakes along my path.

I squint, shielding my eyes with my hand from the bright morning sun that's now peeking through the clouds, and I see the faint hint of what I think is an airplane. "Oh my God!" I cover my mouth in disbelief. "We're saved!"

I watch the plane slowly move across the sky, and it's like a timer counting down the seconds until our ultimate demise. I wave my hands in the air, screaming like a maniac for a few seconds, but the plane keeps flying in the same direction.

Okay, that was stupid. I don't know what I was expecting, but I need to get their attention while I have the chance. I square my shoulders, knowing exactly what I need to do. I sprint in the direction of the waterfall because that's the island's highest point that I know of. Bursting through dense grass and trees, I feel myself earning more whips and cuts on my bare legs with every step I take, but I don't care. I can tend to my wounds on my cushy ride back home, where I will never set foot on a campsite ever again. This will all be behind me, and I'll make Jack swear to never speak of last night... or the engagement party ever again.

Heaving breathlessly, I finally make it to the waterfall. I'm running full speed ahead, ready to shoot my one and only shot, when my foot sinks into a mud puddle. Only, when I try to pull it out, it's like a Chinese finger trap, squeezing my foot harder the more I struggle.

"Are you fucking kidding me right now!?" I scream as I try to yank my foot free, but the plane is moving farther away. I know what I have to do, and although the circumstances aren't ideal, this is my moment to save us.

I stand up as straight as I can, point the flare toward the sky and hold my breath as I pull the trigger on one, two, thr–

"Gwen, stop!" I hear Jack's voice and turn to find him running toward me right before I pull the trigger. My foot sinks lower into an air pocket or something, causing me to fall on my ass in the mud.

In a matter of seconds, our chance at survival is completely lost, and I'm rapidly sinking into a huge pile of what smells like shit, but what my kindergarten education tells me is quicksand. I struggle to pull myself out, but it's no use. The more I fight, the faster the mud swallows me whole.

Suddenly, my fond feelings toward Jack are pissed away, just like our chances of survival. The mud slinks up my neck, and my arms are completely buried by now. "You fucking idiot!" I scream. "You distracted me and ruined our chance of survival!"

Jack's doubled over, clearly winded from his own sprint up

the hill. I'm surprised to hear him chuckling as he clicks on the camera and places it on a tripod across from me.

"Well, Dubbies, it seems our Gwenny-Poo has found herself in a bit of pickle." He squats down next to me as the mud rises to my chin.

"Stop filming me! I do not consent to this!" I spit a disgusting wad of sand from my mouth in his direction. "I was about to save our lives, you jerk!"

Jack laughs again. "Oh, Gwenny, that was a commercial aircraft, flying more than thirty thousand feet high. There's no way they'd even see the tiny flare from that high, much less do anything about it. They're on auto-pilot, baby. You can thank *me* for distracting you."

"You're such an ass!" I say, turning my chin up to keep my mouth and nose above the rapidly rising sand. "Help me out of here. It smells like ass cheese and diarrhea!"

"Ass cheese and diarrhea? That's a unique combo." He's squatting next to me now, no doubt enjoying this far too much. "If you want my help, all you have to do is say, 'Jack, I need you', and I'll save you," he singsongs.

I hurt my eyes from rolling them so hard, and for a moment, I contemplate if being eaten alive by Satan's asshole is how I want to go out, but when the sand rises higher, getting in my mouth, I finally cave. I exhale, repeating his phrase as quietly as possible.

"Oh, babe, I didn't hear you? Could you please repeat that for the viewers at home?" Jack teases.

"Fine!" I scream. "Jack, I need you!" just as the sand rises over my face.

He only waits a moment before I feel his strong arms on me, pulling me out of the shit hole into safety.

As he drags me out, my feelings for the golden man

brimming with sunshine fade to more of a turd-stained skid mark.

"I hate you," I heave once free from the sand-sphincter.

"You're welcome, Gwenny-Poo." Jack laughs as he tells the camera what to do in the event that you find yourself alone in quicksand.

I guess I really should've watched the show ahead of time.

CHAPTER SIXTEEN

Jack

Last night was the most fun I've had in a very long time, and I slept like a Goddamn baby, despite my ever-growing blue balls that seem to be my body's new normal. So you can imagine my surprise when I was awakened by the sound of Gwen digging through my backpack.

At first, I thought she was looking for a snack or something, but when I saw her pull out the flare gun, pointing it around like she was afraid it would go off at any moment just because she was holding it, I had to follow her to see what she was up to.

And I'm happy as fuck that I did.

"I'll take this." I carefully remove the muddy flare gun from her grip, placing it safely in my backpack, saying a silent prayer of thanks that she didn't completely ruin our chances of being saved. "Come on." I offer her my hand. "Let's get you cleaned up. You smell like a turd covered in burned hair."

She rolls her eyes, ignoring my extended hand, and pushes

herself up. "I don't think I need any more help from you," she huffs. "I hope you got the footage you needed."

I know she's being passive-aggressive, but I don't bite. "Actually, yeah, this was great." I gesture to the sinkhole behind me as I gently steer her along the trail I made on the way here. "I never thought I'd get actual raw footage of something like that. Besides, you should've seen your face right before you went under." I laugh. "I can already see the memes!"

"Well, isn't that wonderful? I'm sure Sandra will be so proud to have Éclat representation in the form of near-death by suffocation."

"I agree. I'm glad we're on the same page." I laugh. I know she's mad right now and probably a little embarrassed, but the way I see it, I've just saved her life thrice. How many more times before she stops fighting and finally trusts me?

We finally make it back to the campsite, and I scoop her into my arms and carry her to the ocean to wash off. I drop her into the waist-deep water, calling over my shoulder as I walk away. "Get cleaned up and put on a swimsuit. After your bath, I'm teaching you to fish."

"But... I don't want—"

I hold my hand up, interrupting her. "That wasn't a question. I'll see you in a bit." Then I leave, giving her some privacy.

I've packed my retractable noodle rod, but since I only have one, I've spent the morning carving a spear out of some dried bamboo. It's long enough to keep Gwen from having to go too deep but short enough to control. When I see Gwen walking toward me clad in nothing but a bright white string bikini, my mouth goes dry, and all my blood rushes to my cock. Shit. That's not what I expected.

"Take a picture. It'll last longer," she teases and spins in a circle giving me the full view.

Her perky tits are scantily covered by two nearly-sheer white triangles, and her plump, round ass is completely exposed in the back. "Is that a thong?" I all but shout, feeling jealous and protective even though we're the only two people on this island.

"Yes, it's a thong bikini. Haven't you been to the beach before?"

"It's underwear. You're wearing underwear as a swimsuit? Please tell me you don't wear that in public."

"Jack, have you seen my ass?" She turns around again to make sure I get the full view. "Of course, I wear this in public." She pauses. "Well, at least I *planned* on wearing it in public when I bought it for this trip."

"So, I'm the first guy to see you in this?"

"Um, yeah, I guess."

"Good." I breathe a sigh of relief, not exactly sure what I'm relieved about. It's not like Gwen and I are a thing. We had spontaneous wild sex once in a broom closet. I can't deny I'm attracted to her, but as I've gotten to know her better, it feels like more than just a carnal desire. Protection oozes out of every pore in my body, making me want to pee in a circle around her to make sure no one even looks her way, much less tries to sleep with her.

"Get your sexy ass over here and help me catch some bait. I hope that bikini is comfortable because we've got a long day ahead of us."

She props her hands on her hips in a challenge, "I walk around downtown Chicago in stilettos every day while freezing my ass off in the name of fashion. I think I can handle paradise in a bikini."

"That makes one of us," I mumble under my breath.

I pull my camera from my backpack and motion for Gwen to come over as I secure the camera around her chest. "Because you look like pinup Tinkerbell in the hot little bikini, I have no choice but to put you behind the camera for today's filming." She rolls her eyes but doesn't argue as I strap the camera to her chest.

"Don't you think you'd get more views if I were in front of the camera?" She winks.

"Those aren't the kind of views that will grow my channel," I say as I graze the side of her breast when tightening the velcro. Her breath hitches at my touch. At least I know I'm not the only one feeling sparks around here.

I switch the camera on and begin my intro. "Hey, Dubbies. Today, we're up at the ass crack of dawn for a fun-filled day of fishing. My special guest will be behind the camera today, so I apologize for the video quality in advance." I send her a wink, but the viewers will definitely think it's for them. "As you all know, you've got to have bait to catch fish, so before we get to catching our meals for the day, we're here in a shallow tidepool catching whatever small fish we can find to use as bait."

Last night while Gwen was sleeping, I was busy weaving a couple of baskets with palm leaves for us to use to hold whatever fish we catch.

We wade into the shallow water, and I can't help myself; I glance back, seeing Gwen's nipples harden in the cold water. I'm such a pig, but fuck, I can't help myself. I play it off like I'm talking to the camera and say something about the tides in the early morning and the best places to find bait.

There are several large rocks where we're standing, so I show the viewers and Gwen an easy way to find fresh food.

"Look down at your feet, at the rocks. Do you see those little knot-like things?"

She nods, and I walk over, pulling my pocket knife from my belt. I pry one loose and hold it up to the camera in front of Gwen's tits, having to bend down slightly for the shot. Fighting to keep my eyes on the camera lens, I hold up the crustacean. "You know what they say about oysters." I use my knife to scoop out the meat and make a show of dropping it in my mouth. "Not only are they one of nature's finest aphrodisiacs, but oysters are a quick and easy source of protein. This is something that could literally save your life if you don't have the equipment to fish."

I pry another loose from the rock and scoop it out with my knife, offering it to Gwen. "You'll need your strength today. Eat up."

She curls her lip in disgust. "Uh uh. Nope. I'm not eating a slimy sea booger."

"Would you prefer a crunchy sea booger?" I make a show of looking around, knowing the viewers will love this banter. "Sorry, babe, I don't have any crunchies available right now. I guess we can let it sit out in the sun and shrivel up for a little while, but then you'll probably have to—"

"Uh!" she huffs. "Just give me the damn booger!"

I laugh and dangle it above her mouth, knowing the camera can't see, and this is just for me.

"Open wide." My eyes crinkle as I try to hold in my laugh.

To my delight, she opens up and lets me feed her the oyster. I place the slimy creature in her mouth, and she sucks it from my fingers, rolling her tongue around my finger after.

"You know," she chews it for a moment and swallows, "it reminds me of something… but I can't quite put my finger on it."

Well, I guess that backfired. I turn my back to the camera, so she doesn't catch sight of my erection on film, and I grab another oyster, this time for bait. "It's the first cast of the morning, my favorite time of day," I call over my shoulder.

We collect a few more oysters for breakfast and keep the

rest to use as bait, which we'll use to catch smaller fish to also use as bait.

"How is that not bait? Why do we need to catch more?" Gwen asks.

And I know she didn't mean to set me up so perfectly, but damn, we really work well together. "The oysters will only attract these small fish, which aren't very good for eating." I hold up the fish, showing the camera. "See, there really isn't much meat there, so if we use smaller fish as bait, we can catch something bigger that will sustain us and be better worth our time and energy." I collect the small fish into one of the baskets, then dip the basket in water to keep them fresh. "Of course, we'll have to find some deeper water if we want to catch bigger fish."

Luckily, I've scouted out this side of the island and have a pretty good idea of where I want to try to fish, so we turn off the camera and make our hike.

Gwen trudges along behind me, wearing mismatched flip-flops I found on the beach. Her leather platform sandals have long been destroyed, so we've made do the best we could. Though she isn't complaining, I know after the mile trek, she's got to be in pain.

"How are you holding up back there?" I call over my shoulder.

She grunts in response, and when I peer back, I can see the pain in her eyes. I want so badly to scoop her up, to carry her the rest of the way, so she doesn't feel any pain or have to work for anything. But I know if I want any chance of finding us help, she'll need to handle this. So I go against everything in me. "Buck up, buttercup. What was all that stiletto talk back there?"

She flips me the bird, and we continue our trek to the sounds of Gwen's grunts and swearing.

We finally reach the deeper water, but we're on a cliff of

sorts. We need to climb down to the lower rock if we want any chance of catching something with the rod. I assess the routes we could take, all of which are covered in loose sharp stones. There's no way she'll make it down there without slicing something open, and we don't have time for an injury setback.

"Hey, Gwenny!" I say in my most charming voice. "How good of a swimmer are you?"

Her eyebrows pull together as she looks around the rock as if searching for a nearby swimming pool. She most certainly isn't thinking what I'm thinking.

"Why?" she draws the word out skeptically.

I catch sight of her cut-up feet and wince. The cuts aren't too deep, so she'll be fine, but I need to find her better footwear soon. I rub my palms together and grin. I turn the camera on and bend down, so I'm in the frame. I could really get used to talking to Gwen's tits while filming. I think it's my new favorite thing. "Ok, Dubbies, Gwenny here won't be able to climb down the rocks safely, so I've got a little surprise for her." I walk backward, guiding her by her shoulders toward the cliff's edge. "Do you trust me?" I grin ear to ear.

Once she realizes what I have in mind, she tries to bolt, but I catch her around the waist, angling the camera toward the ocean, and whisper in her ear, "Come on, baby, do it for the viewers. I promise I'll be right there to pull you up."

"Fuck the viewers! I'm not jumping off a cliff for reality television!" She's kicking now, fighting me with every ounce of her strength, and I can't help but laugh because it's really not that far, and it's actually the safest way to get her down there.

"Ok, ok, just relax. I won't make you jump." I set her down, and as soon as her feet touch the rocky ground, I shove her as hard as I can off the cliff, ensuring she lands in the deep water underneath.

Gwen screams like a banshee until I hear her body splash in

the water. I wait a moment for her head to pop above the water's surface, and then I rush down the steep rocky cliff to rescue my girl. I have a feeling she's going to make me pay for that, and I can't say I'm not excited to see her feisty side come out again. I've come to realize that feisty Gwen is my favorite person on this island, and that says a lot because I think pretty highly of myself.

"You bastard! I could have died!" Her flushed face is bright red, and the water is so clear I can see her tiny bikini shifting beneath the surface with every wave. She's struggling to keep her head above the water, her arms flailing, and I'm not really sure what her feet are doing, but I wouldn't call it *swimming*.

"I thought you said you could swim!" I scold her, half laughing but half concerned. She's several feet away from the rock, and as the waves crash around her, she's drifting farther away from me.

"No, you asked me if I was a good swimmer, and I said 'Why'!" she yells before her head goes underwater from a wave.

I wait a moment for her head to pop back up. "You swim like shit! What's with the doggy-paddle bullshit? Kick your fucking legs!"

I see the puzzled look on her face like she's trying to think through the movements, and another wave crashes over her head.

This time, I stand up, shed my backpack and shirt, and dive in to retrieve her. It takes me several minutes before I reach her, and when I do, I pull her to me, keeping her head above the water. Her lips are trembling, not from the cool temperature but from fear, and I feel like the biggest asshole alive.

"Come here, baby." I pull her into my arms and plant a kiss on her temple. "Gwen, look at me." I wrap her legs around my waist, so she doesn't have to work while I keep us afloat. "I'm sorry. I thought you were a better swimmer, and I never would've pushed you if I knew." I hug her to my chest, pressing her body tight against mine as our hearts beat in unison. "I'm so fucking sorry. I feel like such a dick."

She nods, tucking her head back into the crease of my neck and squeezing me around my chest. I spin her around, so she's on my back as I swim to the rock. I don't even bother to lift her onto it. I just climb the rock with her on my back.

When I sit on the edge, she shoves her face between her knees, and I don't have to look to know she's crying.

I give her space for a moment before pulling her into my arms, where I apologize profusely. Promising never to put her in harm's way again. I'm learning there's more to Gwen than meets the eye, and I decide to make it my mission to learn everything there is to know about this amazing woman.

CHAPTER SEVENTEEN

Gwen

I feel like such a fool for trusting him. Of course, he made me feel like an idiot ... again. Falling and crashing into that cold water reminded me so much of one of the worst days of my life. It's why I hate swimming, and it was the first time I lost trust in the people who were supposed to care about me the most.

But Jack didn't know that. How could he?

I wipe the traitorous tears from my eyes and inhale a deep breath in and out, grounding myself. Though it's not exactly as safe of a moment as I'm used to, at least there's solid ground underneath me.

I know Jack would never hurt me on purpose, and what he did was innocent, well, mostly. He thought I was a better swimmer, and under any other circumstances, I am. But something about the falling, being pushed, and the shrill splash of the water sent me back in time. I was ten years old all over again, and all the fear I felt that day bubbled up to the surface.

"Gwen, I really am sorry." Jack places a gentle hand on my

shoulder, and I reflexively flinch. He stops dead in his tracks and squats down to face me. "I know I fucked up, but shit. Did you think I was going to *hit* you?"

"Of course not." I shake my head and stand up, adjusting my bikini that's all kinds of twisted. To Jack's credit, he doesn't even sneak a peek. "I think the water just knocked the wind out of me, and I was stunned. I'm totally fine."

Jack clicks his tongue, studying me, but he doesn't press the subject. "Well, I guess we better get to fishing then, huh?" He passes me his small rod and shows me how and where to cast. Explaining how the fish pool in the tidepools.

"Here," he passes me the bait and rod. "I want to see you do it on your own."

To my surprise, he removes the camera from my chest strap —which has been continuously rolling the entire time—and carefully frames me in the shot. "Sorry, Dubbies. This one'll be a close-up. I can't have you feasting your eyes on Gwenny's goodies, now can I? You know I'm a jealous bastard."

My cheeks heat at his admission, but I'm brought back to the moment when he shoves the small flopping fish into my hand along with the reel. "Have a go of it. I hope your fishing is a hell of a lot better than your doggy paddle."

I can't help but laugh, his teasing blotting out the flashback fighting its way to the forefront of my mind. Jack has a way of doing that, totally encompassing everything and everyone around him. It's like he owns every room he's in—or island, in this case. Right now, I'm grateful for his big, cocky *personality*.

"Eww!" The slimy fish flops in my palm, and I grit my teeth, wanting to get this right. To prove to myself that I can do this, even though it goes against all of m instincts.

I go to jab it in the center and remember his prior instruction just as he says, "Right through the eyeball."

"I know!" I sneer, shoving the small hook right through the

poor fish's eyeball, so he'll wiggle away, and hope some other bigger fish will take a bite at him. I reach back, and with a gentle flick of my wrist, I cast the reel right into the tidepool. The water is so clear I can see several medium-sized fish swimming around, and I hold my breath and wait. As I wait, Jack reels in several fish and collects a few more oysters, and I get more and more frustrated. I see the fish swimming by my line and pausing, but none bite. Finally, one stops, and I feel it.

Tug. Tug. Tug.

My heart races. "Jack! I got a bite!" I squeal.

"That's it, babe!" He moves to my side, talking me through it. "Now, slowly reel it in just as we practiced."

The fish tugs and fights and pulls, and I find myself stepping closer to the edge of the rock to give it a little slack. "I think it's a big one!"

Jack zooms the camera in as I begin to reel in my catch, and he hoots with delight when it finally comes into focus. "Babe! You caught a fish! On a noodle rod!" Bending down to grab the line, he takes the basket and uses it as a make-shift net, so the line doesn't snap.

When he pulls the basket up, he's wearing the biggest grin, and my heart swells with pride. It's a small thing, but I can't help the tightening in my throat as I watch him look at me like that. Like he's proud of me.

He unhooks the fish with some pliers and shows me how to hold it by the mouth. "Here, hold it like this, and don't fucking move. I want to get a shot of you with your first catch, but that goddamn bikini..." He shakes his head, and I don't know if it's in annoyance at my non-existent swimwear. "You know, Gwen, I think you'll be just fine after all. We're going to work on swimming lessons, though."

"What do you mean I'll be just fine?"

Jack hands me the basket of our fish and the rest of the

oysters and lifts me into a cradle as he maneuvers up the rocky cliff that he pushed me off several hours earlier.

"What are you doing? Let me down!" I kick and squirm, but it's no use. He only tightens his grip on my thigh.

"I think I've caused you enough pain for one day. Look at your feet."

I glance down and notice my bleeding feet. I'd hardly felt it before he pointed it out, probably from the adrenaline of being pushed off the side of a mountain and catching my very first fish.

"I'll carry you until we get back to the sandy ground. You just hold on to our dinner, ok?"

I nod and let my head rest on his chest, the rhythmic movements of his steps lulling my mind back to normal.

"What did you mean by 'I'll be just fine'?" I ask again.

"I didn't want to get into this just yet, but we've got some time, so I guess I'll tell you the plan." He pauses, all the playfulness leaving his voice.

"The plan? Like to get home?"

"Yeah. It's not completely final yet, but I've been working through some ideas about how to get us home. That's why I need you to know how to fish, to take care of yourself."

"What do you mean? Where are *you* going to be?" My eyebrows pull together in confusion.

He sighs. "I'm going to build a raft and set out to find help. I've been going over it in my head, and I think I know where we are. If I head north, it should only take me a few days to reach the other island." He pauses. "You'll stay here and stay out of trouble and wait for me to return with help."

I blink several times, trying to process this. I even check the stupid camera to see if he's filming because surely this is a joke and he just needs more blooper footage of me freaking the fuck out.

"No. Absolutely not!" I kick my legs for him to put me down, and when his grip tightens around me, I push my arms away from his chest.

"Watch it! You're going to drop all our shit!" he scolds. "I'm not putting you down until the ground is soft, so you can stop fighting me. You're only going to make yourself sore and lose our dinner."

"Jack, you can't just leave me *alone* on a deserted island to fend for myself. I'm coming with you."

"No. You're not!"

"Yes. I am!"

"Gwen, I threw you in the ocean today, and you froze. That half-ass doggy-paddle shit isn't going to fly in the middle of open water. There's no way we'd make it. I won't be able to keep you safe and get us out of here. You're a liability."

When we reach the sand, he sets me down carefully, one foot at a time, like I'm made of glass. Then continues his trek toward the campsite as if the conversation is over.

"What if a giant chimpanzee attacks the tent while I'm sleeping!? Have you seen *Planet of the Apes*? Jack, I can't fight off a pack of chimps by myself."

This makes him laugh. "If a pack of chimps decides to murder us in our sleep, I'm afraid there's nothing *I* can even do about that."

I run behind him to keep up. "You're not helping!"

"Well, it's not a negotiation, babe. I'll teach you all the basic survival skills you need before I leave. Don't worry about it, okay?"

"How? How am I not supposed to worry about it? What if a shark eats you? What kind of raft are you going to build to survive the ocean magically? What if you get lost at sea, and you never come back!?"

He stops abruptly, and I run straight into his backpack, the force giving me a canvas burn on my forehead. "Ow."

"Gwen, don't you trust me? I've got this. I'll get help, and I'll come for you, but I need you to listen to me and cooperate for this to work." His eyes scan my face. Though for what, I'm not sure. I don't know what comes over me, but I nod.

"Say you trust me," he whispers.

My breath hitches, and my throat tightens around the words. "I trust you." I manage.

A devious smile pulls at his lips, and he places a hand over his heart. "Aw, thanks, babe. You really know how to stroke a guy's ego."

I shake my head and laugh as a kaleidoscope of butterflies erupts in my belly. What is this man doing to me?

After we return to camp, the sun's high in the sky, which Jack says means it's close to noon. We have the leftover oysters for lunch, and Jack finds some edible plants that taste close enough to kale if I close my eyes and pretend. I'm grateful for the seemingly-normal cuisine.

After we've eaten and Jack's purified enough water for us to drink for the rest of the day—a lesson I will never forget—we get to work cleaning my fish for dinner.

"Do you have to keep the head on it like that?" I ask as Jack saws the medium-sized fish in half. "And the tail. That's just gross."

"Well, if we were in the states, yes, we'd cut the head and tail off for a more appetizing experience. But out here, we need all the calories we can get." He gestures toward my stomach, which seems to be shrinking by the day. I've always been on the thin side of curvy, but over the last four days on this island, I've noticed my bones protruding more than usual.

"I just feel like I shouldn't have to look the poor thing in the eye as I eat him. It feels disrespectful."

Jack laughs. "What's disrespectful is that pathetic excuse of a *bikini* you're wearing." His eyes scan up and down my body, and warmth pools at my center. I think about his large calloused hands; how they'd feel roaming my body; how his tongue felt in the broom closet.

What happened to the corporate follow-the-rules Gwen, and who is this carefree woman I'm slowly turning into? Maybe a part of me doesn't actually think we'll ever get off this island, so what's the point of denying ourselves all the pleasure we want? But the other part of me doesn't know what I want even if we *do* make it home.

I'm so confused.

"Penny for your thoughts?" Jack's question brings me back to the moment, and I blush.

"I was just thinking about home," I admit.

"Yeah? Anything in particular?"

"I don't know," I shrug. "It's just all of this." I look around at the cloudless sky, plush trees, and sandy beaches for as far as the eye can see. "This is so simple ... and peaceful. I guess it's kind of nice."

"Yeah?" He slides a skewer through the other half of the fish and covers them with the basket to keep any flies away until dinner. "You're not lonely for your work? You don't miss city life?"

His question makes me pause, and I consider it. I'm surprised when I shake my head as the realization hits me. "Not really. How about you?"

Jack stands, taking my hand to lead us closer to the beach. "Sometimes I think I could spend my whole life out here, alone, surviving off the land." He pauses. "But there's a part of me that wants more." He sighs. "You know the family, the house, the dog. But those are just pipe dreams," he says, his smile fading.

My eyebrows lift, astonished at his confession. "Who says you can't have it all, Jack?"

"I learned a long time ago that I'm not really cut out for long-term commitment. I change my mind too much. I need the freedom of all of this." He gestures around himself. "If I were to settle down, marry someone, start a family, it wouldn't be fair to them, and it wouldn't be fair to me either. I don't want to resent anyone. It's just the smartest move all around."

He leads me to sit down and comes behind me, straddling my body with his legs. Then he slides my hair over my shoulder to massage my back. His touch sends chills down my spine, and my sore muscles cry out in glee as his strong hands work out my knots.

An accidental whimper escapes, and I tense, not wanting him to tease me about being so soft. But he doesn't react. He just keeps his pace, rolling his knuckles in that heavenly motion as I melt into him. "So, no family, then?" I tease, poking him in the side.

He flinches. "I can't even take care of myself half the time." He rubs his brow. "It's not that I don't want a family. Lord knows my mother and sisters would lose their minds if I reproduced." His smile is so big now that I can see all of his perfectly straight white teeth. The contrast is so vivid next to his dark beard. "I just don't want to let anyone else down, ya know?"

"Who else have you let down?" The words fly out of my mouth before I can stop them.

Jack shrugs. "Well, for starters, you're here because of a fuck up of mine." He grimaces. "There's also the minor plane crash—"

"That one wasn't your fault," I add. "I mean, I hate to admit it, but it was my cell phone that ruined your navigation system." I grimace. "I really thought that the whole no cell phones on a plane thing was a myth. They should really emphasize that more, you know?"

This earns me a laugh. "They kinda do, but I suppose you've never been on such an old plane before." He boops me on the nose. "I'll agree. We can share the blame on that one." He straightens his shoulders. "But I could kick myself for causing the swimming incident today." He pulls at his long strands of hair in frustration. "It feels like everything I do puts you in more danger."

"How were you supposed to know I couldn't swim?" I say, trying my best to cheer him up. "Besides, you've literally saved my life like three times already." I lean back and nudge him with my shoulder. "I think you're selling yourself short. You could do anything you wanted to do. I really believe that."

"Anything?" He winks.

"*Almost* anything." I bite my lip. We're wading closer and closer into the unknown here, and I don't know whether I should run away or toward him.

"How about you? You want kids, the house, the dog?" He finds a knot, and I groan as he works it out with his thumb. God, this man really knows how to use his hands.

"I'm not sure." My answer comes out before I can second guess it. "I used to be completely closed off to the idea because my parents are so terrible, but the longer I'm away from the hustle and bustle of the city, I feel like maybe there's room for something else." I shrug. "I guess I'm still figuring myself out right now."

Jack's hands must have some type of truth serum—either that or the midday sun is hypnotizing me because I've never been this honest with anyone, not Elliot or Maggie. Hell, not even with myself.

"Well, I say there's no rush. You've got to follow your heart and let yourself discover what you want through your own experiences. Then when an opportunity presents itself, you'll know what you want because you've actually lived."

A small smile creeps up my face, and I lean into him, letting him wrap his arms around me. "Yeah, maybe so."

A quiet moment passes before I speak. "A dog, huh?"

Jack laughs, "That's what you took away from this conversation?"

"Well, yeah, dogs are awesome. What kind do you want?"

He runs his hands down my arms, which is quickly becoming one of my favorite sensations. I really don't know what I'll do when I don't have him caressing me to sleep every night.

"I think I'd like a Mini Australian Shepherd... named Sparky."

I laugh. "Don't be specific or anything."

"Well, you asked."

"If you know what you want, why don't you just go adopt a dog?"

He sighs, his hands finding my thighs now. "This isn't a steady life for a dog. I never know what country I'll be traveling to, and he'd spend more time with a dog-sitter than he'd actually with me. It'd be pointless."

"Or..." I say, "you could just bring him with you..."

Jack pauses for a moment as if he's considering it. "Nah, it's too dangerous. It's hard enough babysitting the rich pricks who think their social status makes them invincible. But that's not how mother nature works. She doesn't give a shit about who you are or where you came from. She doesn't discriminate." His tone softens to almost a whisper. "I think that's why I love what I do so much. And obviously, it's why Landon hired you in the first place."

I consider his words, and I'm both comforted by them and saddened. It seems like there's always a sacrifice to be made in life, and just when I thought Jack Manning had it all, I find out he's missing something he can't have.

I turn over in his arms, so I'm curled on my side with my head resting on his chest. "Well, personally, I think Sparky the Mini Australian Shepherd would be great for views." I sink into him further as his hand finds its way to my lower back, rubbing and caressing. It's not a sexual touch. Somehow, this feels more intimate than that; it feels safe.

"Fuck the views," he says with a snort. "I started this channel because it allowed me to travel the world and do all the shit I wanted to do. To experience life how I always wanted to live. I love my fans, but sometimes I wonder if I'm wasting my time here. If I'm really living up to my full potential. Like what's the point of any of it, shuffling rich pricks around the world like some kind of circus monkey? I want to empower people to take chances, embrace nature, and slow down to savor what's really important in life. Sometimes I feel like I'm missing the mark, like I'm just another sell-out trying to make a buck off views. Maybe I should just give it up and settle down like a normal thirty-three-year-old man."

The idea that Jack would give up on his dreams for something so ordinary makes me sick to my stomach. "Jack, you can't possibly think you're not making a difference. There are so many fans who look up to you. I can see your passion every time you turn on that camera. You were born to be in front of it, as a leader." I nudge him on the shoulder. "You inspire people, like it or not.

"Please don't ever doubt that you're making a difference because, from where I'm sitting, you're the one who seems to have this whole life thing figured out." I sigh. "Promise me you won't give up so easily. It would break my heart to see it."

He rubs his hand through his beard as if in thought. "Yeah. I guess." His hand glides up my arm. "What about you, mystery woman? What would you do if you weren't repairing people's images at the drop of a hat?"

I think for a moment, but nothing comes to mind. "I don't really know. I've always seen myself in Corporate America. I've dreamed of making VP since I graduated high school and started my career. I love the galas and working with celebrities. I love spinning a shit-storm into a brand deal. Sure, the work is constant, and I'm basically always on call." I sigh. "I barely have time to do anything other than work, and I feel like I'm chasing this promotion on a treadmill, not sure that I'll ever actually make it. Is that sad? Am I just a boring stick in the mud?"

Jack laughs. "Gwen, there's nothing boring about you, but why are you so set on making VP if you're not even happy in your current position? Wouldn't a promotion just end up being *more* grueling work? What's so broken that you need a fancy title to fix it?"

"We can't all galavant around the world chasing fun, Jack. Some of us have to grind because we've got shit to do and people to prove wrong." I cut him off before this goes any further, and I turn back around to sit up. "I'm going to go get cleaned up for dinner." I gesture to the ocean, and thankfully, Jack takes the hint.

Clapping his hands together, he stands and rubs the sand from his legs. "Yeah, I'll see if I can find us some more *salad*."

I nod, closing my eyes before turning toward the vast ocean in front of me. The world is so big, and yet this island feels like a world of its own. If only life really could be so simple...

CHAPTER EIGHTEEN

Jack

Gwen's mood has been kind of off ever since I pressed her about the promotion last night. She even curled into a ball in the tent, sleeping as far away from me as possible. I can take a hint; she needs some space. I just wish she'd be more open with me. I know there's more she's not telling me, but today, I've got to focus on building the raft and our escape plan.

I send Gwen to collect some oysters for breakfast while I boil some herbs in water to make us tea. It's not coffee, but I'm feeling extra tired today since I slept like shit last night. I was keenly aware of the cool air in place of Gwen's body. I kept waking up to make sure she was still in the tent and not wandering off and getting into *more* trouble.

I'm busy chopping bamboo shoots for the raft when she comes up behind me. "How can I help?"

I think for a moment, not wanting to give her a task too dangerous.

"Jack, I'm not that fragile, and I promise not to go near any weird plants or wildlife." She points to her eyes. "I'll be on constant alert. Now, just tell me what I can do to help," she says with a sharp tone.

I laugh. "Fine. Why don't you carry these bamboo stalks toward the beach and stack them in a pile? I'll be cutting these down most of the day. After that, you can start braiding palm leaves into a rope. I'll show you if you want—"

She holds her hand up and rolls her eyes. "I think I can figure out a simple braid. No need to mansplain it."

"Ok, then, well... have fun," I call out and then get back to work on another bamboo shoot. I don't know what crawled up her ass, but at least she's offering to help.

But I may have a sneaking suspicion... Only time will tell.

Gwen and I spend most of the afternoon on our separate tasks, staying as far away from one another as possible, which isn't hard since we're the only two people on this island. To my surprise, she's managed to move most of the bamboo to the beach, though it took her five times as many trips because she can only carry two shoots at a time. I grab the last ten logs and make my way to the beach, dropping them into the pile with the others. I may need to collect more once I start building, but this will be enough to start a solid base.

"Nice work. Someone must've had their Wheaties this morning." I come up behind her, admiring the pile of neatly tied ropes.

She squints her eyes, staring daggers at me, and returns to her braiding.

"You know, if you pull a little tighter like this," I show her, "the rope will be stronger—"

"I think I can manage to braid a rope. Why don't you worry about your task and let me worry about mine?"

And... I guess we're back to her wanting to kill me. Perfect timing.

I hold my hands up in surrender and slowly back away. "Alright, alright. I'll just leave you to it, then. Let me know if you need me for anything. I'll just be over here minding my business, and not having pleasant coworking conversations with the only other person around," I tease.

I've managed to tie the base of the boat together with the bamboo and rope we gathered today, but I'll need to add another layer tomorrow. I haven't seen Gwen since she stormed off earlier, but I figure I'll grab some footage of the raft as I build it so the viewers can see it come together.

I walk back to the campsite to get my camera, and when I get back to the beach, I see Gwen fighting with a long bamboo shoot, trying to draw something in the sand.

I turn my head to the side, trying to make out the giant spaced-out letters. She's wearing a red bikini top today with a pair of my shorts and a survival blanket tied around her waist.

HELP WE ARE STRANDED

I have to walk several feet to get the entire message, and she's finishing up the last D when I reach her. "What the hell are you wearing? Aren't you hot in that?" I gesture to the metallic sheet tied around her middle.

"Do you think I'd be wearing it... if I *were* hot?" she snaps.

Ok, so I can see she's still got her panties in a wad. I really wish I knew what I said yesterday to cause the attitude.

"You know you could've saved yourself some time and just spelled out SOS, right?"

"I just wanted to make sure they knew our circumstances," she snaps. "It's better than your stupid boat idea."

"The boat idea is literally the only thing we have going for us." I'm starting to get annoyed because I need her on board for this plan to work. I can't leave her here alone if she's not prepared to take care of herself. "The chances of a plane flying close enough to see this message is so minimal that I'm better off doing the back-stroke to Costa Rica than waiting on someone to find us."

"Well, at least I'm trying!" She crosses her arms over her chest.

"Yeah, good job writing a message on the shoreline. The tide will wash it away within five hours."

I strap the camera to my chest, turn it on, and make my way to the boat, explaining how I made the raft and my plans for the rest of it. "Hey, Gwen, come here real quick."

To my surprise, she listens and hesitantly walks toward me, making sure to stay out of the camera's view. I reach up and tug the emergency blanket free from her waist, and she covers herself with a gasp as if I've stripped her bare.

"What the hell! I was wearing that!" she shrieks.

"And I needed it. Thanks, by the way. I wouldn't have even thought to use this as a sail if you hadn't been strutting around in it like a tin-foil runway model," I add, laughing at my joke. I can totally see Gwen as an emo/scene girl in high school.

"What did you look like in high school, Gwenny?" I ask her on camera. She's crouching now, hiding behind my backpack.

"Wouldn't you like to know!"

"Yeah, I would. That's why I asked." I poke her playfully, and she waivers in her squat. "I played soccer in high school. College, too, actually. I got a full-ride playing striker." I offer even though she didn't ask, and I waggle my eyebrows as I spin the camera to face me. The viewers love shit like this, getting to know the real me, and I like to sprinkle it in whenever I get the chance.

I just wish Gwen would give me a little more. I'm dying to know what she's hiding underneath her hardened exterior. She may not realize it yet, but I will get her to open up to me if it's the last thing I do.

"Of course, you did." She rolls her eyes. "The golden boy made out of sunshine and rainbows," she huffs under her breath.

Am I sensing a note of... jealousy?

I make a mental note to come back to this conversation because I'd love to dig deeper into it, but right now, I've got too much work to do.

I tie the last rope to the raft and note how many more pieces of bamboo I'll need to finish, then switch off the camera. I don't want to build the sail until the day I leave, just in case another storm comes through. It's my only blanket, and if a strong enough wind hits it, I'll be paddling my ass off to get anywhere.

I walk toward Gwen, extending my hand to help her to her feet, but she just shakes her head. "I'm good right here. I think I'll stay here until dinner tonight."

Now that I'm really looking at her, she looks pale, even more porcelain than usual, with dark circles under her eyes.

"Are you feeling ok? You look... off."

"I'm fine. Just go back to camp."

"Why are you being weird?" I cock my head to the side and study her.

"I'm not."

"Whatever you say." I roll my eyes and pull the hem of my shirt over my head. Extending my hand once again, I say, "Come on, it's time for swimming lessons. I'm not taking no for an answer." I pull her up and grab my spear, hoping to kill two birds with one stone. I can't leave Gwen alone on this island without knowing for certain that she's able to swim if she needs to. And if I can give her a spearing lesson, we won't have to worry about dinner either.

"You're really not going to let this go, are you?"

"Nope. But the faster you learn, the quicker I'll leave you alone so you can growl and hiss in peace."

"I don't hiss, but if you're not careful, you may get scratched."

"Trust me; I can practically feel the murder in your eyes right now," I admit. "Are you sure you're feeling okay?"

"I'm fine. Can we get this over with already?"

"Sure thing." I lead the way, and she follows a few steps behind me, huffing and puffing the whole way until we reach a shallow tidepool just past the shore.

We have to wade through the clear waist-deep water to get to the tide pool. It gets deeper before it's shallow, and the waves crest over Gwen's head as she struggles to keep up with me.

"Come on," I grab her around her small waist and pull her toward me until we finally get to a spot she can easily touch her feet on the ground. I look down at the white sand beneath our feet. Various shells and sea glass float by, and that's when I see the most beautiful coral reef I've ever encountered. I dunk my head under water to get a better view, taking in the vibrant colors of nature. I'm so happy I have my camera with me. I've only got one fully charged battery left after this one, and I hope to use it for at least some of the escape plan. I'd like to document my time at sea when I'm in stable water, and it'll keep me occupied.

"Gwen, hold on to my neck. There's a coral reef a few meters ahead, and I think it's shallow enough for you to touch."

"I don't think that's a good idea..." She sucks in a shaky breath as a wave crashes into us. "Won't there be fish, and... I don't know, predators near the fish?"

I hold up my spear. "I've got a weapon. Come on," I plead. "When do you think you'll ever get another chance to see something so incredible?"

She thinks it over for a minute and eventually nods. I can't help but grin. This is exactly the kind of shit I live for. It's the reason I do this. While everyone else learns about the earth from the Discovery Channel, I'm wading in the ocean and seeing it firsthand.

I swim toward the reef with ease as Gwen clings tightly to my back. Once we're within a few feet, I set her down, testing to see if she can stand. It's close, but if she stands on her tiptoes, she can keep her mouth above the water.

"Just stay here for a second, ok? I'm going to swim under the surface and see if I can get some shots of the reef up close." I place my hands on her shoulders, steadying her. "I'll be right back up. You can even watch me; the water's so clear."

"Just hurry up. It's freezing, and something slimy just touched my leg."

"Ok, why don't you practice your breaststroke while I'm down there. Remember, it's like this." I show her, and she rolls her eyes.

"Fine. But hurry."

Without answering, I dunk underwater and make my way toward the reef.

Mountains of bright pink coral weave through the water, and many different fish swim in and out of the coral's crevasses. I see anemones and eels and even some clownfish. When I make it to the very bottom, I'm startled when a bright pink octopus shoots its ink and jets off away from me. The ink pools together and then fades as if it's drawing a circle around something. I maneuver a little closer and find a large clam shell sitting alone as if it were placed there just for me. I quickly shove it into my shorts pocket. I'm never going to pass up an easy source of protein. I swim up for air for a brief moment and make my way back down, bringing the spear with me this time. If I see a big enough fish, we may actually get full tonight.

This time I circle the reef on the other side, still filming, and set my sights on a dolphin fish that probably weighs twenty pounds. That could easily keep us fed for three days if I smoke it overnight and preserve it.

I'm just about to take my shot when I glance to the side and see Gwen kicking her legs and a very large nurse shark heading straight toward her and the trail of fresh blood seeping through her bikini bottoms.

Oh fuck.

Even though I know the shark likely won't hurt her, I'm afraid she doesn't know that. And if she freaks the fuck out, as I expect her to ... then it may react.

I abandon the dolphin fish, pushing off from the bottom as hard as my legs can kick, launching up. The shark is alone, and he's probably just curious, no doubt attracted to us by the blood. I knew she was acting weird earlier, and my *only-brother-senses* were tingling when I saw her pale face. I can't believe I didn't put the pieces together sooner. Of course, she'd get her period eventually. I guess that explains her moodiness this morning.

I don't want to hurt the shark. The best thing to do is to lure Gwen away from it without telling her why. Though, if she would only look down, she'd see it circling her feet in this clear water.

And there it is. I see it the instant she realizes it. I've seen a lot of crazy shit during my time as an adventure guide, but none of it could've prepared me for this...

CHAPTER NINETEEN

Gwen

"Holy-mother-fucking-shit-balls!" Something slimy grazes the side of my leg, and it's only then, when I look down, that I discover I'm being circled by the biggest shark I've ever seen.

Its body is long and brown with speckles, and it saunters through the water, circling around me, just waiting to bite off one of my legs.

Adrenaline floods my systems, and my vision goes blurry for a minute. I close my eyes and try to breathe. *Just stay calm*, I tell myself. Isn't there something about them being able to smell fear? *Is that a real thing, or am I thinking of wasps?*

I try to slow my kicking, though, with each wave that crashes over my head, I struggle to keep my footing on the rough sandy ocean floor. Where the fuck is Jack when I need him?

I look around at my surroundings, and since we're in this shallow tide pool, I'll need to swim at least fifty feet to reach the closest rock, and I'll still have to figure out how to climb out of the water by myself. I see Jack come up for air in the distance, and I wave my arms to get his attention, but he drops back down under the water's surface.

Here I am, literally about to be eaten alive, while Jack's getting a boner over the coral reef. Sounds about right.

I knew I shouldn't have let him talk me into swimming today. I fucking knew something like this would happen to me with the shit-luck I've had on this island. I started my period this morning, and don't you know, I only had three tampons in my bag.

Three.

Three measly regular-sized, medium-flow tampons that I need to last me at least five days. I'll never think of shark week the same. The first day is always the worst for me, and I'm practically bleeding out in the middle of the ocean, just begging to attract predators.

I look down and confirm my suspicions. My tampon is leaking, and it doesn't take much to notice the trail of bright red blood seeping from my vagina. This is a new level of betrayal from the cruel bitch. I'm sorry I didn't have you impregnated this month. Must you literally throw me to the sharks!?

I bite my lip and consider my options. I could doggy-paddle my heart out toward the closest rock, but there's still the blood trail to consider. My frantic flailing will probably attract more attention, and that, with the fresh blood, may make the shark more excited.

I think of my dad's old joke about how if a bear was chasing him, he didn't need to be faster than the bear, just faster than the other guy. Since there isn't another guy ... well, not really, the only thing I can do is try to lure it away with something it wants.

Before I can talk myself out of it or think of any other option, my survival instincts kick in. I slide my hand down my bikini bottom and rip the oversoaked tampon free from my body and throw it as hard as I can in the opposite direction.

I hear the faint sound of a plop as the tampon hits the water, and suddenly, there's blood everywhere, a trail directly from my body to the dilapidated tampon that the ocean's decided to return to me with the push of a wave.

Goddammit.

I dive for my life, chest heaving, as I try to swim the way Jack taught me. Kicking frantically, arms flying over the water's surface, I make some headway toward the rock. My foot makes contact with the beast, and I kick as hard as I can, hoping to push it farther away from me and continue my journey to safety.

When I'm finally close enough to the rock, I reach out my hand to grab its sharp surface, but instead, I'm met with a large hand. And then Jack's there, pulling me up from the sea as if he'd been waiting for me the whole time.

I collapse in his arms, sobbing and shuddering at my near-death experience, when I notice he's shaking, too.

I look up to see his forest green eyes shining with tears, but upon further inspection, I notice his blazing white teeth and his trademark rolling laughter.

"Why... why are you laughing?" I wipe my eyes with the back of my hand, still pressed against his chest.

He pulls me in tighter, squeezing me. "Because that was the funniest shit I've ever seen... and I got it all on film."

I tear myself away from him, "I almost died!" I scream.

"You were fine. It was a nurse shark. They're harmless." He sits down, buckling over in laughter. "You yeeted that fucking tampon and kicked the shit out of a shark and somehow managed to swim all the way here." He wipes his eyes. "Just when I think I've seen it all."

I shove him and stand up. "If you weren't down there

jerking off to the coral reef, maybe you could've *told* me that," I hiss.

"Babe, I tried to tell you. I was filming it because I've never seen one up close, but you freaked out before I could get to you." He tries to hide his smile, "I really am sorry."

Looking down at my bottoms, he gestures to the blood that's now flowing freely down my legs. "I should've known you'd got your period when you were so pale—and grumpy—this morning."

I try to cover my crotch with my hands, but there's no use. The blood is everywhere. "How would you have known?"

"Four sisters, remember" He taps his temple. "I have a Spidey sense for menstruation. Are you anemic or something? That seems pretty excessive."

I nod, feeling completely and utterly humiliated. I don't even have the strength to fight him when he wraps his arm around me to lead me back to the camp. "Come on, Bloody Mary. Let's get you cleaned up."

***

Just when I'm ready to wring Jack's neck for filming perhaps the most embarrassing moment of my life and teasing me relentlessly about it, he goes all gooey on me.

After we get back to the campsite, he orders me to rest in the tent while he makes me a cup of tea—that's what we're calling the hot leaf water these days. The sun's starting to set, and we're once again feasting on a handful of oysters and a small fish. Jack didn't have a lot of time to hunt today after the whole tampon/shark escapade, and I try to ignore my stomach's cries of hunger.

I grip the half-filled soup can and slurp my hot beverage,

pretending it's a cup of coffee and savoring the warm liquid as it coats my throat.

"Fuck, I miss coffee," I say between sips. I'm curled up by the fire, trying not to focus on the fact that I've got a wadded-up old t-shirt shoved between my legs. Not only did Jack embarrass me by laughing, but he's been doting on me all day long and even gave me his shirt to use as a wilderness maxi pad.

"Usually, I bring instant coffee with me on my survival trips, but I thought I'd have time to restock before we headed back out." His voice trails off, and his soft eyes meet mine. "I'm sorry I wasn't there for you today, Gwen."

He pulls my feet into his lap and begins to massage each foot, applying the perfect pressure. He rolls his hands up my arch like he's mastered the art of massage, and I fight my eyes from rolling back in my head in sheer pleasure.

"It's ok." I look down at the ground between us, unsure of where the tension I'm feeling is coming from.

"You know, I'm proud of you for thinking on your feet." He nudges my chin so I can look him in the eyes. "But don't ever throw a blood-soaked tampon in a body of water again, ok?" He laughs. "You're really cute when you fight back like that."

"*Cute?*" I roll my eyes. "No one has ever called me cute before. I am not *cute*."

"What adjective would *you* use to describe what happened today, then?" he asks mockingly.

"Um, I don't know... fierce? Badass? Scary? Just to name a few off the top of my head."

He grins and resumes his foot massage, switching to the other side, and I have to hold in a moan. "You are pretty scary... but do you know what I think?" His eyes twinkle with mischief, and I'm afraid to go down this road and let my guard down with him.

"What do you think?" I ask, letting my curiosity get the best of me.

"I think you put on this hard shell to push people away from you because you don't want them to see what's on the inside."

"And what makes you think my inside is any different?"

He pauses as if considering this. "It's how your eyes change from curious to guarded so quickly. How your breathing hitches when I move too quickly toward you. How you sometimes flinch for no reason." He rubs his hand up the side of my leg, stopping just above my knee before sliding it back down.

Butterflies erupt in my stomach as I focus on him picking me apart piece by piece.

"Don't worry, your secret is safe with me," he teases. "You have to really pay attention to notice it, and lucky for you, you're the only person here for me to analyze." He picks up my foot and plants a gentle kiss on top. "Besides, you're not so bad to get to know. I have to admit, you never cease to surprise me, and you've kept our footage incredibly interesting."

I take the opportunity to kick him in the balls, knocking the wind out of him. "Oof," he coughs, "Hey, what was that for?"

"For trying to figure me out." I reach up to grab his nipple, but he catches my hand before I can give him my signature purple nurple, which he remembers all too well.

"Not so fast, sweetheart." He pulls me into his chest by my hand, a little rougher than I'd have expected, and wraps his arms around me tight. "Why must you always be so feisty?" He kisses me on top of my head. "You're like a little feral kitten. You think you're big and scary, but deep down, all you want is for someone with a little patience to rub you the right way in all your favorite spots."

I try to protest and squirm away, but he only holds me tighter.

"Nope. You're going to lay here and let me snuggle the hell out of you... No pun intended." He laughs.

"Jack," I whine. "I'm bloated and bleeding out everywhere. It's disgusting. I need my personal space," I say as I try to shove him away.

But it's no use. Fighting Jack's snuggles is like trying to pry your mangled foot out of a bear trap. Once he's clamped his massive muscular arms around you, there's no escaping until he's done. I hate to admit it, but he does make me feel somewhat... safe.

"There you go, just relax and enjoy the oxytocin."

"The what?"

"It's the love hormone. Of all the feel-good hormones, it's my favorite." He plants another kiss on top of my head and gives my thigh a firm squeeze.

"I don't know if I consent to this hormone swapping. You see, I have a firm no-love policy."

He narrows his eyes. "Why on earth would you ever have a no-love policy?"

"Because I don't need any distractions," I say as if it's the most obvious of answers.

Jack looks around the forest surrounding us. "It's a good thing there aren't any distractions out here, then."

I slap him on the chest. "I'm serious, Jack. My work is important, and I've only made it this far because of my sharp, distraction-free focus."

"So, that's all you want in life?" he challenges me.

"Well, yeah. I guess." I think for a moment. "I've always wanted pure financial freedom so I can do what I want when I want. I never want anyone to dictate my future or hold anything over my head."

He ponders this for a moment and then speaks. "So, what

you're saying is, you're a workaholic, so you have the financial freedom and power to do things for yourself?"

I nod. "Exactly."

"Uh huh." He places a finger on his lip mockingly. "And exactly *what* do you do for yourself? What's so important to you that you need the freedom to do it?"

I try to think but don't have an answer, so he continues. "And when do you do it? I assume you have to take off the time you work so hard to get, so you can spend it relaxing and enjoying yourself somehow."

I look down at the ground.

"It sounds to me like you've got it all backward. You work like a dog so you can have the freedom to relax, but you never take advantage of the freedom because you don't want to lose the power you get from your work." He spins his finger in a circle. "It's an endless cycle. And you're going to wake up one day when you're sixty years old and realize you spent all of your youth chasing something that you weren't ever supposed to catch."

I'm stunned. No one has ever seen through me so well and certainly never called me out on it. Memories of my childhood flash through my head, images of my father screaming over B's on my report card, the way they completely freaked out when I decided not to go to law school or medical school. The way they just let me go, without even putting up an argument. "You don't know anything about me, Jack." I dig my nails into his arm to pry it away from me. "Don't assume just because you're being nice to me and cuddling me," I hiss, "that you know anything about me or why I am the way I am." I want to stand and storm off, but I can't really do that with the wadded-up t-shirt underneath me, so I scoot away from him.

"That's because you haven't told me." He lays back, resting his head on his palms, looking up at the evening sky. "But don't worry, I'm not pressuring you. I'll be here to listen whenever you're ready."

"Ugh," I turn over onto my side in frustration. "Don't hold your breath on that one."

"I think you'd be surprised at how long I can hold my breath." Then he closes his eyes as if everything and nothing has changed between us.

I scrunch my eyes close and will myself to drift off to sleep under the bright full moon night sky.

CHAPTER TWENTY

Jack

The past couple of weeks have melted together in a blur as I've busted my ass finishing the raft. I've spent most of my days hauling bamboo downhill to the beach. My muscles scream as I drop the last load onto the firm sand. I knew building a raft wouldn't be easy, but I underestimated how tedious of a job it would be. I begin braiding more palm leaves to fasten the large pieces together, and my stomach rumbles in pain. I glance down at my abs, which are disgustingly chiseled. The kind of definition you can only obtain through eating zero carbs and utter dehydration.

Fuck, I've got to step it up if I want us to make it out of here. In the last few days, I haven't recorded much footage, only grabbing some B roll of sunrises and sunsets to use as filler. I want to make sure I have at least one full battery when I'm alone on the raft, if for nothing else than to document my last moments on this earth.

I think the solitude is getting to me. I hang my head and

scrunch my face, trying to reset my mind. I don't have time to think like this. I can't afford it right now.

Pushing the fear back down into my gut, I stand, grab my fishing rod and spear, and make my way to the sea. Today, I'm determined to catch something, anything, to take the edge off our hunger pangs. I don't think Gwen's got much body fat left to lose, and it's killing me to watch her soft curves melt into angular edges.

Things have been different between us lately, almost like there's been a shift. Rather than fighting me tooth and nail on everything, Gwen's really stepped up and helped around camp. She's different, and although our interactions have mostly been pleasant, I find myself missing her spunky sass and sarcasm. I think the isolation is getting to both of us, forcing us to look a little deeper into our lives and what we really want. Isolation does that to you. There are no other distractions to keep you ignorant of what's stirring beneath the surface.

I cast my line to the shallow wave pool and wait; it's something I've learned I have a knack for.

The problem most people have trying to survive in the wilderness is that they don't have patience for the process. Sometimes you've just got to cast your line and know that mother nature will provide and be open to all the possibilities in which she can do so.

I think the same thing applies to Gwen. I've just got to be patient with her, and when she's ready, she'll open up and let me in.

I wade out a little farther until I'm waist-deep and squat down, sinking my head beneath the water. The cool water rushes over my sun-heated skin, and I let it wash away the worry coursing through my veins. "Patience," I mutter under my breath as I rise and shake the water from my long hair.

I cast my line again and watch my small bait fly in the wind with ease against the still morning sky.

It lands with a small plop, and I reel it in a little and wait. Then a hard tug pulls my attention back to the moment. I stand my ground, digging my heels into the shifting sandy ocean floor, and slowly move with the fish as I reel in my line. I catch a glimpse of my fish and have to stop my jaw from sinking under the water, as I'm now nipple deep. I raise the rod in my extended hands and crank as hard as I can, pulling the monster closer and closer.

Once it's within arm's reach, I reach back, grabbing the spear tied to me, and yank the line with my left hand as I stab the fish with the spear in my right.

I hear a crunch and push with all my strength until I see my spearhead piercing through its other side.

"Fuck yes!" I pump my fist and hoot as loud as I can in celebration. Howling and yelling nonsense for no one to hear but me. I wave my arms wide, spear and all, and lift my head to the sky, savoring this moment. It's a Dolphin fish, and it's so big, we'll be eating like kings for the next week. I wish I had my camera with me, but a part of me thinks this moment was just supposed to be for me. Mother nature proves to me once again that every little thing is going to be all right.

I heave the enormous fish over my head and make my way back up the shore.

If I can't get Gwen to open up through talking, maybe I can get to her through her stomach.

The smell of citrus sizzling over the flame makes my mouth water. We haven't had a real meal in almost two weeks—two weeks tomorrow, to be exact—and this smells better than any five-star restaurant I've been to during my travels.

"God, that smells good!" Gwen practically growls as she joins me by the fire.

Today, she's wearing some tube top thing with low-rise bikini bottoms. The dinner cooking isn't the only thing making my mouth water. Her skin glows from the fire, and a gust of wind rustles her wavy hair, sending leaves and flower petals in a spiral around us. I look around, half expecting a crab to pop out and start singing to me.

"Whoa. The wind is so crazy here." She finger combs her messy strands. She's acting different tonight, and I can't figure out why.

"Should I kiss you now or wait until after dinner?" I tease. I kind of feel like antagonizing her a little since she seems so happy to have a decent meal.

"If that tastes anything like it smells, you may not even have the choice." She licks her lips.

I jump back in shock and eye her up and down. "Who are you, and what have you done with Gwen?"

She scoots closer to me and bumps our shoulders together. "She's gone. I've eaten her. Now you just have this scrawny bag of bones that will do just about anything for a meal." She opens her arms, gesturing to her protruding hip bones.

"I still think you're hot, boney ass and all."

"Yeah? Well, this bikini is certainly humbling." She clasps her hand over her chest. "I miss my perky boobs and ass."

I pass her a serving of piping hot fish, and I don't miss how her eyes light up as she takes it, digging in without any abandon.

"I promise your ass and tits will be perfectly plump in no time once I get us out of here."

A lump forms in my throat, and I try to choke it down as I

take my own piece of fish. I don't know if it's a promise I can keep, but I do know I'll die trying if it means making her happy.

We pick at our food, savoring the smokey flavors, and I glance around the brightly lit campsite and realize I have everything I need right here. A sun-kissed Gwen sits to my right, finishing her second helping of fresh dolphin fish. I woke up to the sunrise, took a swim, and fished well into the afternoon. And the sky is clear, speckled with bright stars as a gentle breeze blows a fresh hint of salty air. If only the girl were actually mine, and if only things were ever this easy.

"How about we play a game?" I say, breaking the silence.

She studies me through narrowed eyes. "What kind of game?"

"Truth or dare... obviously," I say, matching her posture.

"Orrr... we could play spin the bottle?" Her eyes light up at her suggestion.

Interesting. So she's feeling horny. I was wondering—after I discovered dead vibrators lying around. I knew she'd eventually break, though now that that seems to be what's happening, I'm not sure how I feel about it. I don't know if it'll mean the same thing to her as it will to me, but I suppose a little fun can't hurt, especially considering how hard we've both been working.

I'd be lying if I said my body wasn't screaming to feel her again, to be inside her again while I'm totally sober. I've never had such a strong pull toward anyone, but there's something about how I feel when she's near me. It's like there's this extra set of lungs in my chest and the weight of the world doesn't feel so heavy.

Of course, I'm not telling her that... yet. I'm going to be patient, but I may as well torture her while I wait. Hell, it'd be great if I could get her on the same page, too, but I know in my bones that this fight will be one of the hardest in my life. I'm a cocky motherfucker, and I've never met a challenge that scared me as much as Gwen.

"You ready?" I waggle my eyebrows.

"Sure," she sighs.

"Ok, I think you know how the game works. Gwen, truth or dare?"

"Dare," she says, throwing me an evil smirk.

I see how she's playing this. I tap my finger to my chin as I think of something exciting. I'll play along for a few rounds.

"Gwen, I dare you to dance with me." I stand and offer her my hand.

Eyeing me up and down, she obliges. "But we don't even have any music–"

I pull her into me, not speaking a word, and place my left arm firmly at the base of her spine, answering her question with my body language. My palm almost covers the entire bottom half of her back, and I pull her in close, tucking her head to my chest.

She's tense at first, unsure of what to do, so I caress the span of her small back with my hand as we sway to the rhythmic waves. Then as if my body has a mind of its own, I begin singing "Lady May" by Tyler Childers in the crook of her neck. My voice isn't amazing, but I can carry a tune well enough, and I can't deny how spot-on the lyrics feel. This woman captivates me, and I'll spend the rest of my life chasing her until she realizes how much. I can only hope she feels the same way under her calloused exterior.

I finish the chorus and hum the rest of the song, finishing our dance with a twirl and dramatic dip. Gwen's eyes close, and I gently kiss her lips. Then I lead her back to the fire.

"Well, that was interesting," she teases. "I didn't know you could sing. A triple threat. Your mother must be so proud."

"She is actually. But I attribute most of my charm to my

older sisters. I think I'll always have the upper hand against most men because of them.

"I can see that." She bites the corner of her lip as if she's assessing me, and I can't help the rush of hope that shoots through my body.

"Your turn. Truth or dare?"

"Truth," I say, trying to fight back my laugh.

"Ugh, why are you so boring? Ok, let me think, what can I use to take advantage of you?"

I don't want to take advantage of you, Gwen. I want you. I swallow the admission down because she's not ready to hear it. I have to play fair... for now.

She quirks her lips to the side as she thinks. "Is it true that you think about me when you get off?"

I laugh because, of course, she's going there. "You caught me." I hold out my hands in surrender. "I think about my hands on you and how you whimper when you come." I make the gesture of the shocker as I scratch my leg, and I see the moment her eyes hone in on the motion. She glances from my hand to my mouth, and when she tries to pounce on me, I have to hold my hands out to stop her.

"Come on, Jack. Just give it up already!" She grunts as I shove her flying hands back.

"Someone's hormones are raging this evening." I make a show of pulling away from her and straightening my t-shirt collar. "If I didn't know better, I'd think you were trying to bait me into doing very naughty things to you, Gwenny." I wink, and she throws her head back in frustration.

"Where is the neanderthal that I came here with, and why have you suddenly developed morals?"

I shrug. "I don't know. Maybe I just need you to woo me before I give it up. I'm a sensitive guy, baby. You can't just go straight for the groin." I wink. "Maybe I need you to rub my back first, or at least buy me dinner."

"You are insufferable!"

"And you're only just now realizing this?" I laugh. "Truth or dare." I lift my chin to encourage her.

"Dare." Her eyes sparkle with mischief.

"I dare you to get on your knees and say, 'Jack, I promise to listen to you from now on because I *need* you.'"

"I'm not saying that!"

"Why not? It's true." I laugh, trying to keep a straight face.

"No, it's not true! I'm an independent woman, and I don't *need* anyone." She lifts her eyebrows. "*Want*, however, that's a different story."

I pull my lips to the side in a smirk. "Listen, if you want to lose the game, have at it." I pretend to get up, acting like I'm clearing out to go to bed.

"You can't lose truth or dare, asshat," she snaps. She still hasn't budged from her place in front of the fire.

"Whoa." I look around in concern. "Baby, I hate to tell you this, but losing truth or dare is real. Sounds to me like you haven't played the official game before because where I come from, if you don't fulfill your choice, there are consequences." I pin her with a stare.

Her breath hitches for a moment, and her eyes sparkle with mischief. "What kind of consequences?"

My balls clench in response. It takes every fiber of restraint I have to keep up this charade. "Well, that depends on the other players." I look around again. "And since I'm the only one here, I guess it's all up to me. It could be anything from skinny dipping in the ocean to ... eating a beetle. You just never know."

She gags audibly. "You will never make me eat a beetle. Mark my word on that one. I'll starve to death first."

"Let's see, what will your punishment be..." I look around the darkening campsite.

"Forget it, Jack." Her voice is stern, losing all sense of playfulness from before. "I can take a hint. Your testosterone levels have obviously dropped too low to be rational. You should make sure to see your doctor first thing when you get home. I'd hate for your peepee to shrivel up from lack of attention." She pushes my chest away, and I grab her wrist in a challenge. We stare at each other for a little longer than is comfortable as I search her eyes, pleading with my own to stop being so defensive. I don't know if she feels this spark between us, too, or if it's just her raging hormones talking, but even I know I'd be a damn fool to pass up this opportunity. I just hope I can keep my heart intact this time.

"Fine, swimming lessons it is." I stand up and peel my shirt off before offering her my hand.

"Seriously? Can't we relax and have a little fun for even five minutes?"

"Why are you avoiding this?" I raise my eyebrow as I study her. Her face is flushed and her breathing more rapid, like she's nervous. "Let's just go over the basics for like five minutes," I plead. "It'll make me feel better."

"Ok. I'll do it. But you'll have to catch me first." She darts to the side, taking off in a full sprint toward the beach. I'll admit, she's quicker than I expected, but there's no way her petite legs can beat me. Within seconds, I've caught up to her, and we find ourselves in a face-off. I'm on the tip of my toes, watching her, waiting for her to choose a side.

I see her eyes flick to the right, and I lunge, catching her just as her legs kick off the ground.

Her laughter is wild and manic. It's effervescent and explosive, the most beautiful sound I've ever heard. I can't help my wicked grin as I throw her over my shoulder while she tries to kick and punch her way out of my grip.

"Save your strength for your lessons, Baby Spice." I slap her on the ass, my hand easily connecting with her skin since her bikini bottoms are just a few inches shy of being a thong. I swear this woman's swimsuit choices drive me mad.

I wade into the cool ocean water as the waves crash against my shins, and I don't stop until I'm waist-deep. Then, without warning, I pull her down into a cradle and sink us both down under the water.

She gasps for air and pushes me away when I bring us both up. "Dammit, Jack! You got my hair wet!" She splashes water in my face in frustration.

"Oh, stop. You were going to get wet if you did it right anyway." I wink.

"Well, now I guess you'll never know." She plugs her nose and sinks into the water, this time brushing her sleek blonde hair back away from her face.

"Baby, I don't need to feel you to know when you're wet for me. Now come here." I pull her in front of me, so her back is facing my chest, and I grab her arms, moving her through the motions. "Open your arms like this and push against the water while you kick your feet. It'll propel you farther than keeping your hands close to your body." I steady her hips and give her a gentle squeeze for encouragement. "Now, you try by yourself. I'll be right here the whole time."

"You promise not to swim off and film a shark, leaving me to fend for myself?"

I grin. "That sounds nothing like me. Now go."

I watch as she pushes away from me, gliding through the water. She starts strong, mimicking my arm movements exactly, but when a bigger wave crashes over her, she falters. Before she can panic in the current, I'm by her side, lifting her. "Very good." I steady her and let her catch her breath. She's shaking now, and it kills me to force her to do this, but it's for her own good. I have to know she'll be ok when I'm gone. I shake the thought from my head because I can't worry about that right now. Right now, I want to focus on Gwen. I want to watch her overcome this and I want to be by her side while she does it.

"You've got it," I whisper in her ear.

She nods but doesn't say anything. A few moments pass, and she takes off again without me having to ask. This time she's more confident, and I can see she wants it.

"Kick your legs," I remind her as I watch her swim away. It's getting too dark to see her in the distance, and I start to worry.

As I'm about to take off to go after her, I feel her arms wrap around my waist as she presses her face against my back. "Thank you," is all she says.

"For what?" I spin around to face her, pulling her flat against me so I can feel every curve of her soft body against my skin.

"For being patient with me. For teaching me something I should've been taught a long time ago. For giving me a better memory to replace the old one with."

I lift her chin and meet her eyes. "Can you tell me about the old memory, Gwen?" I push her hair behind her ear and whisper into her neck. She's in my arms now, her legs wrapped firmly around my waist, and I don't even know how we got like this. It's like she is supposed to be in my arms. It's so natural for us.

"I think it's your turn, Jack. Truth or dare," she says breathlessly.

Even though my heart aches because she dodged my question, I don't pry. I want her to open herself to me when she's ready, but that doesn't mean we can't have some fun tonight. "Dare."

"I dare you to take off your shorts."

I lift my eyebrow and loop my fingers underneath the hem of my shorts, slowly sliding them down before I flip them onto my shoulder. The cool water sends a rush over my exposed cock, and I'm so hard. I want to reach up and tug that bikini top off her and take one of her sweet pink nipples in my mouth, but I resist. Instead, I pull her closer to me so she can feel my hardened length against her skin. Her breathing hitches, and when she reaches for me, I pull away before she can touch me.

"Wha—what are you doing?"

Laughing, I swim toward the shore. "You said to take off my shorts. You didn't say I had to let you touch me." I grin as I swim away, and she chases after me, grunting in frustration.

But you know what? She swam the whole way.

I guess she just needed the right motivation. I smile and pull on my sopping wet shorts, struggling to pull them over my bare ass before Gwen reaches me.

"You're no fun! Why are you being such a tease?" Her annoyed voice is suddenly loud and clear.

"Why are you so cagey?" I challenge back.

She doesn't answer me; instead, she wrings out her hair and stomps back up to the campsite to sit by the fire.

"Aw, come on. Don't be like that." I reach out and pinch the peak of her nipple through her bikini, and she squeals at my touch.

"Are you enjoying giving me a lady-boner and matching blue balls to go with it?" she snaps as she scoots away from me.

"Actually, I am. It's so refreshing to see you in your natural feral state."

She hisses in response, and this time, I'm the one laughing. Fuck, she's so cute, and she doesn't even know it. I'll be damned if I tell her, though, because I know she'd shut it all down the moment she thought she was perceived as weak.

No, I think I'll keep this thought to myself.

"Truth or dare?" I ask.

"You're not going to give it up until I say the truth are you?"

I pretend to look at my invisible watch. "Baby, I've got all night."

"Fine, truth."

"Is it true that you're happy?"

"What kind of question is that?" She laughs. "Let's see... am I happy right now? Well, no, because I'm all worked up, and I need the real thing." Her eyes glare at my crotch. "And you're being a prude and holding out on me." She picks at her fingernails, "I really thought we had something in the janitor's closet, some real sexual chemistry."

I stalk toward her, bending down so our lips are so close I can feel the warmth radiating from her skin. "You know that's not what I mean." I run my finger over her plump bottom lip and let my hand drift to her nape, where I brush my thumb over her slender neck. Holding her like this sends a wave of testosterone through my veins, and my eyes dilate with carnal need.

"Then what do you want me to say?" she whispers.

"I want you to tell me if you're happy or not, so I don't fuck things up."

She bites her lip, and I don't move my hand, just holding her gaze as I wait for her to finish. "I'm happy enough."

"Not good enough." I urge her to keep talking, tightening my grip ever so slightly around her pulse point, and her eyes are so hungry with need. It's killing me holding off like this, but I need to know where we stand. I need to know how she really feels because the last thing I want to do is risk one or both of our careers trying to chase something that will never work out.

"Fine, she sighs. "I've been happier in the last two weeks here with you than I've ever been in my life. Even though I'm scared and I don't know what's going to happen. I trust you, and I know you're going to figure it out."

I breathe a heavy sigh, and she continues, "And even if you don't, and it's just the two of us alone here for... forever. I don't think it'd be that bad either."

My lips crash into hers before my brain even registers what we're doing, and she's climbing in my lap, straddling me, hungrily scratching down my back, and pulling my hair.

God, I want this. I want this so fucking bad, but I've never slept with a woman I had feelings for, and I can't deny how I feel about Gwen anymore. She's chaotic and feisty. She'll argue with me for the hell of it, even if we both agree. And she won't fucking listen to anything I tell her, she's so damn stubborn, but when I look at my life, at my future, she's the one I want riding next to me on all my adventures, however that may look.

"I don't have any condoms," I say between kisses.

"I don't care, Jack. I need you."

"Fuck," I gasp as she wraps her sexy as sin legs around my waist. I don't have any fight left in me. I'd give her the moon if she asked me right now.

CHAPTER TWENTY-ONE

Gwen

"Whoa, whoa, whoa." Jack tries to pull away from our kiss, but I fight to keep our connection, biting and pulling his hair as I grip his strong, lean frame with my thighs.

"Baby," he huffs out a sigh in between our frantic kisses and squeezes my ass. "Baby, I love... that you're so excited right now, but... Gwen, we can't do this without protection." He pulls on my waist, placing me on my feet, but I've got a death grip around his neck, and I won't let go.

"I'm so sorry, babe." Jack drops to his knees, and before I can interrupt him, he links his thumbs through the top of my bikini bottoms and pulls them clean from my body. A rush of warm island air blows against my tender flesh, and he doesn't miss a beat before his hot tongue slides across my slick sex.

The moment his tongue touches me, my head sinks back in pleasure, and my knees buckle from the shock. We've been stranded on this island for over a month, and my vibrators were all dead within the first week. Every time I tried to take care of things myself, something scary would crawl near me, or I'd think I'd hear a predator waiting for my most vulnerable moment to attack. Once I even got sand stuck under my clitoral hood during a particularly sexually frustrating moment with my vibrator. Needless to say, that was a mood killer. It took me three days before I worked up the nerve to dig it out, and I damn sure wasn't going to crawl to Jack for help with my *situation*. It's a wonder I didn't create the world's first fresh-vaginal pearl. I shake my head at the memory as Jack's hot tongue swirls me back to reality. He brings my knee up to his shoulder, and his kiss sinks in deeper as he rubs his hand up my ass.

God, he's hot. I bite my lip to suppress a moan. He's barely touched me, and I feel like I could come at any moment. I grip his hair, pulling it taut between my knuckles.

He growls in response, and I swear to god, electricity shoots between my nipples.

"You taste so fucking good." He sucks my clit into his mouth, sending another electric wave up my spine, and chills coat every inch of my skin. "I may not be able to fuck you, but this is just as good to me." He laps me slowly, finding just the right rhythm. Knowing I'm close, he scoops his arms under my legs, so he doesn't have to pause his feast as he walks us the short distance to the beach. He slowly squats down until he's on his knees and then glides me down on the soft, dry sand.

The sand is still warm, and the rough grains scratch against my back, giving me the most delicious erotic sensation of pain and pleasure I've ever felt. Out here on this secret island, I'm invigorated at the thought of being completely and utterly alone with the wild man I never knew I needed.

My thighs grip his head in response, and he flips us over, so I'm sitting on his face.

I can't help my grin when I see the joy in Jack's eyes underneath me, his sultry gaze and a roguish smile lit by the faint glow of the campfire. I know that even if we were in the middle of Times Square, surrounded by thousands of strangers, Jack's eyes would still only belong to me. He pulls my thighs down tight, sinking me deeper onto his face as if to encourage me. Assignment understood.

I flick the back of my bikini top open and let it fall to my legs, also covering Jack's face. I have a feeling he won't mind having any more breath restrictions, and I sink into him. He really seems to be enjoying himself, and I can't help how my heart flips in my chest at the thought of him worshiping my body. I begin riding his face as Jack very gently works his tongue in all the right places. He pulls me down to apply pressure as he sucks and licks me. My body is damp with ocean air and sweat, and I feel like a goddess soaking in all this pleasure under the moonlit sky. It's like all my senses are heightened, and every touch or change in temperature has me writhing against Jack's hot mouth.

Fuck, this man is handsome, and now I'll never be able to look at his face and not remember this moment.

My toes begin to curl, heat pools in my core, and my orgasm is so close when I feel the slight pinch of a finger fill my ass. And then I lose it.

My back arches, and I scream my cry of pleasure so loud I hear it echo in the distance. My body shudders from head to toe, and I collapse in a trembling pile on his chest.

"Oh god, that was even better than I remembered."

He laughs and flips us, so we're facing each other on our sides. Everything feels quieter now as my heart finds its natural rhythm. Our heavy breathing blends with the gentle sounds of crashing waves, creating a symphony that instruments could never rival.

"Same," is all he says, but he's looking at me with hearts in his eyes.

He pulls me into a hug, nuzzling his face in the crook of my neck, breathing in my scent. My heart does that weird flip thing again. I snuggle into his side, our bare skin pressed against each other, coated with a light sheen of sweat and sand. I don't know if it's the post-orgasmic high or the fact that I feel like I owe him after giving me the oral of a lifetime, but I actually feel like opening up and telling him the truth.

"When I was ten years old, I almost drowned–" I swallow the lump in my throat at the memory.

Jack grips my hand before running his fingers up the length of my arm. "You don't have to tell me if–"

"No, I want you to know." I suck in a breath and slowly let it out, just like Maggie taught me all those years ago in college.

"We'd only been on the cruise ship for a couple of days. It was the vacation of my dreams—my tenth birthday trip—and I was dying to see dolphins. It was all I wanted. My parents had promised me they'd take me on one of those side excursions, but they just kept putting it off, finding other adults to mingle with and talk business. My dad was notorious for making everything a networking opportunity.

"I didn't like being ignored—if you can imagine—and decided to take matters into my own hands. One afternoon while my parents were away at brunch, I snuck off alone. I was leaning over the ship's side, trying to spot a dolphin, and tumbled over the side into the freezing ocean water.

"The water was so cold. It knocked the breath from my lungs, and I tried to scream, but I couldn't make a sound. The waves just kept crashing over my head each time I tried to take a breath. I'd never had trouble swimming in a pool before, but somehow, when the ocean fought against me, pushing and pulling me in every direction, my body just froze. I didn't know what to do."

I pause, taking a moment. "I thought I was going to die."

"I don't know how much time passed before someone saw me. Luckily, I was wearing a white tennis uniform that day, and I was easy to spot. Otherwise, I don't know if I'd have had the same fortune. One of the crew members jumped in and pulled me to safety. They had to give me CPR for ten minutes before I finally responded. I was airlifted to the nearest hospital with hypothermia and a respiratory infection, and I haven't been swimming since."

"Oh my God, Gwen, I'm so sorry." Jack pulls me into him, squeezing me tighter, and I can feel him trying to take the pain away from me, but I continue.

"The worst part was that my parents were so mad at me for ruining their brunch. Apparently, my dad was just about to make a pitch to some high-rolling investor when the crew interrupted them, telling them what happened.

"He didn't speak to me for weeks, and my mother stood beside his decision, and my regular spankings suddenly got more intense. He took out his anger on me, and I had the bruises to prove it. They eventually sent me off to boarding school, and I welcomed the feeling of safety I got from the built-in distance. I could finally let myself breathe, not having to walk around on eggshells around them constantly. After that, they doubled down on their expectations of me, always moving the mark no matter how hard I worked to make up for my childish mistake."

I wipe the tears coating my cheeks with the back of my hand and see Jack's broken heart shining through his eyes. "So when I graduated high school and told them I wanted to work in PR, to go out on my own rather than going to law school or med school like they'd always dreamed I would, they cut me off. Not just financially. My parents told me I was a waste of time, energy, and, most importantly, money. They said they were done with me since I was so willing to throw away all the opportunities they worked so hard to give me."

I hold out my arms. "So I've spent every opportunity since trying to prove them wrong. Trying to prove to them and myself that I could be successful and the very best on my own terms."

I sit up, covering my chest, feeling vulnerable in every sense of the word. "After that, I swore I'd never depend on anyone for anything ever again. That I'd make my way in this world on my own, without the help of anyone or anything."

Jack's stunned eyes stare back at me, and he doesn't hide the tears he shed during my story. "Gwenneth Peirson," he pulls my chin up to meet my eyes, "you are the strongest person I've ever met, and I am so sorry that happened to you." His fingers graze down my cheeks to my neck, where he traces the delicate skin of my collar bones. "I'm sorry I pushed you to swim." He sighs, pursing his lips in frustration. "Fuck, if you'd have told me sooner, I wouldn't have taken my eyes off of you, not for one minute."

"It's not your job to take care of me, Jack. You didn't know, and you sure as hell couldn't have guessed. I'm a big girl, remember?" I try to cheer him up because the last thing I want to do is dampen the mood with my little sob story. I climb into his lap, so we're face to face, and I wrap my legs around his waist, planting a gentle kiss on his swollen lips. The taste of my sex in his mouth sends a swirl of desire through my body, and I deepen the kiss, sliding my tongue to meet his with feverish need.

"I have a IUD," I say in a raspy whisper, and in an instant, Jack's rock-hard body flips me onto my knees. I have no idea how my childhood sob story could be such an aphrodisiac, but our bodies move on their own as if this is the natural response to end this conversation.

"Jack, I need you to fuck me." I plead. "I need you to make me forget—"

"I know what you need, sweetheart," he growls in my ear, and my goosebumps are back, coating every inch of my flesh. "I know exactly what you need, and I promise after I'm through with you, this memory will overshadow everything you told me tonight." He slides his fingers through my hair and gives me a not-so-gentle tug, telling me who's in charge, and I melt against him like a hot knife through butter.

A feral moan escapes my lips, and his rough hand presses against my low back as I feel a warm silky wetness brush against my sex and the all too familiar scent of coconut fills my lungs.

I can't help but smile at the most unpredictably hot gesture. "Are you using coconut for lube?" My voice trails up in surprise, and I'm delighted when the soft head of his cock brushes against my entrance.

Jack doesn't answer me. Instead, he slides his large cock in with such haste that the sensual sting of my body stretching to accommodate his sudden presence sends a jolt of heat to my core. Then he slaps my ass hard enough to take my breath away.

And if I never have sex again, I'll die knowing that it doesn't get any better than this.

A few more slaps, and I'm panting from the adrenaline. He knows just how to mold me like a piece of clay in his very capable hands. He thrusts into me deep, and my knees sting from our combined weight against the rough sand, but I don't mind at all. The smell of sex, coconuts, and sea salt overwhelms my senses as he grips my hips as if he's trying to keep himself from floating away.

"Oh God, yes." I moan, and he gives me another smack followed by a gentle rub. I'm all mixed up with pain and pleasure, a sensory overload that I never knew I needed until now, and Jack Manning is the only one to deliver.

"Fuck, Gwen, you're so perfect. Do you know that?" His breathing sends chills down my spine. "I think your body was made for me, handpicked by God himself," he growls before flipping me over so I can ride him.

The rush of being topless on the beach, having each and every one of my senses amplified to the max, gives me a high I've never known. Our sex is dirty and rough. It's tender in its own special way, and all I know is that I'll never be the same again. It's like Jack's climbed inside me and altered my DNA, taking all the bad memories and replacing them with something so close to *love*... No, that can't be right. Can it?

Our bodies sway and move together, and Jack can't take his hands off me as I ride him. I can tell he's barely holding it together when I bend down, laying my body as close to his as I can as I grind.

"Fuck, baby. I'm so close," he growls.

"Me, too." I whimper.

He lifts my chin with that cocky as sin smirk and says, "Smile." And that's when I see the camera with that blinking red light strapped to a palm tree pointed straight at us.

An impish smile covers my face, and I throw my head back and laugh. "Now, how did you know I had an exhibitionist kink?"

"Just a lucky guess." His scratchy voice sends another jolt through my nerves, and I lose it. Head thrown back with abandon, I lose myself in Jack Manning and succumb to the most glorious orgasm that shakes me to my core and, dare I say, rewires me into something completely new. Something wild.

"Let me take you on a proper date." Jack kisses the tender spot beneath my jaw a few minutes later once our breathing has slowed. "Are you free tomorrow night?"

I can't fight the grin and simply nod as my head rests against his bare chest. "I'll have to check my calendar, but I think I can work you in."

"Good." He plants a kiss on my hand and wraps himself around me tighter. Covered in perspiration and sand, we lay in each other's arms with only the full moon's gentle glow shining down on us like a spotlight, like we're the only two people in the world.

CHAPTER TWENTY-TWO

Gwen

"I swear if I ever get off this island, I'll never order another Pina Colada for as long as I live!" I slap the dinosaur-sized mosquito on my arm, leaving a trail of blood behind.

"What? You're sick of coconut?" Jack winks. "I don't know. I think it's becoming one of my favorite smells." He leans in and bumps me in the side. "It reminds me of you."

I smile as I remember the exotic coconut slippage between us. "I'm so sick of it. I eat it, drink it, use it to keep from burning in the sun ... Hell, last night, we even used it as lube! I'm basically a walking coconut at this point."

"I can't tell you how much I enjoyed my Pina Colada last night." Jack pulls me into him and sniffs the top of my head. "I love you. I'd drink Pina Coladas every day of my life if you'd let me."

His walk comes to a stop, and he pulls me closer to him as I suck in a sharp breath at his words. "Shhh." He places his finger over my lips. "You don't have to say anything back. I know this is intense. I just wanted you to know how I feel about you." He pulls my hand up to meet his mouth and kisses it.

Butterflies swarm in my belly, and my heart aches at his words like a swirling ying-yang of fear and joy. I knit my brows together and bite my lip, suppressing a smirk.

"I know you do, Tarzan." I press up to my tiptoes and plant a soft kiss on his lips. "I'm going to get ready for our date. I'll see you when the tree shadow is over here." I point to the tree above us and then to my right—which I've recently learned is West.

Jack laughs at my caveman time-telling technique since, technically, he at least has a real watch and knows what time it is—in Costa Rica anyway. "Ok, Jane. I'll see you then." He shuffles as he looks down at his muddy bare feet and wiggles his toes, "I guess I better go clean up myself." Turning to head in the opposite direction, he calls over his shoulder, "I hope you're ready to be swooned. You have no idea how hard it was to reserve the whole island for just the two of us."

I laugh at his joke because even though we've been trapped here alone for forty-five days, I wouldn't trade our first date for any big city high-rise restaurant—even if I could properly curl my hair or wax my vagina. Somehow, Jack makes the simplicity of island life appealing, not just tolerable. If I didn't know better, I'd think this was his master plan all along.

———

I've done the best I can to get ready by using a small compact mirror to apply my makeup. Luckily, my sun-kissed skin has a golden glow that could never be achieved using a sunless tanner. Even though it'll take me a year of laser treatments to reverse this sun damage, I can't help but notice how happy I look... and feel.

Since my face is already glowing, I add a little highlighter to the apples of my cheeks and apply my favorite pink glittery lip gloss for a subtle pop of color. My hair has decided to do her own thing, so rather than fight the natural waves, I dipped my head in the ocean this morning and finger-curl my waves for soft, beachy waves that I also couldn't create with all the hair products in the world.

I stretch my arm as long as possible, holding the tiny compact mirror as I try to take in my look. Since I don't have any real clothes—thanks to Jack's emergency decision-making when the airplane crashed—I've put together a simple white thong bikini with a floor-length red and pink Moroccan print swimsuit coverup. Each side has a giant slit exposing my leg to my waist. It's a bit scandalous for a first date, but I have a feeling Jack won't mind at all.

I'm almost finished fluffing my hair and decide to add a tiny bit of mascara because why the hell not. This is a special occasion, and I don't know when I'll have another chance to get all fixed up again.

My stomach swirls with nerves and excitement... and a little bit of sadness. Part of me wishes we could recreate this date in the real world, in our real lives, but the other side of me wants to keep this precious moment right here on this island where it belongs.

I snap my compact shut and exit the tent. I'm not sure how much time has passed exactly, but I'm getting better at noticing how the sun moves across the sky. Who would've thought Jack would make a survivalist out of me? I certainly didn't. I swipe my arm to push away the hanging palm leaves that make the door to our hut and find Jack waiting for me. He's sitting on a log, gazing around as if there's nowhere else he'd rather be.

His eyes light up when he sees me, and my heart flutters when I see he's also dressed up for me—well, as much as a man stranded on an island can.

I chuckle when I realize his dressed-up island date outfit isn't much different than how he looked when I first met him in the real world. It's a refreshing thing to see someone who's so sure of who he is, no matter the crowd. I envy him for that.

Jack's wearing mid-thigh length floral swim trunks—a different pair than he usually wears—and a contrasting floral short sleeve button-up that's left open, revealing his sculpted, masculine chest. I let my eyes roam over his massive frame, and a smile tugs at my lips when I notice he even brushed his hair. His usual man bun is intact, but it's a little tamer than usual. It looks like I'm not the only one trying to make a good impression here.

"You look... Wow," is all he says as he takes my hand, helping me climb out of the hut.

I grin, tucking my wild waves behind my ear. I can't fight the blush that creeps up my cheeks. Who is this bashful woman? I'm practically melting under his gaze, and for the life of me, I can't wipe the smile away. I feel like myself but in another dimension or something.

Jack's Gwen is the same woman with the same heartbreaking childhood in her past, but she's come out stronger on the other end. She's confident, sure of herself, and, most importantly, *happy*.

"You clean pretty nicely yourself, Tarzan." I wink, and my skin tingles from his touch.

Christ, he's just holding my hand. What's going to happen when he touches me for real? I'll combust because no one deserves this kind of happiness. Certainly not a girl like me.

"So, where do we begin? I hope you called and made reservations? I'd hate for us to put in all this effort just to be turned away at the door," I tease.

"It's your lucky day. I know a secret place. The food's subpar, but I promise the view makes up for it." He squeezes my palm, reminding me that we've not let go of our hands. Yep, that's another first for me. Holding hands isn't something I normally do, but I clench my small hand around his rough, calloused one and allow him to lead me away.

I think I like this version of myself. Who knew?

I allow Jack to lead me through the overgrown trees, and I notice a trail that wasn't there before. He must've prepared it ahead of time, cutting a clean path, so we're not being smacked in the face by the dense vegetation.

We're walking up a small incline. It's so subtle I probably wouldn't notice, but my thighs begin to burn after only a mile or so. It's such a familiar pain now, and I don't totally hate it.

I smile, thinking of Elliot and all our runs through Millennium Park back home. It's a similar feeling, giving me comfort mixed with a twinge of sadness. I miss my friends so much, but I can't think like that right now. I want to be present where my feet are, and that's here on this island in paradise with the wild man I never knew I needed.

"You ok back there?" Jack calls over his shoulder. We're walking step in step, he's slightly in front of me, but I'm close on his tail, allowing him to lead but also not letting his hand loose from my grip.

"I'm perfect." I exhale a sigh and breathe in the fresh air around us.

"Good. We're getting closer." He comes to a stop, glancing up at the steep rocky terrain in front of us. "We'll have to climb the rest of the way to get there." He turns to face me. "I can carry you on my back if you're tired—"

"I can do it," I interrupt him. "You don't have to baby me, Jack." I flex my emaciated bicep. "I fought off a shark, remember?"

Jack's throaty laugh sends a soothing vibration through me. "You're right. I don't know what I was thinking. In any case, I'll let you go ahead of me—you know, so I can check out your ass. It's totally not because I want to make sure you don't fall."

I step up the rock and stretch my arms, grabbing the first protruding stone and lifting my leg to push my weight up the mountainside.

Stretch, reach, push, pull. I'm finally getting the flow of this. My muscles are screaming for me to stop, but I know the top is so close. I squeeze my eyes shut and refocus my breathing. I can do this.

"Just say the word if you need a break," Jack's calm breathy voice calls from behind me. "It's only a little ways farther." I feel the heat of his hand on my ass cheek as he gives me the little boost I need to reach the next stone.

After what seems like an eternity of rock climbing— something I swore I'd never do when Maggie suggested we try it back in college—I finally reach the edge. I place my hands on the flat surface and pull myself up to sit on the edge, and nothing could've prepared me for this view.

Poor Jack's on his own now since I'm way too preoccupied to offer any help.

I gasp as my eyes roam over the quaint scene before me.

Jack's laid a bed of palm leaves along the ground and has somehow managed to build torches that form a semi-circle behind us. There's a small campfire in the middle and two coconut cups decorated with various leaves and berries—the only thing missing is the paper umbrella.

He's woven a small basket covered in one of his t-shirts, where I presume he's storing our dinner.

"Well, what do you think?" I jump when I feel his voice on the back of my neck. I was so distracted with the setup that I almost forgot about my date.

"When? When did you have time to do all this?" I think back to the two-hour window it took me to get ready and try to imagine Jack making this happen while I combed my hair and applied mascara.

He scratches his head and shrugs. "It's something I've been working on for a while. I wanted it to be perfect before I showed you." He saunters toward me, bringing my hand up to his soft lips, and plants a gentle kiss on my hand. "Do you like it?"

"I love it, Jack. It's perfect." The beginning of tears burns behind my eyes, and a knot forms in my throat. "You're perfect."

"I made you something." He rushes to his homemade picnic basket and rummages through it until he finds what he's looking for.

"You got me a gift?"

"It's just a little something, don't get too excited. I'm no jeweler, but when I found this shark tooth, I knew it was meant for you."

He wraps a small twine bracelet around my wrist and ties it. When I turn my arm over, I see a large, sharp shark tooth in the center. He made me a charm bracelet.

"I love it!" I blurt out. The tooth is so large it takes up the entirety of my wrist, and I feel so powerful wearing it.

"It's not from a nurse shark, like the one we saw, but it reminded me of how strong and tenacious you are. I wanted you to have it, so you always remember what you've overcome, what you're capable of."

"I'm never taking it off," I promise. "Besides, it's like having a built-in weapon. Now I'm ready for anything."

"Slow down now. I don't need you picking fights with anacondas anytime soon." He laughs.

"I can't make any promises."

"Here, why don't you take a seat." He gestures toward our picnic set up by the fire, and I follow his lead.

"Jack, I think you've outdone yourself here. This must've taken hours."

He removes the shirt from the top of the basket and pulls out the fish he no doubt caught this morning. Mahi mahi, my favorite. Well, it's my new favorite anyway. Before crash landing on this island, I was never much of a fish eater, but now after eating the freshest catch every single day, I'm afraid I'm becoming accustomed to the finer things in life.

"Oh, and you're in luck. I had just enough rum left to make us a few rounds of these." He hands me the elaborately decorated coconut, its weight heavy in my hand.

"Cheers," I say as we clink our coconuts together. When the warm liquid touches my lips, I savor the tropical flavors mixing with the flavorful rum. "Oh my god, how did you manage actually to make a Pina Colada out here?" I take another hurried sip because I was so wrong about this drink. It's perhaps the best thing I've ever tasted.

"So, you do like it?" He laughs. "I found a pineapple tree a few days back, and I was waiting for the right opportunity to woo you with my bartending skills."

I drain the rest of my drink and slam it down on the ground beside me. "Consider me woo-ed." Then I take his cup and drain it.

"It's a good thing I packed extra, then, isn't it?"

I simply nod and lean back on my hands, admiring the golden afternoon sun that'll be setting soon as Jack begins cooking our meal. He really knows how to impress a lady. Better yet, he knows how to impress *me*, which is actually a whole lot better.

We sit there soaking in each other's company while the fresh fish sizzles against the fire and he prepares me another Pina Colada. A girl could get used to this.

After we've eaten the most delicious mahi-mahi and fresh citrusy salad known to man, I'm sated in the best way possible. My belly is full, and my heart is overflowing with adoration.

No, it's more than that. My feelings for Jack have grown. They've multiplied like a gremlin soaked in water—ocean water—to a point where I'm consumed mind, body, and soul with this man. Maybe it's the Pina Coladas talking, or maybe I've finally found the other piece of my soul, but this night has been nothing short of magical.

"Tell me something about yourself that no one knows." My question breaks our gentle silence, and Jack looks up for a beat.

"Sometimes, I wish I could go back to the early days when I started the vlogs just to teach people how to thrive in nature. Once I started taking on the guided tours, it seemed like my passion for exploring turned into more of a job. Having to keep sponsors happy and clients alike constantly." He shrugs. "I don't know. I kind of just miss doing it for fun. But I guess that's a pipe dream, and you can't have it all."

"Sure you can." I nudge him with my shoulder. "Maybe you just haven't found the right way yet, but that doesn't mean it doesn't exist. Maybe you just need to think outside the box?"

He scratches his beard, considering this. "Yeah, maybe so.

This evening has been one of the best nights of my life, and I want Jack to see me for who I am. I want him to want me still, the good, bad, and even the ugly parts of me.

"I want to apologize for how careless I've been since I've met you. My whole life, I've carried this chip on my shoulder about not needing anyone, and by not letting you help me, I've put both of us in harm's way too many times to count." My throat tightens as I choke out the words.

Jack softly laughs but nods his head, encouraging me. I love that about him, how he always knows when to be silent and when to speak. I don't feel like he's waiting for me to finish talking to respond. He actually listens.

"I need you to know that I'm sorry for being so stubborn, and I think I was just annoyed by how happy you always seemed to be, no matter the circumstances." I look down at my wringing hands as I speak. "I've spent my whole life chasing external validation to make me happy, and seeing you choosing happiness even when things didn't go your way, it almost felt like you were holding up a mirror revealing all the parts of myself I hate the most."

He scoots closer to me, wrapping his large arms around my shoulders and pulling me into his chest. "Aw, baby, I never want to make you feel bad about anything. You've overcome so much, and you've become a strong, independent woman all on your own. That's something you should feel proud of. Don't ever doubt that you're anything less than perfect in my eyes."

"I guess I just want to say thank you for being so authentically you. You've inspired me to let my guard down and challenged me to think about success and life in a whole new way." I laugh because I don't even recognize this version of myself. "This has been the hardest thing I've ever lived through, but if it had to happen, I'm really glad you're the one I was stuck with on this island."

A warm smile pulls at his lips, and rather than answering me, he glides his fingers over my heart as if he's writing something in invisible ink.

"What was that?" I ask almost breathlessly.

"Just signing my name where it belongs. Don't worry. I've made a space for yours, too."

Tears well in my eyes, and I can't fight my grin as he guides my hand over his heart. I use my pointer finger, forming each letter of my name as I brand him with magical invisible ink. It's a promise, and even though it's invisible, I know this bond is something that will stand the test of time. No matter how long our time may be.

Then he pushes my bikini top aside, and I suck in a breath at his smooth, warm contact.

Tears fall from my eyes. This time there's no stopping them as I look at Jack, taking all of him in, too. We're two imperfect people when we're apart, but somehow, when we're together, our pieces line up perfectly, and I feel whole. For the first time in my life, I feel seen.

"Let's do something crazy!" I wipe my tears with the back of my hand and pull Jack up to stand with me. He humors me as he lets me lead him to the cliff's edge. It's the first time I really look at how high up we are. The sun's just fading into the horizon, filling the sky with pink and orange hues straight out of a painting.

"Is it safe?" I ask as I look down at the wild ocean waves crashing against the rocks below.

He considers me for a moment. "If you jump out at a forty-five-degree angle, this way," he gestures with his arm, "it'll be plenty deep enough–"

"I love you, Jack." I pull his head down, so our lips meet and wrap my legs around his waist. Jack doesn't miss a beat, cradling me under my ass as our kiss deepens. Our kiss goes from frantic and needy to soft and sensual. I can feel his hard length hardening against me, and I'm nothing but a beating heart and hormones as I let the rush overtake me. Then he sets me down and clasps his hand in mine. Before I have time to protest or change my mind, we're flying off the cliffside lit only by the sunset in a rush toward the sea. I barely catch my breath before the cool ocean water encompasses me, and Jack never lets go of my hand.

Thrills and butterflies swarm in my belly as I kick my legs, pushing myself up to the ocean's surface. I gasp for air just as Jack's head peeks above the water, and I can't help the enormous laugh that escapes me. At this moment, I feel brand new, like a free woman, baptized in the ocean with nowhere to go but up. I cling to him, wrapping my cold legs around his waist as we kiss again. The salty water only adds to the sensualness of the moment, and I know he can either take me here in open water or get me to dry land because what happens next is only a matter of where and not when.

"Make love to me, Jack. I need you." I plead between our kisses. My tears mingle with the ocean water, and I've never felt more exposed in my life.

Before I can untangle myself from him, Jack swims toward the shore, pulling me into his lap. We collapse in a heap on the beach, not worrying about finding a more comfortable spot as Jack begins undressing me right there for no one but God to see.

"I love you," he says between muffled kisses.

"I love you, too."

He manages to whip off my drenched swimsuit cover and flings it to the side before uniting the strap of my bikini top. Ever so slowly, he pulls the top away and gasps at the sight of my heaving breasts. It's not that he hasn't seen them before. Hell, last night, his mouth touched every last inch of my skin. But this, this is a whole new feeling. Jack looks at my body like he's seeing it for the very first time. His touch is delicate and purposeful, like he's trying to memorize every inch of my skin. Every one of my senses is heightened, and I'm beginning to wonder what if the secret ingredient in the Pina Coladas was more than just rum. Somehow, I know the difference we're feeling can only be explained by one thing.

We're just two imperfect people finally meeting our match.

He climbs on top of my body, freeing us both from our respective bottoms, and pushes into me like it's the only thing left to do. Our bodies work together in their own rhythm, and the only thing in the world that exists is us and the love we share.

"Oh my God." I throw my head back in a moan as Jack

pulses his cock inside me. "It's so good, like record-breaking good," I pant. "How can this feel so perfect?"

Jack grunts in agreement, his lips finding my ear. "You should feel how good this is. Fuck, I wish you could feel this." His grip around my waist tightens, and I know he's fighting for control just like me.

I stretch my head back, giving him space to explore my neck, and his kiss confirms his understanding. "Fuck, you look so beautiful. Baby, I could worship your body day and night and never get tired of it."

Another whimper escapes me, encouraging him to lead me further and further into the blissful unknown.

He lifts my leg, bringing it up to rest on his shoulders as I cry out in pure ecstasy. Then he finds that spot just above my pubic bone and presses down with his hand as his thick cock fills me up, pulsing inside me with need.

"Oh, yes! Keep going. Please don't ever stop!" I pant.

"Your pussy is so wet for me, Gwen. I love how our bodies fit together so perfectly. It's like you were handmade by God just for me. You are so strong and beautiful, and I wish you could see yourself through my eyes just once so you know how much you mean to me."

His pulsing slows because we're both so close now. "Jack, I love you," I mew.

"I love you, too, baby." Then he adds my free leg to his other shoulder and drives in with a new force of determination.

Fireworks erupt in my belly as warmth floods me. It spreads from my toes all the way to the crown of my head, and I've never felt such an explosion of pleasure in my life.

I am a puddle, and I crumble into Jack's strong embrace. I feel his climax following mine, and then he collapses on top of me.

We're a sweaty, tangled mess of limbs and sand, and I

delight when the cool ocean tide kisses our heated skin, bringing us back down to earth.

I don't even try to get up. Instead, I just lay there in Jack's arms as he strokes my wet strands of hair away from my face.

"Promise me you'll never change who you are for anyone," he says. "You're perfect just how you are, and I swear I'll kill anyone that ever tries to convince you otherwise."

As gentle a man as Jack really is, somehow I know he isn't lying. I'm strangely comforted by his threat to protect me, and I nuzzle into him, finding the magical place between dreams and reality.

What a day this has been.

CHAPTER TWENTY-THREE

JACK

I cast my line as the sunrise peeks over the ocean's horizon and let the ocean breeze fill my lungs. I've always felt at home near the ocean or, really, anywhere surrounded by nature, but having Gwen here with me has taken my love for this freedom to the next level.

I've been all but skipping with joy everywhere I go. It's like all my senses have been heightened, and the simple pleasures of life have given me an entirely new awareness.

I know, I know. Someone get me some Vagisil right now, but I'm a man in love, and I don't care who knows it.

I feel a small tug on my line and smirk as I begin to reel in my first catch of the day. A warm smile spreads across my face because it seems luck has been on my side lately.

The line pulls tighter, and I stand to my feet to get a better grip on my flimsy collapsible rod. The last thing I need is for this baby to break. So far, we've had pretty good luck catching just enough fish to keep us fed and not having to wait around all day to do it. Of course, the foraging for oysters and other crustaceans helps sustain our diet as well.

I'm wading out into the water, trying to get as close as I can to the little fighter so my line doesn't snap, when I see the bright silvery-blue scales of a mackerel. My heart leaps in my chest as I wade in waist deep. I won't be losing this monster without a fight.

Normally, I wouldn't waste my time catching such a large fish because it would go to waste before Gwen and I had time to eat it, and though I may be a fisherman, I don't enjoy killing animals for the sake of it. I'm careful about my kill, and I only do it for sustenance, not pride, but since I'm leaving soon, I'll take every advantage I'm given. I'll need food for the journey, and having smoked fish will keep longer than any fresh fruit I could pack.

The fish tugs harder to the left, catching me off guard, and I roll my ankle in the loose rocky sand beneath me.

"Fuck" I hiss as the searing pain shoots up my ankle, and I tighten my hold on my rod, more determined now than ever.

The fish is giving it his all, swimming side to side like he's dodging a bullet, which isn't too far from the truth of his situation.

"Come on," I mutter, narrowing my eyes as I take another step closer. If I can just get him ten feet closer, I won't have to worry about the nose dive that inevitably comes next. With another slow crank, I pull him into view, and I know I've got him.

"I'm sorry, buddy, but you're going to be my ticket out of here." With one final reel, I draw him close enough to grip his mouth with my thumb.

This mackerel is so large I can't help but hoot in delight as I wade backward to shore. When I finally get to the beach, I lay him out and gut him to lighten the load before carrying him back to camp. I say a silent thank you to the fish and the universe for providing us with such a bountiful catch and make my way back to camp.

When I arrive, I find a beautiful sleepy-eyed Gwen hovering over a freshly lit fire. She's got this radiant, authentic beauty about her and the fact that her hair is standing up on all ends tells me she hasn't been awake long.

"Good morning, gorgeous." I lay the fish on the large flat rock we've been using as a table and rush to kiss her on her forehead. If I've learned anything about this woman, I know she needs her space in the morning and can't stand morning breath kisses—even if it's her breath that needs the attention.

"Did you make this all by yourself?" I gesture to the fire.

"Yeah." She rubs the sleep from her eyes with the back of her hand, "I, um, I was going to surprise you with tea when you got back." She passes me one of the large conch shells we've been using as cups, filled with fresh piping hot tea.

I shouldn't be surprised, but somehow, I am. Gwen has learned so much in our short time here. Not to mention, after learning about her past, I shouldn't be surprised by any survival skills she has. The woman is resourceful in every sense of the word.

I take the hot conch shell, and we sip our teas together in silence—just the way Gwen likes to wake up.

After she's done with her first shell of tea, I grab my camera and begin setting up the tripod.

"Whoa, Wombat Willy. I didn't realize we were still filming content. You've got to warn a girl before you break out the camera!" She attempts to smooth down her bedhead, which is the cutest thing I've ever seen.

"Trust me, babe. You're adorable right now, but I'll try not to get you in the shot."

She rolls her eyes and pours another shell of tea. I think, by this point, we're both unsure of what the future actually holds for us, so minor things like being camera ready and making a good appearance are literally the least of our concerns.

I start the camera and back up to frame the shot. "Hey, Dubbies! Today I'm going to show you how to preserve a large fish by smoking it. This can definitely come in handy in a long-term survival situation." I glance over at Gwen. She's paused, slowly sipping her coffee, but I know I've piqued her curiosity. "Now, you all know I usually don't even try to catch large fish like this beauty." I stand up, holding the fish by the tail to reveal just how large it is. It hangs from my shoulders all the way to my knees. "Today, we're learning how to smoke a fish, but you could do this with any wild game. As always, I'll list instructions in the show notes below." I slap my hands together and rub them eagerly. "So, let's get started, shall we?"

Since I'm down to my final battery, I had to be strategic with instructions and film time, only showing the absolute most important steps in the process. Smoking meat is an all-day endeavor, and by the time I've got it all set up, all we need to do is wait.

I'm exhausted, having spent the whole day building a smoke hut, cutting meat, and maintaining the fire. I've just laid down to rest when Gwen curls up next to me with a cup of water.

"You look exhausted."

"Yeah, I forget how tedious the whole process is, but it'll be a lifesaver when I set out next week. Having meat will help me keep my stamina more than coconuts and oysters ever could."

She stills at my words. "Next week?"

Since we've been in the honeymoon phase for the last couple of weeks, it's sometimes hard to remember that we still need to escape. I know I'm guilty of letting reality fall to the back of my mind, and I guess Gwen is, too. "Yeah, babe. I think we need to make a move soon." I lean on my elbow, so I'm facing her. "The season's changing, and I don't want to be stuck here when the storm season hits." I point to the gray sky above us. I can see the tides changing, the waves getting bigger, and the temps turning cooler at night.

She nods her head silently before curling into me closer. "So, you're leaving next week? That's what all this food prep is for?"

"Yes."

"I'm scared, Jack. I don't know if I can do this alone, and every time I think about you setting out on that flimsy raft in the middle of the ocean, it makes me sick."

A lump forms in my throat, but I do my best to talk around it, to be strong. "Don't worry about me. I just need you to remember all the things I've taught you, and before you know it, we'll be on a plane back to Chicago. You'll get that promotion, and we'll take the internet by storm with this story." I kiss her soft lips. "Do you trust me?"

"Of course, I do." She rolls her eyes.

"Then let me worry about the plan." I pin her hands above her head, and she lets out a little squeal. "I know just how to melt all this stress away. Now, if you'll excuse me ..." I kiss my way down her body, leaving a trail of goosebumps coating every gorgeous inch of her.

Gwen's body has quickly become my favorite source of distraction, and I have to say, I don't think she minds it too much either. We make love, leaving all our worries behind.

Little does she know I've spent the last couple of weeks in

nothing short of a panic about it, but I'll be damned if I let her know. I feel like it's my duty as her protector to keep as much of the scary stuff away from her as I can.

Smoking the mackerel was tedious as fuck, but as I begin to pack the dried meat into my bag, I know it was the right move. I divide the meat into two portions. One for me while I'm traveling and one for Gwen while I'm gone. I can't stand the thought of her being without food, and even though she'll have the whole island to forage for her meals and I won't, I can't let myself leave her with nothing.

"Ohhh, is it done?" Gwen reaches over my shoulder and takes a small piece of dried meat. She shoves it into her mouth, and I watch her reaction go from unsure to pleasantly surprised.

"Well?"

"It's not bad, actually." She laughs and takes another.

"Whoa, now. Slow down. These are our rations for when I'm gone, remember?" That comment earns me a pout.

Every time I've mentioned leaving, Gwen gets all tense. I can tell she's worried, but she doesn't want me to see it even though I can read her like an open book. The thought of leaving her here alone kills me, but we both know that right now, it's our best chance of survival.

I just wish there was some other way, but we've got to work with the cards we've been dealt, no matter how scary it may seem.

A crash of thunder breaks my trance, and I look up to see dark clouds on the horizon. There's a cool wisp to the air today, leaving a bad feeling in the pit of my stomach. We've been lucky so far with only minor rain storms. Apart from the big one that rolled in after we first landed, the weather's been pretty mild, actually. But I'm not naïve. I know what the storm season out here looks like, the complete and utter destruction that can happen without a moment's notice, and that realization is what's got me on edge.

"A storm's moving in," I tell Gwen as I snap my backpack shut and place her portions in the only waterproof ziplock bag I have left. Even though I was fortunate to be prepared for an excursion of this extent, I know we won't be able to survive like this for much longer on what we have.

"Yeah, it looks pretty nasty out there. Do you think it's going to be a bad one?"

"I don't know. There's definitely potential. We'll just have to be prepared. We probably won't get much sleep tonight."

"Ok, well, I found some berries this morning. I thought we could make a salad for dinner with some of the oysters we have left over from lunch. That way, we won't have to worry about fighting to keep a fire alive."

"That sounds perfect, actually."

"I know." She kisses me on the cheek as another crack of lightning lights up the sky. Gwen jumps in surprise. "Come on, let's go inside and eat."

"Sure thing. Let me just move the raft under some trees just in case. I'll be right there."

"Want me to help?"

I smile at her offer. "Yeah, actually, that would be great. I'll grab the front."

She walks behind me and lifts the raft, and together, we slide it, pinning it between two palm trees. They may not offer the best protection from the rain, but they'll at least keep the raft from blowing away in the wind.

"Thanks for the help. Why don't you go inside and get the food ready while I try to tie this off as best I can."

"Don't stay out here too long, Tarzan," she teases. "I don't want you blowing away out here."

I smirk, watching her walk away as another clap of thunder echoes in the distance, a cruel reminder of just how not in control I actually am.

"Yeah, yeah. I hear you loud and clear." I say aloud to mother nature. "Just give me a week to get ready, will ya?" I get my answer when a light sprinkling of rain begins to fall.

"Fucccck."

I'm drenched by the time I make it to the campsite, where I find Gwen hunkered in our flimsy lean-to with two salads laid out and ready. "It's really coming down out there. Is this normal? Should we be worried?" Her eyebrows pull together in concern as the heavy wind whips our shelter back and forth.

I take a seat, sitting crossed-legged next to her, and begin shoveling my salad into my mouth. I don't speak because I'm afraid I may scare her. I eat my salad and oysters and mentally prepare for what I know is coming. A bead of water leaks from the roof, landing directly on my forehead. The cold liquid slides all the way down my face before dripping into my empty bowl.

Gwen's eyes go wide, and she glares at me with concern, "Oh, shit. The roof's leaking! Do we need to patch it or something?"

Just as the question leaves her mouth, a gust of wind blows through the shelter, taking the roof with it.

"Gwen, listen to me. You need to get to the overhang where we had our first date. There's a small cavern on the side. It's only big enough for one person. Go right now, do you understand me?" My words come out as a command rather than a suggestion, and I can see the fear bubbling up in Gwen's eyes from the change in my demeanor. She nods her head in understanding and bolts as another wide gust rushes over us.

I steady my breathing and get to work. I've got to collect all of our things, the things we both need for survival. I throw on my backpack and do my best to shove our food supplies and what's left of Gwen's clothing into a hollowed-out tree trunk. Her things will be wet, but the fish I dried will be fine ... as long as the wind doesn't blow it away.

The rain pelts against my face like bullets, stinging every inch of exposed skin as I rush to find Gwen. But when I see the huge waves crashing against the rock, my heart sinks. Not only could this ruin our chance of escape, but we also may not even live through the night to try.

"Fuck!" I scream as I squint my eyes, trying to make sense of where I am. I know I'm close to the rocky overhang, but the rain is flying around me in every direction. "Gwen!" I call, cupping my hands around my mouth. My heart's racing so fast I think it may spontaneously combust. "Gwen!" I yell again as I climb the shallow rocks, stumbling and falling with every other step I take. Blood spills down my legs, and I know I'll be digging out fragmented rocks for days. I just hope Gwen made it in time. "Gwen!" My voice cracks, and a wave of nausea courses through me, mixing with the adrenaline, and I feel like I'm going to be sick.

"Jack, I'm over here!" Her scared, shaky voice is music to my ears, and I turn toward her voice. That's when I see her, hunkering behind a rock, her white blonde hair slicked back as her small body curls in on itself.

"Baby, I'm here." I rush to her, pulling her shivering body into my shaking arms. "Baby, I told you to hide in the cavern! Goddammit, you scared me."

"I... I... I couldn't find it, and then a gust of wind blew down this tree right in front of me, and I panicked." She sobs into my drenched t-shirt. "I thought I was going to die, Jack."

"I've got you." I take her hand and give her a firm squeeze.

I'm not letting her out of my sight until we're safe. "We'll make a run for it, okay?"

She nods her understanding and squeezes my hand even tighter.

"The cavern is just ahead. I want you to go in first, and I'll follow you." Gwen's face is white as a sheet, but she steadies her gaze and nods.

"We go on three, okay? One. Two. Three."

CHAPTER TWENTY-FOUR

Jack

Last night was the worst night of my life. Gwen scared the shit out of me when she wasn't where she was supposed to be. The muscles in my back scream and ache from lying on the hard rocky surface of the narrow cavern.

The small cavern we slept in is barely big enough for one person, so I used my body as a shield to cover the opening, protecting Gwen from being pelted by the storm. She still shook like a leaf in my arms all night, but at least I was able to shield her from the brunt of it.

The only reason I know the time is because of my watch. I didn't sleep a wink, and the hazy sky is blocking most of the sunlight. I climb out of the cramped cavern, and the vision before me steals my breath.

Our small little paradise is unrecognizable.

Everything we've built to sustain ourselves has been destroyed. Palm trees lay uprooted in every direction, and I try my best to keep my composure. I don't want to scare Gwen because the last thing I need is for her to know how scared I am right now.

I suck in a long steady breath to slow my racing heart and take her hand. "Come on, let's go check on the camp."

She nods her head and furrows her brow. "Jeez, look at all of this mess." She kicks a stray log away from the path, head wandering around in every direction. "Was that like a monsoon or something?"

"Or something," I say, not wanting to get into the details right now. I know I'm being short with her, but I have to be careful with my words here. I need to see the camp and assess the damage so I can figure out our next move.

When we finally make it to the campsite—or where the campsite used to be—there's no evidence of the last two months of our lives.

I let out a heavy sigh and crouch to the ground, folding in on myself as I try to think of any solution, but my exhausted brain is coming up empty.

I make a mental list of the things we have—my camera equipment, what's left of our clothing, the basic survival tools I keep in my bag, and my collapsible fishing rod. I've got the dried fish that I thankfully finished smoking yesterday, but all the other food reserves are gone. We don't have a shelter, and all the firewood is drenched.

It's going to take me days to rebuild a shelter, and we'll have to survive off coconuts and oysters—that is, if we can even find them with all the flooding.

At least we still have water.

As soon as the thought comes to my mind, a jolt of fear shoots through me, and I dart off toward our stream as fast as my legs can carry me.

"Jack!" Gwen screams, trying her best to keep up with me. "What are you doing? What's going on?"

I'm breathless and heaving when I reach the small stream and take in the destruction before me.

Everything is flooded, and what was once a small freshwater stream is now just an extension of the ocean. It's as if it was never there in the first place. Suddenly, this island is a lot smaller than it was just twelve hours ago.

"No, no, no." I rush to the water and cup a handful to test it, and my worst fears are confirmed. The water is salty, it's been contaminated by the ocean, and there's no way it's drinkable.

"FUCK!" I scream, sinking to my knees as I let out the feral cry I've been holding in for so long. I scream in anger as hot tears brand my face with fear. Every semblance of composure I've held melts away, and it's as if I've just turned on a firehose of emotions. This is what rock bottom feels like. All this time, I've been clenching a tiny bit of hope in my chest. Knowing we at least had plenty of water gave me some confidence that we could make this work, but now, seeing everything we've worked so hard to build laying in shambles around us, I feel like our fate is a ticking time bomb just waiting to explode.

Without clean drinking water, we won't survive. There won't be an island for Gwen to wait for me on because she can't stay here without a water source.

I never thought I'd see a challenge I couldn't overcome, but this... this is my undoing.

"Jack, talk to me. You can't just shut down." Gwen's pacing in front of me, and I'm aware I haven't moved from this position for what seems like hours. "I'm really freaking out here, and I need you to tell me we're going to be okay."

Her shaky voice breaks my heart, and white hot rage courses through my veins. I'm supposed to be the professional here. I'm the protector, and I've got nothing. I've failed at the most important job in the entire world.

"I'm sorry, Gwen. I've got nothing." I pull myself to a wobbly stance, towering over her. "I fucking failed us, and we're screwed. Is that what you want me to say?" Her chin wobbles, but she doesn't back away as I let it all out. "Our only source of fresh water is gone. It's *gone*! Do you know how long humans can survive without water, Gwen?" I pause for the full effect, "Three days! Three fucking days, and that's assuming we're both fully hydrated—which we're not." I add because why not hit her with the brutally honest truth of the matter. It's best she knows what her future holds, and I hope she hates me as much as I hate myself right now because that's the only way I can live with myself for the next three days.

"But... that can't be right." She glances around as if some magical new fresh water source will appear. "Can't we keep looking—I mean, we haven't seen the other side of the island. I bet if we keep searching–"

"Do you really think I haven't thought of that? There's no other water source. I've walked this entire island ten times through searching for it," I snap, my words cutting through her small amount of hope like a dagger. "While you were sleeping or bathing or doing whatever the fuck you do all day, I've been scouring this island trying to find any resource that could help us. Is that what you want to hear? It's over. We'll be dead soon, and it won't matter." I sit back down on the fallen tree trunk and fold in on myself, letting all my fears fester like an open rotting wound.

"Why are you acting like this?" Tears fill her perfect green eyes, and she backs away from me. "Where's the boy scout I came here with who could build a fire with a toothpick and a strand of hair?" Her exaggeration stings like salt on my open wound.

"I guess he's gone, and you just have me." I open my arms, exposing all of myself. "Jack Manning, the biggest fuck up of all time, at your service." I take a bow for an added blow.

"No!" Gwen stomps her foot and charges toward me, grabbing me by the ear like a schoolboy. Before I know it, she's in my face like a drill sergeant, commanding my full attention. "You don't get to give up now just because it got hard. This is *your* life, Jack. It's *my* life. I know you feel defeated right now, but I need you to pull yourself together." I feel the sharp sting of a slap against my cheek, and the surprise takes my breath away.

I rub the tender skin, eyes wide in shock as Gwen continues. "I have overcome too much to die on some island in the middle of nowhere." She pokes me in the chest with her finger, "Now you go take a walk and use your Tarzan brain to come up with a better plan than both of us dying of thirst on this island, do you understand me?"

I nod, rubbing the small wound she just inflicted with the tip of her index finger, and hang my head in shame. I have to bite my tongue to keep my southern manners from further insulting her with a "Yes, ma'am." Somehow, I feel like that would render another physical wound, and I'm afraid my balls may be her next target.

"I'll meet you back here when the sun's over there." She points to her designated tree shadow, and it's just what I need to bring me back to my senses. "You come back with solutions. I'm going to... *let off some steam*!" She turns back and snaps, "And that is *not* an invitation!"

And just like that, I've been scolded, motivated, and put in my place by the only woman in the world who can give me a semi while I'm scared shitless. Just another confirmation that she is, in fact, the woman of my dreams.

I meet Gwen back at the stream at our agreed meeting time with a newfound pep in my step. Not only did I rethink my original plan, but I feel confident that she can fend for herself without me—especially after that whole dominatrix show back there. We're really going to have to revisit that fantasy when this is all said and done because seeing Gwen boss me around like that made me feel some kind of way, and I'm not mad about it.

"I hope you've come back with a solution." She crosses her arms over her chest in a protective stance, giving me another opportunity to make things right.

I scratch the back of my head and shuffle my feet. "I did. Um, first of all, I just want to say thank you for what you did back there. I... I've never lost it like that before, and I certainly shouldn't have taken my frustration out on you."

She nods her head, "You're right about that."

I take that as an apology accepted, so I continue. "This is just the beginning of the storm season, so there's no point rebuilding the campsite. It'll just be ruined again in a matter of days—"

"That doesn't sound like a solution, Jack—"

"Hold on." I hold my hands up. "Let me finish, ok?"

She nods her head, and I continue, "Water is our main concern, right? So, since we don't have the stream anymore, you'll have to collect your own water from the rain and morning dew each day. I think I've figured out a way to make a funnel with the palm leaves, and we'll dig a well to collect it when it rains."

"Okay, that sounds easy enough. See, I knew you'd think of a solution outside the box." Her voice sounds hopeful.

"You'll have to rebuild the funnel after every storm, so we'll have to practice setting it up. I need to know that you can do this on your own—"

"Why would I need to be on my own?" she asks, but deep down, we both know the answer.

"Because I'm leaving to find help first thing in the morning." I pause to let it sink in. "I'll leave the rod behind with you so you can catch and cook fish when it's dry. I'll take most of the dried fish with me on the raft since I can't make a fire. It's the only shot we have at making it out of here alive."

She presses her lips together and nods as a silent understanding passes between us. "Then I guess you need to show me how to build that funnel."

"Yeah. We don't have much daylight left." There's so much left unsaid, but I don't think either one of us can handle thinking of saying goodbye so soon or what our future could hold. So I grit my teeth and lead the way.

Spending our last day together digging a well wasn't exactly the romantic goodbye I envisioned, but I'm not really sure I believed we'd ever have to make a decision like this. I think a part of me always thought we'd live out the rest of our lives on this island in peace, no matter how long that actually was.

"Come on. I'll show you the spot I have in mind."

CHAPTER TWENTY-FIVE

Gwen

My back aches, my hands are bloody, and I'm exhausted from digging a giant hole in the ground to store my water. This may come as a surprise, but manual labor isn't exactly my strong suit.

We spent all night digging the well and preparing the rain funnels, and I'm mentally and physically drained. Every muscle in my body is on fire, but I know this is the only way I'll survive until Jack can find help. I caught a couple of hours of sleep before sunrise, mainly because Jack took one look at my emaciated body, a far cry from where it was when we crash landed on this island, and demanded I get some rest.

Since the shelter was destroyed and Jack is convinced this is only the beginning of the storm season, I've been ordered to sleep in the godforsaken cavern tucked away in the side of the cliff. As I roll to my side, squeezing my eyes closed as if I can fend off the sunrise by choosing not to see it, my back cracks against the hard rock. If I thought sleeping on the scratchy sand was uncomfortable, this is a whole new level of hell.

If we survive this, I promise never to complain about my mattress being too firm ever again.

The chirping birds are wild this morning, acting as mother nature's alarm clock.

"Ugh, ok, fine. I'm awake! Are you happy, you fucking birds!?" I make a mental note to attempt to spear a bird for dinner tonight. It's the only revenge that'll make me feel the tiniest bit better about my current circumstances.

I army crawl out of my shit-hole new shelter and squint my eyes as they adjust to the offensively bright sun. That's weird. I look around for a tree and notice the shadow's on the wrong side. That means it's at least nine in the morning. Why didn't Jack wake me sooner?

I stand up, stretching my back as best as my stomach grumbles its dissatisfaction. Yeah, yeah. With all the intense physical labor last night, we didn't exactly have time to eat a proper meal. Grabbing a single coconut from my small collection, I strike it against a rock and begin eating my breakfast. It's not much, but the sweet flavor has my mouth watering for more, and when I'm finished, it takes all my strength not to break out another one from my emergency stash. It's so quiet this morning—with the exception of the squawking birds. I wonder where Jack's run off to.

I head toward the beach and see him working on his boat in the distance. He's hunched over, probably double-checking his knots, and I notice he's added my long swim coverup as a sail. Dammit, that was Chanel, and now it's being used as a boat sail. My past self would've died if she'd seen this treachery, but I smile as I watch him.

His strong back is more defined than ever, though it's more of starvation and dehydration sculpted. The kind of definition men think women like when we would really rather have a little meat on the bone. I glance at my boney hips, then turn to examine my almost non-existent ass. I suppose I can't really talk about Jack being too thin when I'm smaller than I've ever been in my life. For a moment, my vanity gets the best of me, and I mourn my old, healthy self as I try to pinch the nonexistent fat on my stomach. It'll all be worth it. I tell myself. When we get out of here, I'll eat all the carbs and gain back the weight. I'll be strong and healthy, and I'll never look at the flesh on my stomach and think I'm too heavy ever again. I'll eat dessert with every meal and... fuck...my stomach cries out in hunger again. I've got to stop lusting over food. It's not helpful right now.

I shake the thought away, reminding myself to use that determination later tonight to hunt the squawking bird that still won't shut up... *after* Jack leaves.

"Why didn't you wake me up?" I say as I come into earshot of the beach. He's fooling with his sail now, and I can see he's just about packed up and ready to leave.

"You needed the rest." He pulls me to him, planting a long soft kiss on my forehead, and I breathe in his masculine scent. God, he smells good. I know it's weird to say that someone who hasn't properly bathed in two months smells good, but I'm addicted to everything about this man. I don't know how I'll survive without his warmth, his goofy jokes, and overall chipper attitude balancing out my bitchiness.

"Why do you have to leave today?" I whine, gripping him into a tighter hug.

"You know why." His voice is stern, and he squeezes me tighter. "You've got everything you need here. Luckily, all the downed trees made it easy for me to repair the raft." He cracks his neck, and I know as sore as I may feel, Jack must be ten times more exhausted. He stayed up all night, and now, he's about to set sail out into the middle of the ocean.

I swallow the lump in my throat. This whole situation is crazy. But we both know it's our only hope. There's no other choice. I just have to trust that he'll make it out alive, that he'll find help. I squeeze my eyes closed, savoring the feel of his warm hard body against mine, and say a silent prayer it won't take very long.

"And you're sure where you're going?" I ask him again, for the millionth time.

"Yes... well... hopefully. I think I have a general idea of where we've landed, but I can't know for sure." He pulls away, throwing his backpack over his shoulder. "I need you to keep your head straight and take care of yourself. Try not to worry about me."

I notice he's rigged up a stand for his camera, "Are you seriously still worried about content at a time like this?"

"Something like that." He pulls me closer to him, and my body shakes with nervousness. "Keep the well full of drinking water, and don't forget to boil it," he commands. "And remember, when you're fishing, you need to head back before dusk just in case you get caught up."

I nod my understanding.

"You've got the torches I made you for signaling, right? And don't forget this." He places the flare gun in my hand, and I carefully wrap my fingers around it, reminded of just how stupid I was last time I held it.

I won't make the same mistake again.

"Make sure to keep a lookout for any aircraft and use this if you see something close enough. Just like we practiced."

I nod again and roll my eyes.

"Don't let the torches get wet. Keep them in the cavern."

"Yes. I know." I purse my lips together to keep from crying because I know this is goodbye.

"I love you. Keep yourself safe, and don't do anything dangerous." He grips my shoulders and stares into my eyes. "I will come back for you. I need you to be strong and take care of yourself, okay?"

"I love you, too." Hot tears wet my cheeks, and I don't try to wipe them away. "Now go get on your damn *Castaway*-raft and save our lives."

"I will come back for you," he promises, and his mouth crashes into mine with a whole new emotion; it's not love or lust or anything in between; it feels more like a goodbye, and my chest aches as I take him in, loving him with everything I have to give. If he's the last person I ever touch, ever kiss, then I can live with that.

We finally find the strength to break away from each other, or rather, Jack does, and I watch him step on his shoddy raft and set sail into the wide unknown ocean. I wave goodbye, and when he's finally out of sight, I fall to my knees and let myself fall apart. I cry and heave. I wail and plead and beg, but he's gone, and now, all I can do is hope that he'll come back to me. Though hope isn't my strongest virtue, I'm learning.

CHAPTER TWENTY-SIX

JACK

"Hey, Dubbies. I've gotten myself into some new shit I've never experienced before, and I'm not even going to try to pretend I know what I'm doing," I say to the camera securely fastened at the front of my raft.

I'm down to my very last battery, and it's only got a half-life, so I make my message quick. "I've just set out to find help, and I'm not going to lie, I'm fucking terrified. The water's choppier than I expected, and I've only got enough food to last me a week, and that's if I eat a half ration. My water supply isn't looking good either, so as much as I hate rainstorms, I'm going to have to do a rain dance or something before long. So far, all I can see is blue water in every direction." Gesturing to my watch, I continue, "Thanks to this guy, at least I know I'm headed west, which is what I think is the right direction. Hell, at this point, I just need to find land. It doesn't matter where I find it. I'm signing off. Have to save my battery for when I have something to update you on. Bye for now."

I click the camera off and shove it back into my waterproof backpack, which I've got strapped to my back like it's my lifeline. It is, really. Everything I need to survive is in this bag, including all the priceless footage I've taken. I can't risk losing it, and at least it'll act as a floatation device if shit gets really bad. I tighten my grip on the oars and adjust my pathetic excuse for a sail. *Just stay west,* I tell myself, unsure if it's a prayer or a reminder, but it's the only mantra I have to keep going.

It's been two days at sea, and the sun's scorching rays burn my tanned skin, but I don't even mind. It's a nice reminder that I'm alive. A refreshing breeze blows every now and then, kissing my sun-scorched skin and providing me with a refreshing break from the heat. I breathe a sigh of relief as I check my watch to make sure I haven't gotten turned around. Last night was rough, and I'm exhausted from paddling. I was only able to catch a few broken hours of sleep, and I'm starting to feel delusional. Maybe it's the sun or the dehydration, or maybe I'm finally losing my mind, but when my eye catches something massive in the distance, I stand to my feet to get a better look.

Is that a—no, it can't be. I paddle furiously to get a better look, my muscles aching with every push and pull through the dense waves, and I'm actually making some headway. I yank off my backpack to retrieve my binoculars, and my suspicions are confirmed when the enormous tail of a blue whale appears right in front of me. Excitement rips through me in a burst, and I decide this is definitely film-worthy. I'm giddy now, pulling the camera out of my bag and positioning it so that the whale's in the frame behind me. I don't know what to say as my small raft floats closer and closer, and when a second whale comes into view, it takes everything I have not to fall off completely. I tell the camera what I'm seeing and how rare it is to see not one but two of these massive creatures.

Here I am, all alone in the middle of the ocean seeing animals I never dreamed I'd encounter up close and personal. For a moment, I question whether or not I've actually died and this is some out-of-body experience before I transcend the other side. But when the raft floats close enough to the animal that I can reach out and touch its side, I feel like it's the universe's way of telling me I'm going to make it.

I can't help myself as I extend my hand, gently touching the slick wet flesh of the largest creature known to man.

"There's a big world out there, Dubbies. I hope you're able to see this footage. Fuck, I hope you can see this." I pet the animal again as I struggle with what to say to capture the magic of this moment. "I'm scared to death right now, and I don't know if I'm going to make it out of here alive, but if you're watching, just know that I gave this life all I could. I took chances, and I lived. It didn't always make sense, and sometimes, I was a little too reckless—hell, I'm on a fucking raft in the middle of the Caribbean right now. But if this experience doesn't kill me, then I know there's nothing I can't do. I hope you find your passion in life and follow it. I can promise you the waters may be rough, but the universe will reward you with the most amazing moments in between, and these moments are what make it all worth it."

I'm crying now, and I know my message isn't just about the whale. I think of Gwen and the short time we shared in paradise, and even if our time is over, I know I gave her all of me. I just can't give up on her because I don't know if she feels the same. There's so much left she wants to do with her work and dreams, and everything comes down to this. I'm carrying the rest of her life on my shoulders, and I won't give up even if it means I die trying.

I put my camera away and thank the universe for the renewed strength; something tells me I'm going to need it.

For now, I'll take advantage of the peaceful waters and rest while I can.

Two days have passed since my encounter with the whales, and I was right to think it was a small calm before the storm. My back aches as I paddle my oars as rough waves crash over the raft. The constant push and pull of the turbulent ocean make me feel like I'm fighting just to stay in place.

"Come on!" I grit my teeth as another wave drenches me and everything I brought.

I don't have much of a shelter, just a small canopy built from bamboo slats, but it helps to break up some of the pressure of the barrage of water coming at me from every side.

After giving it all the hell I can, I decide to hunker down and let mother nature do her thing. The raft's being tossed up and down in every direction, and when a massive wave crashes against me and a piece breaks free from the bottom, I know my time left here is short.

I crawl underneath the small canopy, lying flat on my stomach, and pull out my camera for my final recording. I don't have anything to hold it, so I do my best to steady the shot with my cold, shaking hands. I hit record.

"Listen, whoever finds this, whoever finds me, Gwenneth Pierson and I crash-landed my small plane on an island approximately two hundred kilometers from Costa Rica. Today is June 22, 2022. I've built a small raft that's currently being destroyed by a storm, and I've accepted my fate. Gwen, if you're watching, fuck, I hope you are. I love you so much, and I want you to know you're the only thing keeping me going out here.

The memory of your smile warms me at night when the freezing water is almost too much to bear. I want you to chase your dreams and let go of your past. Trust people, baby. But most of all, I hope you'll trust yourself. You're so strong, and you don't even realize it. I love you so much. Tell everyone about us and our adventures and live your life without fear, because if you can survive the wild, you can do anything you want. This is my message in a bottle. I hope it finds its way to whoever can help." Another crashing wave knocks the canopy clean off the raft, exposing me to the wild ocean in every sense of the word. "Goodbye, everyone. It was a hell of a ride."

A sob escapes me as I hurry to shut off the camera and shove it into my backpack just before the final wave crashes over me, and suddenly, I'm floating. Water pulls me in every direction, and I hold onto my backpack with the tightest grip I can manage. And everything goes black.

CHAPTER TWENTY-SEVEN

Gwen

It's been three days since I watched Jack sail away, and it feels like every minute we're apart, a piece of my heart breaks a little more. I've mostly survived on oysters and coconuts, and I even found a papaya tree with two measly pieces of fruit, but I'm growing weaker, and I know I need real meat if I'm going to keep up my strength. I can see a hint of gray clouds on the horizon, and I'm afraid another big storm may be rolling in soon, so I decide today's the day I'll go fishing and finally make a hot meal.

Jack left me the collapsible fishing rod, and I've been with him enough to know the best fishing spot on the island. I've just got to swim to the shallow sandbar to get there. Luckily, our swimming lessons have paid off, and I'm comfortable enough to swim the short distance.

The water's a little colder than usual, and I suck in a sharp breath as I wade deeper and deeper. Before I know it, I'm on the sandbar, casting my first line of the day.

Jack taught me to fish early in the day because some days, it takes longer than others to get a single bite, and I won't be caught dead out here in the water when I can't see my feet.

I have a flashback of the shark swimming around me, and I giggle despite my immense worry. God, it must've been a sight to see watching that bloody tampon flying through the air. I really don't know what I was thinking. I was an entirely different person than I am now.

How long ago was that? I think back and try to count the days, but they all seem to run together. I know Jack had a mental calendar, but it's not something I've had to think about. I've just been focusing on making it through one day at a time, but ... I can't remember having my period since then.

My heartbeat quickens as I try to count back, but it's no use. It could've been years as much as I remember. I guess I've lost so much weight that my cycle just stopped. I can't give it much more thought because I'm rewarded with my first bite of the day. Instantly, my worry turns to excitement as I reel in a small silver fish, just big enough to feed me for lunch and dinner.

"Score!" I scream and reel in my little lifesaver. I could stay and try to catch more, but it's no use; the rain will come and spoil anything I try to save, and there's no use in killing fish I won't even be able to eat.

My stomach growls, and I can't keep the smile off my face. I'm looking forward to a hot meal tonight, and by the size of this thing, I may even have a distended belly.

"I've got big plans for you, bucko." I shove him in my net sack and cinch it shut as I make my way back to the shore. I may even use my last mango for a glaze. My mouth waters at the thought.

When I finally make it back to the shore, I start building a fire—the easy way that Jack taught me. I may have the survival skills needed to rub sticks together like a caveman now, but I found a perfectly good water bottle on the beach on my way back, and there's no use in expending any more energy when I can use this as a magnifying glass.

I use an emergency cotton ball Jack left me and a piece of my favorite lipstick—who knew lipstick was such a hot commodity in a survival situation—and line my water bottle up to the sun's sparing rays. It takes longer than usual to finally get a flame due to the clouds rolling in, but when I see the ember come to life, I know I've done it.

I pump my fist in the air and blow my tiny kindle as I watch it grow to a true flame. And then I get to work, stacking the wood pieces we prepared ahead of time, and before I know it, my fish is sizzling above the open flame.

I've come so far and learned so much from our short time on this island. It seems mother nature has taught me far more about trust and faith than any lesson learned through school or work. My heart swells with pride when I think about all I've done to keep myself alive since Jack left. I'm capable of so much more than I ever thought possible. It's exhausting working from sun up to sun down, especially all alone, but somehow, I've managed to keep my water supply full, fish, and even maintain a fire all by myself. I know Jack would be proud of me, and I only wish he could see me thriving out here and know how much his survival lessons actually taught me. I don't know if he realizes how much of an impact his videos have, and if I live to see him again, it'll be the first thing I tell him.

I think of Jack floating out there on his dilapidated raft, eating dried fish, and my heart sinks with worry, but I immediately redirect my thoughts. I'll never survive if I'm worrying about him. Jack would want me to focus on myself. That's the only way we both walk away from this.

I cook the fish until it's golden brown and even add the mango for an extra treat. It's no five-star dining experience, but when I taste the hot, juicy fish, I can't keep my eyes from rolling back in my head in ecstasy. I finish the entire portion; leftovers be damned. I'd rather eat coconut for dinner than not enjoy this while it's piping hot and fresh.

When I'm finished with my meal, I lean my back on a tree and take in the beautiful scene before me. A small gust of wind brushes a strand of hair from my face like a whisper of peace. There's no doubt in my mind mother nature is female. How else can you explain how the same wind can be so delicate in one moment and destructive the very next. She's a powerful woman capable of tenderness and peace, but when she's angry, she doesn't hold back her wrath.

A small smirk pulls at my lips. I suppose we both have that in common.

A strong gust of wind whips my hair over my face, waking me from my deep slumber. I look around and notice the sun's beginning to set. I must've passed out from pure exhaustion. How long was I asleep? I push myself up to stand, heading back to my cavern, when my stomach begins to churn in disgust. Suddenly, the thought of the delicious mango and fish I feasted on earlier sounds like the most repulsive thing in the world. I can't make it five steps before I'm doubled over, retching every last bite into a nearby bush. My body shakes as I forcefully heave the entire contents of my stomach, and I can't help the small whimper that follows. Another wave of nausea courses through me, and I curl into myself and cry.

As if things can't get any worse, I can add food poisoning to my long list of misery. I somehow manage to gain enough strength to get up and make my way back to the small hell hole I now call home.

I climb over the jagged rocks into my little cavern and cry myself to sleep.

Jack, please hurry. I don't know how much more of this I can take.

CHAPTER TWENTY-EIGHT

Gwen

I roll over, dislodge the loose rock from the small of my back, and curl into a ball on my side as another wave of nausea rocks through me. The fucking birds are at it again, squawking mockingly, so happy to be alive they have to scream about it.

I'm miserable. I've been puking for three days straight—ever since I ate that fish—and you don't see me screaming it out to the whole island. No, I keep my quiet sobs to myself.

Maybe I should start waking them up and see how they like it? If I had the strength, I'd murder every bird on this island just so that one doesn't find its mate. It's only fair if I can't have mine; I shouldn't have to listen to him calling for his.

I climb out of my cavern and vomit near the closest tree. "I hope you like the smell of vomit and it throws off all your bird-pheromones!" I scream.

I feel like I'm in that movie *Groundhog Day*, only it's ten times more miserable because I don't have the love of my life with me. He's out there, somewhere, fighting for our survival, and I'm stuck here hanging onto life by a thread. How long does food poisoning last, anyway? Fuck, I hope it's not salmonella or some bacterial infection that'll make me shit myself to death. What a horrible way to die, especially after all I've been through.

I gargle some fresh water I prepared last night, then spit it out by my feet before taking a real sip. At least the well has kept enough water for me, and I've collected enough plastic water bottles that I can boil it ahead of time. It's probably the only reason I'm still alive right now—that and the coconuts.

My fragile limbs carry me to the beach, where I write a new message in the sand. It's become a game I play. Every day, I write another obscure message on the off chance an aircraft will fly over, see it, and rescue me. Today's message reads:

FUCK BIRDS PLS HELP

I'm exhausted after writing the giant letters, so I plant my butt in the sand and breath in the fresh island air.

It's actually sunny today, which is a nice change from the weather lately. The warm sun heats my skin, and for a moment, it feels amazing, like a soothing balm to my aching muscles. But then a hot flash sends a wave of heat through my core, and I have to jump in the water to cool down. That's been happening a lot more lately; it must be a side effect of the food poisoning.

After a quick swim, I eat a coconut for breakfast and make my way up to the cliff for a better view.

It's a hard climb, not something I do too often, but today, I'm feeling nostalgic about the night Jack and I made love on our first date. My muscles are burning by the time I reach the top, and I'm panting for air, but the view is so worth it. There's no trace of the elaborate palm leaves lining the ground or anything for that matter, but the vision of us lying together will be burned into my memory for the rest of my life—no matter how long that turns out to be.

I fall to my knees and lay my head on the cold stone, letting the rocky floor cool me. Luckily, the nausea seems to have subsided, so I eat a small bit of the jerky that Jack left me for emergencies. I'd say this is an emergency. I don't know how much more of it I can take, so I may as well enjoy the view.

The bright blue water sparkles in the distance like a sapphire, and if I didn't know Jack was out there fighting for his life, I might even say it looks peaceful. But I've seen the destruction the sea can cause when the storms come through, and there's nothing peaceful about the ocean. It's just as scary as the day we landed. Hell, maybe even scarier now that I know what she's capable of.

I squint my eyes as the sun's glare seems to shine directly into my retinas. I've never been up here in the bright afternoon sun, but something dark catches my eye, a contrast against the blues and golds of the ocean. Is it another shark? I scoot closer to the cliff's edge, and my stomach flutters when I look down. I remember that jump. I never felt so alive and free than when I held Jack's hand and leaped from this cliff. The dark object isn't moving, and it's farther out than I've ever been, past the sandbar even.

What is it? I cover my eyes with my hand in an attempt to see farther out when I notice something that looks familiar.

It can't be.

I'd recognize that backpack anywhere. Before I can talk myself out of it, I'm jumping off the cliff, slightly to the right, just as Jack and I did all that time ago.

My body falls faster this time around, maybe because I'm alone or just because my adrenaline's flooding my system. The water doesn't feel cold when I land. It's like I'm numb to it.

I throw my arms over my head one at a time, pumping my legs with every ounce of energy I have as I fight my way against the current. I've got one thing on my mind, and my instincts take over before I can overthink the distance I'm swimming. I just pray there's still a chance he's alive because he hasn't moved a limb.

Salty water burns my eyes, and as I propel myself past the sandbar into the deepest water I've ever swam in, I'm not afraid. Not of drowning—or sharks—anyway. The only thing I have on my mind is getting Jack. If he's dead, there won't be a reason to fight anymore, and I know I'll succumb to the same fate, let the sea take me out of my misery just as it did for him.

"Jack!" I scream as water rushes into my mouth. I'm a choking and gurgling mess, and his body is cold. "Jack!" I shake him, but he doesn't move, just floats like a lifeless shell of himself.

"No, God, no!" I scream, grabbing the backpack's straps when I realize it's floating. It's a floatation device!

Of course, it is. Jack's such a survival nerd. Of course, he'd carry something so multifunctional. I slide my fingers to the side of his neck and gasp when I feel a faint pulse.

I have to check again on the other side because I'm afraid my weakened state is playing tricks on me, but when I grab his wrist and feel it, I latch myself on to him and kick my legs as hard as I can, pushing him in front of me as his backpack keeps us both afloat.

Now that I have him in my arms, time seems to stand still, and the distance back to the beach seems to have multiplied. When I finally make it to shore, I drag him up on the beach by the pack and lay him on his back.

Think, Gwen. What would Jack do right now?

The only thing that comes to mind is the old episodes of *Baywatch* my dad used to watch when I was a kid. I don't know anything about CPR, but I remember something about pumping their chest and breathing into their mouth.

I do my best to mimic the *Baywatch* babe's movements,

though I'm sure my version isn't nearly as sexy, and I use all my strength to pump his chest. I have no idea how many times I need to do it, so I alternate breathing into his mouth when my arms get tired.

Finally, after three or four tries, Jack turns his head and coughs up seawater.

"Thank God!" I throw myself on his freezing body and kiss him viciously. "I thought you were dead!" I sob into his neck, and when his hand comes up to my face, I pull away.

"Gwen?" he says as he looks around, confusion pulling at his eyes. "Where am I? How did you find me?"

"I saw you from the cliff. I thought you were dead," I sob, realizing I'm probably not being very helpful, but I've been through a lot today, and I'm just so happy he's alive.

He winces at my touch, and that's when I notice his leg. I gag when I see a broken white bone protruding from the skin.

"Oh shit." I cover my mouth and jump to my feet, so I don't vomit on his wound—that can't be sanitary.

He slowly maneuvers himself to a sitting position, looking around like he's been abducted by aliens. "We're still here. We're on the island?" His words come out like a question.

"Yeah," I say as I wipe the bile from my mouth with the back of my arm. "I think we're going to be here for a very long time."

Jack collapses back down in defeat.

"Let me grab you some water," I say, leaving him to his thoughts, so thankful he's alive. I don't even care that the plan failed.

"I still can't believe you're here." I hand Jack the bottle of warm water. He reaches with his left hand and takes the water from me, guzzling it down like he didn't just vomit an entire pool of it. "That looks really bad," I say, gesturing to his leg.

He sits up on his elbows to take another peek and lays back down. "Fuck!"

"Does it hurt? I could get you a coconut or–"

"We don't have the medical supplies to treat this. We drank what was left of the booze–"

"It's going to be ok," I try to reassure him, but I'm freaking out, too. He's lying on the beach after I just revived him. A piece of white bone protruding from his shin... My basic medical knowledge from watching *Grey's Anatomy* tells me it's a compound fracture. And based on how he flinched when I moved him, I think he may have a broken collarbone, too.

"It's fine. Just come here." He reaches for me, and I all but dive into his arms. I've never been so scared in my life. He kisses the top of my head. "I'm sorry, baby. I failed us."

"You didn't fail us, Jack," I assure him, combing my hands through his long wet strands. "We're together, and that's all that matters."

"I won't survive with this wound. It'll never heal right as it is. I won't be able to walk on it ever again, and that's if it doesn't get infected and fester."

"Stop talking. Just hold me, and let's enjoy this moment while we can, okay?"

He looks at me, and his eyes widen as he takes in my emaciated body. "Baby, what the hell happened? You look awful. Have you not been eating?"

"Oh, I think I have some kind of parasite or something. It's nothing compared to this." I gesture at his whole body. "Really, Jack, don't worry about me." I stand up and offer him my hand. "Let's get you out of this sun. I've got one more papaya and the last of the fish-jerky. I can make a fire, and you can tell me all about your adventure."

Tears glisten in his eyes, and he offers me his hand. "Yeah, I'd like that."

Using all my strength, I help him up to stand and let him lean on me as a crutch as I lead him to our old campsite. It's bare of any trace of the time we spent there except for a dug-out pit for our fires.

I show off my master fire-building skills, and even though I know he's writhing in pain, he forces a smile, telling me all about his adventures at sea, petting blue whales, and living to tell about it.

We laugh because it's all we can do to keep from crying. "I guess I can start calling you Ishmael now."

"If you don't call me Ishmael, what's the fucking point in even meeting a whale?"

"You know I've always wanted to fuck a real sea-man." I waggle my eyebrows, and Jack slaps his lap, despite his pain.

"Saddle up, I may be lame, but my dick hasn't gotten the memo."

So I do. Very carefully, we make love by the fire, and as pathetic as we may seem, it's somehow all I need.

After making love underneath the clear starry sky, we fall asleep, wound in each other's arms. I was careful of Jack's right shoulder and his leg. It made for some interesting positioning, but we're nothing if not resourceful.

I wake to the devil-bird's squawking cries as the sun begins to rise, and with Jack by my side, I'm not even angry. I just smile to myself, hoping the horny bird saw me get laid last night. Both times actually.

Revenge is sweet.

I nestle into the crook of Jack's neck, and when I finally open my eyes, I see he's awake.

"Good morning, beautiful."

"Good morn–" A wave of nausea interrupts my pleasantries, and I jump to my feet, so I don't get any vomit on Jack.

"You sure you're okay?" he calls from behind me.

"Probably not, but it's my new thing." I feign with amusement. "You know, you've got a fucked up leg, and I just puke all the time." I return to sit down beside him as I gurgle my water and spit. "I've come to accept it."

"That's so weird."

"I know, it just comes out of nowhere–" The faintest sound of something makes me pause, and I look to Jack for confirmation. His eyes are wide, and I know he heard it, too. "Is that a–"

"A helicopter!" He sits up in a rush and hisses, forgetting about his injured leg.

Our heads sweep the sky, searching for the source of the sound, and when I see it, my stomach flutters with adrenaline.

Jack's pupils nearly black-out his mossy green eyes as he looks at me. "Gwen, this could be our only chance."

"I've got it!" I leap to my feet, not needing him to finish his sentence because I already know what I need to do. We don't have much time, and I've replayed this scenario in my head, dreamed of this every single day we've been stuck on this island.

I grab the flare gun, tucking it in my swimsuit top, and run to the cavern to collect the dry, brittle bundles of leaves and emergency water bottle. Then make my way up to the top of the cliff. It's the best view on the island and our best chance at getting the helicopter's attention.

Just like the day before, I propel myself up the cliffside,

fueled by pure cortisol and adrenaline, ignoring all the aches and pains. I make the climb in record time and gather the bundle of dried leaves. I position my water bottle, but the sun's being finicky this morning, and the clouds are not helping my cause.

I finally give up on my water bottle and pull out my very last tube of lipstick before grabbing two rocks and slapping them together. Moments pass, and I pray it's not too late, but when I see the beautiful glow of sparks, I cry in delight. Immediately, the dried leaves catch, and I blow my tiny kindling to life. Before I know it, my fire's roaring, and I lay out the rest of the leaves to spell out SOS as large as I can on the cliffside.

Hope flares in my chest when I hear the helicopter. It sounds like it's closer, and I wave my hands in desperation, praying they see my sign. I very carefully aim the flare gun straight up. The shot explodes into the most beautiful signal for help, and I hold my breath as I wait.

I feel the wind from the helicopter before I see it, and when it finally comes into view, I see Maggie's long red hair blowing around in every direction. I sink to my knees and cry a sob of relief. My guttural cry comes from deep in my bones as the feeling of safety extinguishes the red hot fear from my chest.

We're saved.

CHAPTER TWENTY-NINE

Gwen

I can see Maggie's beautiful big blue eyes are swollen from crying as she lunges toward the pilot screaming for him to land the helicopter. I've actually never climbed *down* the cliffside. Ironically enough, I've had to jump every time I've come up here.

Shaking on wobbly legs, I slowly scale my way down the jagged rocks. My foot stumbles, losing its grip, and I slide down several feet before I'm able to catch my grip. A sharp pain shoots through the palm of my hand as blood runs down my arm.

The pain is searing, and I know it'll probably need stitches, but I manage to keep going, the spark of hope giving me all the energy I need to propel forward.

As soon as my feet hit the ground, I'm running to the beach to meet a frantic Maggie, who's all but jumped out of the helicopter before it's even landed.

I can see the pilot screaming at her through the glass windshield, but it doesn't slow her one bit. We're running toward each other, and as soon as she reaches me, I fall apart in her warm, soothing arms.

"Oh my God, Gwenny. I thought you were dead! I can't believe it. I can't believe he was right!" We're both sobbing now, and my whole body shakes with relief.

She wraps her arm around me, leading me toward the helicopter when a medic appears. Before I can say anything, they're strapping me to a gurney and moving me inside the aircraft.

"Jack!" I scream. It's all I can manage.

"Ma'am, I'm going to need you to lie down. Let me strap you in. You're severely dehydrated at the very least, and I need to assess you—"

"Jack's back there!" I scream, looking at Maggie. "You have to help him. He's hurt."

"I will. I'll find him," she assures me. "Just lay down, dammit, and do what the medic says."

She and another medic take off in the direction I pointed, and I let myself relax as they put an oxygen mask over my face. The gurney feels like a plush cloud compared to all the surfaces I've grown accustomed to sleeping on, and it's a strange thing, almost too comfortable.

They've just lifted me in the helicopter when I see the second gurney rolling toward us with Jack's unconscious body lying so still that I'm afraid they may have been a few minutes too late. Only when I see the sliver of his moss green eyes do I realize he's awake, just lying still, unlike me.

They load him into the helicopter, and I hear the medic going over his wounds.

"He's got a compound fracture on his right tibia and a closed fracture on the right clavicle. It looks he's got the beginning of sepsis forming from the leg wound."

The other medic spares no time pulling out bags of fluids

and needles. I feel a sharp pinch of an IV needle in my inner arm as the harsh smell of rubbing alcohol stings my nose. My vision slowly begins to dull.

"What's happening? What are you doing?" I fight the straps tying down my arms as I remember something.

I hear Maggie's soothing voice. "Just relax."

But behind the warm, tingling sensation, I crank my neck, searching the inner cabin, when I realize ... "Did you get his backpack?" My screams are muffled by the oxygen mask.

I panic, pulling the mask off my face as I fight through the fog. Making eye contact with Maggie, I plead, "It'll all be for nothing. You have to get the backpack!"

I look over and see Jack succumbed to the medication, his eyes gently shut, and I'm thankful he's getting some relief from the agony he must've been suffering for who knows how long.

The helicopter lifts from the ground, and I plead once more. "Maggie, please. You have to get the backpack. You have to make them stop."

Determination flicks in her eyes, and her protective fiery spirit flares as she leaps from the back seat toward the pilot.

"What the hell are you doing, lady?"

"Stop! I need to get something."

"We've got a critically injured patient back there—"

Again, she flings open the door and leaps the few feet to the ground.

"Motherfucker, who let the crazy lady on the search?" the pilot says to the medic.

"I'd listen to her if I were you. Last week I saw her hit a pilot with some kind of crystal when he refused to make another sweep. She's a feisty one."

I exhale a sigh of relief when I see her climbing back into the helicopter with Jack's backpack. She takes her seat next to me, flipping it over her front. "I've got the stupid backpack. Now get some rest. You look like shit."

"Thank you," I whisper, feeling her warm hand grip mine. "How did you find us?"

"I have my ways. Now please close your eyes and rest." She squeezes my hand. "I'll tell you all about it when we get to the island."

"What island?"

"Puerto Rico. It's the closest island to here."

I let the realization wash over me. We weren't even close to Costa Rica. Jack was on a suicide mission in the complete opposite direction.

I close my eyes and thank all my lucky stars because, without Maggie's rescue, we'd surely have been dead in a week.

CHAPTER THIRTY

A burning ache wakes me from my sleep, and when I open my eyes, I'm lying in a hospital room, surrounded by noisy machines. I make out a hunched-over Sam in the chair next to me before being accosted by the memory of the events that led me here.

My leg is in absolute agony, and I notice an IV thing in my left arm. It's not like any IV I've had before; it's stiffer somehow, and I can barely move my arm.

I lift the thin white hospital blanket to inspect my wounds. Nothing could've prepared me for what I see.

Or what I don't see, rather.

I let out a shrill scream at the realization, like a frightened child, which, of course, startles Sam awake. His fallen head shoots up, and he stands to his feet, rushing to me.

"Oh, shit, dude. I'm sorry. I tried to stay awake, but you were out for like eighteen hours and—"

"Where the fuck is the rest of my leg!?" I yell as if it's somehow Sam's fault.

He opens his mouth to speak, then closes it just as a nurse walks into the room.

"Mr. Manning, I see you've finally woken up." She clicks her pen and makes a note on some paperwork. "By the sound of your screams, I assume you've just realized the doctors had to amputate your leg to save your life."

My heart begins to race even more rapidly at hearing her confirm what my eyes witnessed for themselves. Maybe a part of me didn't trust my own eyes. After everything I've been through, it could have been a hallucination or something.

I reach my aching arm—the one without the tubes—and feel my knee stump to confirm that my leg has indeed been amputated.

My eyes go wide, and I quickly check my second favorite body part and breathe a sigh of relief. Yes, my penis and balls are, in fact, still intact. My leg I can live without, my dick not so much.

"Don't you have to ask my consent for something like that?" I snap.

"With all due respect, you weren't exactly in the best place to be making medical decisions that could impact your life." She scribbles another note. "Besides, your friend here signed the waiver," she says, gesturing toward Sam.

I snap my eyes to Sam, who's staring at his feet.

"So you did this to me!"

He holds his hands up in defense. "Whoa, whoa, you were going to die if they didn't do it." He looks back to the nurse for backup. "Right? That's what they said, isn't it? 'If we don't amputate his leg, the infection will spread to his bloodstream, and there'll be nothing we can do to save him'." He impersonates the nurse's accent as if he memorized the exact words, which is such a fucking Sam thing to do.

I don't know why I'm annoyed with him. I guess I need someone to pin the blame on, and it looks like I'll be riding Sam's ass about my leglessness for the rest of my life.

Fuck. The thought of missing a leg hits me like a boulder in the chest, knocking the wind from my lungs. Memories of my active lifestyle—my career—flash before my eyes, and I know everything will change because of this.

"Fuck you, man!" I slit my eyes at Sam, and he shrugs his shoulders.

"I'm going to take a walk and see if I can find some coffee. Maybe you'll be in a better place by the time I get back."

"Benjamin would've found a way to keep me alive *and* save my leg!" I scream as he leaves the room.

I know I'm acting like a bratty toddler, but shit, you've got to warn a guy before cutting his leg off.

"Are you done?" The nurse's sarcastic voice pulls me back into the moment. "Because I've got to check your pic line." She pulls at the IV bags hanging from the metal rod above my head.

So many different fluids are running through me, and I can't even begin to imagine the damage they're trying to repair.

"Ouch!" I scream when she pulls at the tape on my arm, leaving no trace of arm hair behind.

"Stop being a drama queen. That was just the tape."

I can see this nurse has zero empathy for me. She's young, too. Probably has a whole career ahead of her torturing her patients. "Well," I look at the name on her badge, "Tatiana, I happen to be a hairy gentleman, and I don't remember asking you for a Brazilian wax today."

This makes her smirk. "You're right. The wax was just a bonus. My special gift to you." She pulls out her blood pressure cuff and begins taking my vitals. "Now shut up for a minute so I can concentrate. Then I'll be on my way, and you can finish your temper tantrum."

I want to snap at her, tell her she's the worst nurse in the history of nursing and would probably be a better fit for a prison or something of that nature, but I don't. Maybe this is my karma for all the havoc I've caused by making stupid, selfish decisions all my life. I snap my lips closed and allow her to do what she needs to, giving her the blessed gift of my silence.

Sam appears in the doorway with two cups of coffee just as she finishes.

"I'll be back to remove your catheter in four hours." Pushing her cart toward the door, she calls over her shoulder, "I suggest you have a better attitude by then."

I can feel my penis shrivel up into my body at her harsh words, and my eyes go wide when I see Sam sharing the same sense of shock.

When I hear the door click shut, I lift the blanket and whisper, "Don't worry, buddy. I won't let her hurt you, too."

"I can see you're really flying through the five stages of grief." Sam passes me a cup of coffee. "A peace offering."

I eye him for a moment before taking the piping hot cup, and I don't even wait for it to cool before I take a sip. The hot liquid is strong, burning my tongue, but it's the most delicious coffee I've ever tasted. I close my eyes, savoring the depth of flavor, and I know I must be bad off if I think hospital coffee is suddenly the gold standard.

"So, give it to me. Just lay it on me. How bad is it?" I finally say after draining half the coffee from my cup.

"Well, the good news is, you're going to live. You may have lost part of your leg, but it's a hell of a lot better than the alternative." He sighs before delivering the next bit, and my stomach clenches in anticipation. "The bad news is... I think you'll be here for a while..."

"What do you mean? How long is *a while?*" I say, using air quotes with my one good hand.

"Well, that depends on the infection." He points to the tube in my arm. "You've got a gnarly case of sepsis, and that pic line is the only reason you're alive." He pauses, considering his words, then corrects himself. "Well, that and the amputated leg. You really are a lucky bastard. You know that, don't you?" He has the audacity to laugh before taking another sip of his coffee.

"How's Gwen? Is she okay?"

"She's stable." He holds his coffee close to him like he's hiding behind it.

"Good." I sigh in relief, and my throat tightens with emotion. I don't think anything could've kept me pinned to this hospital bed if he said anything different. Broken memories of our last days on the island flash through my mind. She was so sick and had lost so much weight. I don't know that either of us would've survived much longer on our own.

Bile rises in my throat, and I grit my teeth at the realization that I failed us.

I close my eyes and try to calm my nerves, I've got the rest of my life to beat myself up over this, but right now, I just need to see she's safe. "Where is she? When can I see her?" I look around the room, trying to steal a glance outside the door.

"She's on the, uh—" He clears his throat. "She's on the other end of the hospital. She's dealing with her own health issues."

I tighten my grip around the flimsy paper coffee cup. "What's wrong? Is she okay?"

It's one thing to wake up with a missing appendage but something else entirely to know that the woman I love is suffering and I'm being kept from her.

"Calm down, man. I promise you she'll be okay, but it's not my place to discuss her health. Please, can you just respect that?"

I squint my eyes, searching his face for any sign that he's lying. There's really no reason for Sam to lie about something so serious, but I can't trust my judgment right now. "Yeah, fine, but I want to hear it from Maggie at least." I grab the only thing available in my reach—my half-full coffee—and pelt it straight at his head.

The paper cup hits him in the face as the hot coffee flies in every direction.

Sam's angry face glows red, partly from the hot coffee. "What the fuck, man! What was that for?"

I clench my hand into a fist, then open it, spreading my fingers wide. "Gee, let me count the reasons." I count off my fingers. "You gave the doctors permission to amputate my leg. You left me alone with the she-devil nurse back there. And you just told me my girlfriend was stable, but you're being vague as fuck about it."

He wipes the remainder of the dripping coffee off his face with his sleeve and pushes up to stand. "I'm going to give you this one freakout pass, but you better believe I'm cashing this shit in someday in the future." He saunters to the door, and I give him the bird on his way out.

"Don't come back without Maggie! I want to at least hear it from her," I call after him.

"Sure thing... but first I need to find your nurse to discuss your catheter removal."

"You better not!" I scream as the door clicks closed.

Yeah, I'm definitely going to pay for that coffee stunt, hopefully not in the form of a new pee hole. I shiver at the thought as my head falls back onto the plastic-coated hospital pillow.

CHAPTER THIRTY-ONE

Gwen

I wake up in a stark white room that smells like chemicals and recycled air. Instead of a bird squawking to find love, a constant beep is echoing in my ears. The hospital is so noisy; I can hear the hustling and bustling of nurses rushing down the hallways and muffled conversations. It's such a contrast to my quiet island oasis.

"Looks like someone's finally awake." A nurse walks in wearing a stethoscope around her neck. Her cold hands wrap a blood pressure cuff around my arm, and she sticks a thermometer underneath my tongue. "Hold this here, please."

I oblige, confused about how long I've been here, but I suppose there'll be plenty of time to ask as soon as she's finished with my vitals.

"Good," she says as she takes the thermometer from my mouth, putting everything back into her rolling cart. "Where's Jack? My... my... boyfriend. I need to see him!" I beg as I swing my legs over the side of the bed.

The nurse grabs my shoulders, urging me to lie back down. "Hold on, dear. Not so fast. You're still very weak." She places the thermometer back in my mouth. "You two have quite the survival story. The whole hospital's talking about it." The thermometer beeps, and she removes it, then passes me a cup of pills and a cup of water.

She's right; I am weak. It's the only explanation for why I'm not fighting her right now. I take the tiny pill cup and toss it back, chasing the bitterness with ice-cold water.

Who knew water could taste so good? I close my eyes as I suck down another gulp, savoring its feel on my tongue. What I would've done to have fresh, ice-cold water while on that island. I shake my head at the thought because it's all so wild. Sitting here in this air-conditioned concrete hospital is such a stark contrast to the leafy green island paradise where I spent the last... Hell, I don't even know how long. It almost feels like a dream.

I look back at the nurse, who's staring at me with concern in her eyes, almost like there's something she hasn't told me.

"But he's okay?" I press because I need to hear her say it.

She nods and purses her lips. "He's going to be just fine... but he needs to rest and heal just like you."

I nod as her reassurance washes over me and breathe a sigh of relief.

The loud tear of velcro brings me back to the moment as she wraps the blood pressure cuff around my arm. "Do you need anything for nausea?"

Now that she mentions it, my stomach does feel a little queasy.

"I... um... I do feel a little sick." I hesitate before asking, "Do you know what's wrong with me?"

A warm smile spreads across her face. "Well, you're severely malnourished and dehydrated, and you're infected with parasites." She clicks her pen and scribbles a note. "I'm surprised your tiny little body was able to hold onto the pregnancy at all, but your vitals are looking better today." She pulls her stethoscope down from her ears after listening to my lungs, then hands me the hospital breakfast menu. "What'll it be, red or orange Jell-O? Or I can call for some warm broth if you'd prefer?"

"I'm sorry." I swallow the lump in my throat. "Did you just say I'm *pregnant*?" The word lodges in my throat like the most unnatural thing I've ever said.

She pulls the stethoscope out of her ears and scribbles another note on her chart. "Yes, dear. I'll be taking you for an ultrasound shortly, and we'll have a better idea of how far along you are."

"So, you haven't done an ultrasound?" Hope flutters in my chest. "So, maybe you're wrong... I mean, how could you know that—"

She smiles, placing a warm hand on my arm. "How about I get you something to eat and let you process this."

I nod yes, then shake it no as tears sting the backs of my eyes. My chest feels heavy as I try to process how this could be real. I pinch myself on the arm and wince. Okay, so this isn't a dream, but how can something like this happen?

I mean, I have an IUD. I've never planned on starting a family, and maybe I should've thought about it more before this moment, but I've always been so focused on my career. Hell, I've never even had a steady relationship. I'm about three heaves away from going into a full-on panic attack when a quiet knock on the door, followed by a smiling Maggie, breaks the tension.

I let out a breath at the relief of seeing a familiar face, but then the tears start falling.

"Gwen, what's wrong?" Maggie rushes to my side, and I

catch a whiff of her shampoo. The familiar scent is a warm blanket to my battered soul, and I cry harder.

"What's going on? Why are you so upset?" She comes to sit by me, propped on the side of my bed, and rubs my back.

"The—the nurse." I gasp a lungful of air. "She told me I'm—I'm pr—preg—pregnant," I finally manage to say and look up to see Maggie's eyes wide in shock, which only prompts another wave of tears. Great, even she thinks this is terrible news.

"Shhh, it's going to be okay. Just take a deep breath," she reassures me as she rubs my back.

"Maggie, what am I going to do?" I wipe my swollen eyes with the back of my hand, and she bites her lip in thought.

"Listen, sweetie." She pulls me into a hug. "Let's just slow down and take a minute before we rush any decisions. You're in shock right now, and that's a completely normal response. Let's focus on getting you feeling better." She pulls away and pushes the hair out of my face as she studies me. "We're going to figure this out, but we just need to take one thing at a time. Do you want me to see if I can call Jack—"

"No!" I interrupt as a fresh wave of tears burns behind my eyes. "I can't tell him right now. Mags, promise me you won't tell him," I beg. "I need you to stall until I figure out what I'm working with." I bite my thumbnail as I try to think. "I'm going to tell him," I assure her. "I just need some time to figure out how all of this works. Do you promise to keep this a secret just between you and me?"

Maggie's eyes go wide, and she looks around the room, then down to the phone in her hands. "Gwen, you know I hate lying," she whispers.

I grip her shoulders, forcing her to look me in the eyes. "I need you to keep this a secret. It's just between you and me, understand? No one else can know ... not even Elliot. Please, Mags."

She nods her head and grips the phone tighter.

"I've got cherry Jell-O and bone broth!" The nurse calls from behind her cart, cutting the tension like a hot knife through butter.

"That's my cue!" Maggie singsongs. "I'll just step outside and give you some privacy." She walks backward and gestures over her shoulder.

I take the cup of cherry Jell-O as guilt pricks at my chest. I feel terrible about keeping this from Elliot, but there's no way I can trust her with a secret like this. She's too much of a loose cannon.

———

A few hours later, I'm lying in my hospital bed staring at the ceiling when the nurse appears in front of me with a wheelchair.

"Miss Pierson, it's time for your ultrasound."

I try to push myself to a sitting position, but my arms are too shaky, and the nurse jumps in to help me. "You poor dear. Here, let me help you." She pulls me up and helps me move to the wheelchair. It's only then, when I'm looking down at the contours of my legs in my hospital gown, that I realize just how sickly I appear. How could Jack find this version of me attractive, and how could this fragile body support another life? It all just feels surreal.

I zone out as she leads me through the hallways, passing windows and doors that all look the same. Jack could be behind any of those doors. It's strange that he's so close but might as well be miles away.

"Here we are." The nurse scans her badge, and the lock beep as the door opens, revealing a small dark room, only lit by a sonogram monitor.

I suck in a breath and climb on the examination table with a racing heart and sweaty palms. The heaviness of this moment is not lost on me as I realize no matter what we find, my life will forever be changed.

"This may be a little uncomfortable, but I'll be gentle." The ultrasound technician pulls a long thin wand from her rolling desk and squeezes some kind of gel on the tip.

"What are you going to do with tha–"

My question is answered as she guides the wand right into my–

"Whoa now!" I flinch. "Where do you think you're going with that?"

She laughs. "I take it this is your first time having a vaginal ultrasound. "Just relax. This is the best way for us to see what's going on in there."

I squeeze my eyes shut and do my best to relax as the cold, lubed-up wand goes inside me. This is so strange on so many different levels.

A rushing swooshing sound plays through the speakers, and I peel my eyes open to see what she's discovered. There's a small white bean on the screen, and confusion pulls at my brows. A sinking feeling pools in the pit of my stomach, and I feel an overwhelming sense of sadness. It was silly to actually think I could be pregnant. I should've known they'd gotten it wrong. I let my head fall back as I remind myself this is good news. Now nothing in my life has to change. Maggie doesn't have to keep any secrets, and everything can return to normal.

"Ah, there we go," the ultrasound tech says. She clicks a few buttons, drawing lines on the bean-looking thing before she continues. "There's your baby, Miss Pierson. That's the heart over here." She clicks again, and I sit up in a rush, knocking my paper blanket to the floor.

"What do you mean?" I gasp, pointing at the screen. "It

doesn't look like a baby. Are you sure that's not my bladder or something?"

She laughs. "You're full of jokes today, aren't you! It's the beginning of a baby. You're measuring just over eight weeks." She pulls the device from me and cleans it off as I process this new information.

"Eight weeks?" I do my best to calculate back, but it's no use. I barely have any reference for time on the island, especially after the last few days when we were as good as dead.

"Everything looks great. You did a good job taking care of this little bean, mama." She rolls back in her chair as my nurse helps me back to my wheelchair.

Mama? The word hits me in the chest like a boulder, and I blink several times as she leads me out of the room and into the hallway. There are many titles I've carried over the years. Friend, enemy, employee, daughter, and my newest title girlfriend... but never did I ever expect to be called a mother.

I try to swallow the lump in my throat, but it only grows larger.

"Oh shit, listen, Tatiana, I'm sorry about my attitude earlier, but if we could just talk about this—"

I hear Jack's cocky voice pleading with the nurse behind a door, and I sit up a little taller as I scan the hallway, trying to figure out where it's coming from.

"Ow! Ah!" Jack screams.

"Give me one second, dear." My nurse pushes down on my wheelchair's brakes. "I'm just going to grab you a new gown to change into after your shower."

She's parked me in front of the nurses' station, and my eyes go wide with panic at the realization that Jack is on the other side of the door.

"Hold still and stop fighting me!" a muffled female voice calls.

"You said you'd be gentle, and I believed you!"

"Stop being a baby before I give you a second urethra!"

"Fuck! Ouch! You didn't have to rip it that hard, and you know it!"

"Trust me, Mr. Manning, that was gentle. Now take your pain medicine. I'll be back in an hour to check on you." I grit my teeth and hunch my shoulders, wishing I could blend into the wall as a broad-chested nurse with a dark unibrow steps into the hallway. She's grinning ear to ear.

I'm so close to him. I could get out of the wheelchair and push open that door, but I'm paralyzed by fear. Before I can make a decision, my nurse decides for me.

"Here we are." She drops a warm gown on my lap, then pushes me in the opposite direction. My heart aches more and more with every step she takes, but I can't make myself protest.

When we finally get back to my room, she helps me out of my gown and into the shower, where I wash away the final remnants of the island. Everything except one tiny little secret.

CHAPTER THIRTY-TWO

Jack

"Jesus Christ, I definitely think my pee hole is bigger." I adjust my wounded dick and tuck him delicately back against the side of my leg. Dropping the blankets, I find Sam staring at me with a look of bewilderment.

"You good?" He quirks a brow.

"I've been better," I retort. "Is there something I can help you with, or did you just stop by to mock me, Samuel?"

He rolls his eyes and tosses me a cell phone. "Here. I grabbed you a new phone." He scratches his head. "It's a... it's got Gwen's new number programmed in it. And Benjamin's, too."

I clench the phone to my chest. "I take it this is a peace offering? Considering all you've put me through."

He opens his mouth as if to argue but snaps it closed. "Yeah, something like that. We, uh... we just thought you should have something to keep in touch with Gwen." He shoves his hands in his pockets and looks down at his feet.

Why the hell does he look so damn guilty? "What's going on? What are you not telling me?"

His eyes meet mine, and there's a mix of something like guilt and sympathy. "I heard from Maggie... She said Gwen's being discharged from the hospital today." He winces. "She's ... she's going back to Chicago." He sits on the chair next to my bed and lets out a long breath as I try to understand.

"She's leaving?" I ask out loud, but it's more to myself. "Does she know about my *situation*?"

Sam shrugs. "Listen, dude, I think you should talk to her and figure things out. It's not my place to get in the middle of your business."

"You didn't answer me." I push my tangled hair away from my face and grit my teeth in frustration. "Does she know about my leg? Is that why she's running away?"

Sam just shakes his head. "I don't know if Maggie told her. All I know is she's on a flight back to Chicago as we speak. Maybe she just needs some time to process everything, you know?" He stands and claps his hand on my shoulder. "Try not to freak out about it. You've still got a long road of recovery ahead of you." He grabs his duffle bag tucked away in the corner, sliding the strap over his shoulder. "The good news is, I talked to your care team, and they're letting you finish your antibiotics off-site. I've arranged for a home health team to come to one of my rental properties on the other side of town. We'll be able to chill out and relax in the privacy of my home. I'll load this in the car and pull it around."

"Why would she just take off and leave me like this?"

"I don't know, but I'm sure she has her reasons." Sam points to the phone. "Why don't you send her a message and ask her yourself?"

He turns to leave, and I'm left with a sinking feeling of betrayal. Surely she wouldn't care that I was disfigured from the accident, would she? But I can't think of any other explanation for her running off without saying goodbye. I toss the phone on my side table and stare at the white paneled ceiling.

Just when I thought my life couldn't get any better, I had to go and fuck around and find out. That's what I get for trying to be the hero. We could've lived out the rest of our lives on that island as far as I cared. Maybe we were never on the same page after all? Maybe it was the island and the sun playing with our emotions? Maybe it was all a lie, and I let myself get so wrapped up in it that I actually believed it was real.

I grab the phone and type out a text.

> So you're just going to leave without saying goodbye?

> Are you mad about the accident? You know I'd take it back if I could.

> I hope this doesn't change anything …

CHAPTER THIRTY-THREE

Gwen

I stare at the phone in my lap and read the text messages for what seems to be the millionth time.

I wipe the fresh tear away before Maggie sees me, then shove the phone into my back pocket. The words *accident* and *take it back if a could* jump off the screen as if they're taunting me, and it takes everything I have not to respond by telling him to go fuck himself.

I want to throw this phone into oncoming traffic as if all my problems would disappear with the destruction of the device.

We just landed in Chicago, and Elliot's driving us home from the airport. I was surprised when the hospital discharged me this morning, and I wanted to wait there for Jack, but I needed space to process everything. By the way he's handling the news, I guess I was right to leave.

Fucking Sam must've told him about the baby. I'm so mad right now I could strangle him.

I had it all planned out. I was going to fly home and figure out a game plan, maybe get some balloons and cake, and throw a surprise party to tell him the news. Taking out my phone again, I stare at my background photo, an image of the sonogram, I wonder if any of it was real at all. Maybe the Jack I grew to love on that island was just another alter-ego for him, like Wombat Willy.

I guess I've got to find a new plan now, one that doesn't include the three of us living happily ever after.

"Oh, and my in-laws are in town. You're going to love them! I'm hosting brunch on Sunday if you're feeling up for it..."

Elliot's voice pulls me from my trance when I realize she's talking to me.

"Gwen's probably exhausted," Maggie answers for me. "Why don't we just play it by ear and let you know."

She meets my eyes in the rearview mirror, and I mouth a silent *thank you* from the back seat.

"Oh my God, it's so good," I moan. I grab the ramekin of honey and drizzle it over my slice of pizza before shoving half of it into my mouth. I've slowly been stretching my stomach back to its normal capacity, and I'm so grateful because it's prepared me for this exact moment. Right now, it's just my girls, this delicious pizza, and me.

We're settled on Maggie's teal velvet couch in her modest studio apartment conveniently located near all the great restaurants in town, one of which is Tony's pizza, which is why I'm close to having my first foodgasm.

Yeah, I didn't know that was a thing until this moment.

She's recently downsized to save up for the downstairs studio, which she plans to renovate into her own yoga studio.

"I know it's tiny, but the studio will be right downstairs when I get it up and going."

"Maggie, this is perfect. Are you kidding me?" I take in the lush greenery covering every bit of the room's surface and feel a peace wash over me for the first time since I got in that helicopter.

Who knew Maggie's plant addiction would be the thing that pulled me out of my anxiety spiral? I make a mental note to get more plants once I find a new apartment.

A rush of anxiety floods my system at the thought of finding a place to live. The world didn't stop just because Jack and I were MIA for three months, and I don't blame my friends for moving my things out of my luxury high rise when my landlord evicted me after the bills weren't paid for two months in a row.

A memory of Jack curled into my side, watching the sunset flashes in my mind, and I close my eyes and shake away the memory. I can't think about him right now or what any of this means. I just need to focus on keeping myself healthy, fed, and safe.

A rush of gratitude warms my heart when I take in my best friends. Without their searching, I know I wouldn't be sitting here right now. "I don't know why I haven't asked you this before, but why did you keep searching after so much time had passed?" I nuzzle into to soft velvet couch, caressing the soft fabric. It's such a contrast to the gritty sand I'd been so accustomed to.

Maggie bites her lip as her eyes find Elliot's, and Elliot gives her a nod of encouragement. "Go ahead, Maggie. Tell her." The corner of her mouth pulls into a grin.

Maggie sighs and rolls her eyes. "Okay, I'll tell you, but you're just going to think I'm weirder than you already do..."

I reach out and place my hand on top of Maggie's. "Babe, I am so damn happy for your weirdness. You saved my life."

"There's this guy at work," Elliot chimes in. "He was my first client. You may remember him from that night at Terry's when you threw me the party—"

"Is he the beauty influencer with the high cheekbones?" I squint my eyes, trying to remember.

"Yes," Maggie confirms. "His name is Damian." She cuts herself another piece of pizza. "Well, we got to talking at a work dinner Elliot hosted, and when we mentioned you and Jack were missing—"

"He told us not to give up. He could sense your energy and that you were both still alive." Elliot's eyes well with tears. "I don't know if I ever would've believed him if he weren't right about something he said to Benjamin and me before we first got together."

"So we pulled up a Google Maps, and he pointed to the area he thought you were."

They exchange a glance and look at me, and I almost can't believe it, but after everything that I've seen and lived through over the last three months, who am I to doubt anything.

"Wow." My eyes go wide as I take in this information. "Mag's, you may have just made a believer out of me." I clap her on the shoulder as tears prickle behind my eyes. "I don't know if I can ever thank you enough for saving us."

"You don't have to thank me, Gwen." Tears well in her honey brown eyes, and she pulls me into a tight hug, breathing a sigh of relief into the crook of my neck. I return her hug, squeezing her as if I'm afraid one of us will disappear, then Elliot joins, wrapping her arms around us both.

"Who are you, and what have you done with Gwen?" Elliot shrieks, and we all laugh. I've never been much on feelings, but somehow, realizing you were so close to death makes you appreciate everything and everyone around you that much more.

Maggie pulls away and clears her throat. "I hope you're okay staying here. The couch folds out to a queen, but I don't mind giving you my bed until we can get your things out of storage. I don't want you to be uncomfortable."

"Maggie," I hold up my hand and stop her, "stop apologizing. This is perfect." I snuggle into a throw pillow and inhale her familiar scent of peaches and vanilla. Everything about this place is so cozy and warm.

"So... you don't have to answer if you don't want to," Elliot takes a gulp of her wine, "but what's the deal with you and Jack?"

"Elliot!" Maggie gasps. "Gwen's been home for two hours. Can you at least let her warm up before you bombard her with questions about her sex life!"

Elliot's eyes go wide, and a smile breaks across her face. "Sex life!?" She points to me and then to Maggie. "Who said anything about sex life?" She grabs a throw pillow and shoves it in her lap. "You better talk, missy. I have a feeling this is going to be good."

I stare daggers at Maggie, and her face turns a pale shade of green. "Dammit," she whispers before looking up to meet my eyes. "Sorry, Gwen."

Elliot's eyes bounce between us as she tries to piece together what we're not saying. "Wait a minute!" She throws the throw pillow down and stands, grabbing a fresh bottle of wine. "What's going on here? What are you two keeping from me?"

Her eyes scan me as she pours herself a fresh glass of wine, then she gasps so loud you'd think she witnessed a crime.

"Did you want a glass of wine, Gwen?" She pours me a cup and pushes it toward me.

I take the wine from her gingerly, "Oh, yes, thank you." But I don't take a sip.

She slowly sips her wine, staring daggers at me over the rim of her glass as if in a challenge.

I purse my lips, then lift my extremely full glass of wine to my lips, turning it up so the liquid touches my mouth. "Mmmm. That is really good."

She repeats her gulp, still eyeing me.

I take another fake sip.

Maggie stares between us, her eyes darting back and forth as sweat starts to form on her upper lip.

"This wine is so good. Isn't it Maggie?"

"Oh, yes, it's delicious." Maggie takes an exaggerated sip.

Their eyes land on me as if it's my turn in this silent drinking game. I take another fake sip. "You know, I can already feel this buzz going to my head." I set the glass down. "I haven't had a drink in so long. I better slow down before I get a headache."

Elliot slams her wine glass down so hard that wine spills out of the top of the glass. "You lying bitch!" she screams, pointing at me.

I feign ignorance. "Elliot, what are you talking–"

"You haven't drunk any of your wine, Gwenneth." She eyes me suspiciously before walking over and plopping next to me on the couch. "What's going on? Why are you being so weird? And why aren't you drinking?"

We both jerk our heads, and she looks to Maggie as if she holds the answer. But Maggie's jaw is clamped shut, and her neck is splotchy red.

Elliot sucks in a gasp. "Maggie's lying about something!" She points between us. "You two have a secret you're not telling me. Maggie's neck is giving it away!" She looks back at me, scans her eyes up and down my body, then lets out another exaggerated sigh. This time, her hands cover her mouth, and tears well behind her eyes.

"You're not?" She shakes her head. "You can't be?" She looks to Maggie for confirmation, and the traitorous bitch looks down at her hands, a dead giveaway that we're lying.

"Oh my God!" Elliot shrieks before pulling me into a hug.

"I'm going to be an aunt!"

"So let me get this straight ..." Elliot recaps for the third time. "You and Jack had sex on the island... several times. Your IUD somehow dislodged in your uterus. And now you're pregnant?"

I nod. "Yeah, that's the cliff notes version, at least."

She bites her lip and smiles. "You dirty, dirty girl. I can't believe you thought you'd be able to keep this a secret from me!" She throws the throw pillow in her lap, sending it flying at my head, and I duck as it barely misses me.

"I needed some time to think before I made any rash decisions," I huff. "It's not like this is anything I've ever expected, and I just freaked out."

"What the hell, Gwen? Why are you here in Chicago and not with Jack right now... especially with everything with his–"

"Oops!" Maggie squeals as her entire glass of wine topples over onto my lap. "I'm so sorry! I'm such a spaz. Here let me help you." She pulls me to my feet and ushers me to her bedroom, giving me a clean t-shirt and a pair of shorts.

"At least it was white wine," she says as she scoops up my

wet clothes and passes me my phone from the pocket before shoving my clothes in the washing machine.

The phone feels heavy in my hand, like a foreign object. I turn it on, hoping there's a new message from Jack that erases the last one from my memory, but I have no such luck.

I excuse myself to the bathroom for a moment alone. I've always been an extrovert, but being thrown back into the real world after living alone with one other person for three months is getting to be a lot. I lean over the sink and splash cold water on my face, staring at the phone beside me, daring it to do something other than taunt me.

I'm contemplating throwing the damn thing out the window when a familiar number lights up the screen.

I don't think I could forget that number if I tried.

I glance around the bathroom as if someone's going to pop out and offer me some guidance, but I can't be so lucky. Biting my lip, I exhale a sigh and click answer.

"Sandra, is everything alright?"

"Oh, good, you are alive. You know I've heard the rumors that you were back in town, but I didn't believe them. I thought you'd surely have called me by now if you were..."

I swallow a gulp, unsure of where this exchange is leading.

"Well, it's only been a few hours... I've been pretty busy reacclimating to life, and—"

"Oh, pish posh. Listen, Gwen, I need you back at the office like... yesterday," she sighs. "This whole Pheobe Thornstein scandal has gotten completely out of control. Pantone is in over her head, and I simply don't have time to step in and fix this for her." She pauses a beat, letting her words sink in. "I was hoping you'd be able to help. I know it's been a while, and you're getting reacclimated after your *vacation*, but I'm hoping you remember at least *some* of your responsibilities..."

Only Sandra can call asking for a favor while baiting me

with a backhanded compliment. I'm tempted to hang up on the spot and leave that piece of my life severed… but this job is all I've ever known, and it does feel good to be wanted.

I quirk my lips to the side and roll my eyes, letting out a long sigh before answering. "What exactly did you have in mind?"

"I knew you were a smart girl," she coos. "I'll need you in my office first thing Monday morning. We've got a mountain of HR paperwork to sort through, so if we want to make any headway on this, you'll need to be ready to get your hands dirty. Can I trust you with this, Gwen?"

I nod as if I'm convincing myself, then say, "Of course, you can, Sandra. I'll see you Monday."

"Excellent. I knew I could count on you. Goodbye, dear." She ends the call before I can respond, and I look down at the phone in my palm.

Maybe this is how it's meant to be? Who was I kidding when I thought my life could be any different? At least Sandra *wants* me… I don't know if I can say the same for Jack.

I type out a response to his text.

> Of course, this changes things. I need some time to figure out what I want.

I tuck the phone into my bra—old habits die hard—and make my way back to my friends to tell them my news.

One thing's for certain, no matter what changes in my life, I can always count on Sandra to keep me grounded. Maybe this is the stability I need to navigate this new season of change.

I'm not completely convinced, but at least it's a start.

CHAPTER THIRTY-FOUR

JACK

Hobbling through the doorway of our two-bedroom bungalow on the beach, I stub my good toe on the entryway. "Shit," I hiss as I try to cradle my leg while keeping balance on the devil-sticks digging a hole in my armpit. "Who the fuck invented these things?" I yell as Sam pushes past me, causing me to lose my balance and fall headfirst into the doorframe.

"Oops, I didn't see you there," he calls over his shoulder as he drags his suitcase and my small tote bag into his rental property, where we'll stay for the next three weeks.

I'm not going to lie, this place is much better than recovering in that torture chamber of a hospital, but I can't help but wish Gwen was here with me instead of Sam.

I narrow my eyes and shove the crutches back under my armpits, making a beeline for revenge. By the time I finally reach him—running through a house on crutches while adapting to your missing appendage is no easy feat—I'm exhausted, and I don't even have the energy to retaliate. I'll just have to wait until he least expects it. Play smarter, not harder. I'm pretty sure that's what the saying means.

Terracotta tiles line the floor, and one wall of the living room wall is made up of a giant sliding glass door that overlooks the ocean. It's a hell of an upgrade from the hospital, where I've spent the last week being poked and prodded every time I turned around. I still have this stupid IV line administering antibiotics around the clock, but at least now I've got a better view.

I look over and see Sam ruffling through the kitchen. Then I hear the familiar hiss of a beer bottle clinking open, and like Pavlov's dog, my mouth is salivating uncontrollably.

"When did you have time to get beer?" I make my way into the kitchen to grab my own.

Sam may be one of my very best friends, but we've got a bit of a love/hate relationship, especially when Benjamin's not here to even out the group.

Sam plops down on the tan leather sofa and props his feet—yes, both feet. That's something I now notice about people—on the coffee table before taking a long pull of his beer.

"I had a grocery service delivery this morning when you were filling out your release papers."

I nod my head in approval, not that he can see me. He's too busy kicking back and enjoying his right leg to notice me struggle to balance my body weight while bending to retrieve my beer.

Not much of a caretaker, that one. I think Sam could give nurse Tatiana a run for her money on worst bedside manner.

"Don't worry about me." I wince as I knock my stump against the counter before making my way to the living room with a cold beer in hand. "I've got this. I don't need any assistance."

Sam laughs. "Oh, good. I didn't want to emasculate you. I

know how important it is for you to have your independence." He takes another pull of his beer and flicks the TV on, finding the local soccer channel.

I want to take a swing at him with my crutch, and for a moment, I actually try to calculate if I could hit him from where I'm sitting, but I decide against it. I have to face the facts; I'm weaker than him in my current condition. It's a hard pill to swallow.

I direct my attention to the TV, and a sense of calm floods my chest. Soccer, the universal language. It doesn't matter that my favorite teams aren't playing or that the commentators are speaking Spanish. The game speaks for itself.

I let the cold beer flow down my throat, savoring the first sips of something so delicious, and let myself get lost in the game. I thought I'd never get to indulge in either ever again.

Sam may be a total tool at times—not that I don't deserve it. I mean, I think I'll be paying for that hot cup of coffee to the face for a while to come, but he knows me, and he knows this is exactly what I need.

I take another sip of my beer and glance at the white bandage covering most of my thigh. I'll never be able to play my favorite game in the world again. The realization hits me like a boulder to the chest, and all I can do is drink and mourn my past life.

I don't know what happens next or even what's possible for me, but nothing could've prepared me for this outcome. I was okay with dying at sea, being swallowed up by the ocean. I was okay with spending the rest of my numbered days dying of an infection on the island with Gwen. So, why is this so difficult to deal with?

My emotions have been all over the place as I've tried to grapple with the new way of life, but I can't seem to get a handle on my new identity.

What does this mean for my career? Can Wombat Willy still give guided tours and travel the world without a leg? Will Gwen still want me when she finds out I'm damaged goods?

Every time I settle my brain down on one thought, a new wave of confusion starts to ruminate.

I miss Gwen so fucking much my heart actually aches, but I need to get to a better headspace before I let her see me like this. I asked Sam and Benjamin to make sure she didn't find out just yet. I know it seems selfish, but I want to get my shit together, so I won't be so broken when I see her. So she won't feel sorry for me.

I drain the rest of my beer and slam it down on the coffee table, startling Sam.

"You okay, dude?"

"Yeah, I just–" I hang my head and sigh as I try to pull myself back up on the crutches. "I just need another beer."

"I got you. I've got the perfect snack just for this occasion," Sam says, getting up before I can protest. I really do hate the pity I see in his eyes. It's probably why he's been such a dick.

My head starts to spin as the warm buzz washes over my frazzled nerves. It gives me a new sense of determination, and when my bladder screams from all the beer, I attempt to make it the few short feet across the hall to the bathroom.

My arms and leg are wobblier than ideal, but I manage to make it down the hallway and relieve myself before Sam's finished preparing our snacks in the kitchen.

I'm almost back to my spot on the couch when I check my phone for the hundredth time.

Still nothing.

I check the time, and even with the time difference, she'd surely have landed in Chicago by now.

"Dude, are you sure this is Gwen's number, and you're not just fucking with me? Because that's fucked up, man. I know I threw the coffee in your face, but I'm going through a lot right now, and–" The phone buzzes in my hand, and I toss it in the air in surprise. It falls to the ground.

"Fuck!" I scream as I look at the phone lying face down on the tile floor. I balance myself on the crutches, wishing I had X-Men superpowers so I could pick the phone up with my mind... But, alas, I am a mere human and have no such luck. The crutches dig into my armpits as I try to maneuver myself down, a physical reminder of just how weak of a human I am. I can't even pick up a phone off the floor by myself, for Christ's sake, and the phone lays there taunting me.

I grit my teeth and steady myself as I attempt to lower myself in a pistol squat. There was a prior version of me who could do this with ease, but that was before I lost thirty pounds of muscle mass... and almost died of an infection.

Slowly but surely, I sink down until I'm in a one-footed squat and grab the phone. I click it on and see Gwen's name with a new text message.

GWEN

Of course, this changes things. I need some
time to figure out what I want.

My heart drops to my stomach as a wave of nausea rips through me. I read the text again, trying to understand what she means— if she's saying what I think she's saying.

"Hey, man, I hope you like your nachos spicy because–" Sam's voice stops short when he sees me on the floor.

"Whoa, dude, what's going on? Did you hurt yourself?" Sam rushes to help me, but I wave him away.

I stare at the screen, blinking, and sigh. I guess Maggie told her... I close my eyes and sink lower until I'm sitting on the ground as a fresh wave of tears falls down my cheeks.

"Gwen finally answered me," I sigh. "I just need a minute to think."

"Oh shit, I'm sorry, man. I guess you two weren't on the same page about things after all?"

I look at him, confusion pulling at my eyebrows. "What are you talking about? You knew about this?"

He shrugs. "I told you I didn't want to be in the middle of your business, but you need to respect her wishes, dude. This isn't just about you."

Why would I want to be with someone who left me when things got hard? As if I can fucking help what happened to me out there. I guess this is my penance for being so horrible at my job that I couldn't even save us. I type out a response.

> Take all the time you need because I'm out.

I squeeze the phone, then send it flying across the room.

"Why don't I trade these beers for some tequila?" He spins on his heel before I can answer.

Is the solution to my shattered heart and bruised ego at the bottom of a tequila bottle? I guess we're about to find out.

One hour later, my head is buzzing, and my vision is blurred as Sam and I stare at the empty bottle of tequila and assortment of half-squeezed lime wedges polluting the coffee table.

"You know, I love you, man," I hiccup and pat Sam on the shoulder.

"I love you, too." He ruffles my hair back and forth. "Even if you've got a peg-leg and a weird job that doesn't sound real." He laughs and hiccups, then jumps back as if he's surprised himself.

"We both have the hiccups!" I shout excitedly. "That's because we've bonded. I won't tell Benjamin if you don't." I quirk my head to the side and eye him.

He squints so he can hear me better. "Ha! Benjamin would never approve of getting you this drunk to deal with your heartache!" Sam offers me a wide grin. "But Benjamin isn't here!" He motions to himself with his thumb. "That's why I'm in charge, and Sam says tequila heals all wounds!"

I hold up a final shot. "I'll cheers to that!" Then I throw it back and laugh.

"Who needs women or legs!" Sam shouts. "You're better off without her, and personally, I think you have so many more options for costumes now—"

"That's what I was going to say!" I interrupt. "Just think of all the different attachments ... I bet there's one for rock climbing, running..." I think for a moment...

"Pirate costumes!" we say in unison.

"Fuck yeah. How cool is your kid going to be, having a real-life Captain Hook for a dad!" Sam chuckles.

I'm sucking on a lime wedge when his joke plays back in mind, and I choke as the juice coats my right tonsil. "What the fuck is that supposed to mean?" I laugh through choked coughs.

He lays down on the arm of the couch, pulling his legs into his chest. "Oh, you know exactly what that means, you dirty breeder."

"Dirty breeder? What the fuck were you drinking, man?" I laugh, "If I'm a dirty breeder, then so are you."

"Fuck, I think I'm going to puke—" Sam jumps off the couch, and I sink deeper into the soft leather as the world spins all around me.

CHAPTER THIRTY-FIVE

Gwen

It's been a hell of a first week back in the office, and Sandra hasn't held back any punches. I've heard pregnant women are easily exhausted, but there's nothing that could've prepared me for the pain of keeping my eyes open while working twelve-hour shifts each day.

Yesterday, I fell asleep in my desk chair sitting up. I was in the middle of typing an email, and I just conked out for an hour before someone burst through my office door and startled me awake. I bowed my head and said, "Nameste," pretending I was meditating. I'll have to thank Maggie for that little trick because if she didn't force me to go with her to that maternity yoga class last week, I don't know if I would have been able to play it off as I did.

Sandra wasn't lying when she said the Pheobe Thornstein job was all kinds of screwed up. I've been up to my eyeballs doing damage control. It's the same old stuff that never seems to change. A few carefully crafted scheduled tweets, some social media posts, a planned run-in with the paparazzi, and some talk show interviews. We're leaning hardcore into the victim angle. I think we may even get her a book deal to tell her side of the story.

It's exhausting, trivial work, and the more time I spend inside those glass walls, the more I realize how utterly insignificant it is. It's like I've dedicated my entire life to polishing trash cans ... Not that the people don't matter, but who really cares about any famous person's reputation? How is any of this contributing to society as a whole or making the world a better place?

I huff. Now I really do sound like Jack... or Wombat Willy... whichever version of himself he allowed me to see.

For a moment there, he really had me, but I guess if something seems too good to be true, it probably is. What did Maya Angelou say? *"When people show you who they are, believe them the first time."*

I roll my eyes. Of course, he was so full of his good guy talk, but when it really came down to it, he ran away, leaving me high and dry to deal with everything all on my own. I guess all men really are the same, aren't they?

Tonight I'm meeting Elliot and Maggie for after-work drinks to plan Elliot's bachelorette party and put some finishing touches on the final wedding details. Even though I'm still staying with Maggie until I can find a new apartment—something more suited for a baby—I feel like I haven't seen her in days.

I've been so busy working ten- and twelve-hour days that I haven't had the energy to do anything else, pregnant or not.

I suck in a breath to compose myself and steady my shoulders as I open the door leading into the familiar bar, Terry's, where it all began for Elliot, Maggie, and I. Somehow, this place feels like home just as much as anything else. The stale scent of popcorn and booze stings my nostrils, and my stomach recoils at the stench.

It's no island oasis, that's for sure, but it's comforting nonetheless.

Elliot and Maggie asked me to meet them tonight to discuss some wedding things and decompress after a long work week. I don't know how much help it'll do, but they know I'm struggling and trying to help things go back to how they were before.

I catch sight of Elliot and Maggie holding down our favorite corner booth .

"Gwen! I'm so glad you came!" Elliot jumps up to greet me, pulling me into a hug.

"Well, it's not like you would've taken no for an answer..." I sneer.

"Oh, stop, just because I hacked into your work calendar and blocked off time–"

"After hours!" Maggie adds.

"Yeah, well, Sandra's been demanding as hell, and it appears that the office indeed cannot function without me, so..."

"You're pushing yourself too hard, Gwenny." Maggie scans me up and down, her expression concerned.

"Yeah, Gwen, we're really worried about you," Elliot adds.

"Listen, I'm not the first woman in history to work a stressful job while pregnant, nor will I be the last. The world doesn't revolve around me and my problems, and it's naïve to believe it ever would." I pause when I see the waitress come into view to take our drink orders.

"Hey there, ladies. We're running a two-for-one special tonight on Pina Coladas. What can I get you all to drink?"

"Ooh, I love a good Pina Colada!" Elliot claps her hands together. "I'll have that, and could you give me extra pineapple on the side. Ohh, and a cherry on top, please!" Her eyes glimmer with excitement over the smallest things. It's one of my favorite things about Elliot. My ears grow hot, and I don't know if I'm angry or sad. Somewhere along the way, the two feelings seem to have fused together in my body, and I can't trust my basic feelings anymore. Everything is amplified by hormones. There's no way Elliot could have known how painful of a reminder that drink could be for me, but damn, I feel like I've just torn open some of the stitches around my fragile heart.

"I'll just have a glass of red wine, please." Maggie passes the menu back to the server. "Oh, and could we please get two orders of fried pickles for the table?"

I take a calming breath. It's as if Maggie can read my mind.

"And how about for you, miss?" The young server's innocent eyes meet mine, and even though she just needs my drink order, I feel like she's asking me something else entirely.

I pause for a moment, considering my options. I can't drink alcohol. I don't want soda ... I close the menu and pass it back to her, deciding why not let myself relive one of my favorite memories. "I'll take a virgin Pina Colada with extra coconut, please."

"Very well, I'll just put in these drink orders and be right back with your fried pickles and some waters." The server takes our menus and leaves, no one realizing the gigantic step I just took in letting myself think back to the beautiful moment where Jack and I very well could have created a new life.

I swirl my fingers around each other, contemplating sharing the story, but when she places the frozen drink in front of me, I take one sip and decide to keep this memory to myself. It's too special.

"So, when will your apartment be ready?" Elliot asks as she chomps down on the best fried pickles in Chicago, a new discovery on my part; kudos to Maggie for paying attention.

"The first of the month," I answer.

"You know, if you ever get tired of sleeping on Maggie's sofa,

Benjamin and I would be happy to host you in one of our guest rooms."

Elliot is sweet to offer, and now that her in-laws aren't staying with her anymore, I should probably take her up on it. But there's just something so cozy about Maggie's place. I think it's all the plants or the big windows. I feel like I'm outside, so it's not so stuffy like most buildings in the city. It's a new quirk I've noticed about myself. Ever since I've been back, I feel so trapped when I'm inside buildings.

"Thank you for the offer. I'll let you know if I change my mind." I shove a dripping hot fried pickle in my mouth, and my eyes roll back in my head at the salty explosion of flavor. "Damn, food tastes so much better. It's unreal."

"When do you go back to the doctor?" Maggie asks, interrupting my foodgasm.

"Um, I'm not sure. I think next week or so?"

"You've still been taking your prenatal vitamins, though, right?"

"Yes, mom." I drag out, rolling my eyes in defense. Maggie seems to have made my prenatal health her top order of concern.

"I still can't believe you're having a baby!" Elliot squeezes my hand, and I force out a smile.

I'm so thankful for her eternal optimism. The truth is, I've struggled with my decision, going back and forth, contemplating all my options. I've even been looking into open adoptions as of late because who knows where life could take me. Of course, I'm not going to tell her that just yet.

Elliot and Benjamin are three weeks away from getting married. This is the most exciting time of her life, and I don't want to be a Debbie Downer with the raincloud over my head everywhere I go. No, this is not anyone's concern but my own. I won't let Jack's silence impact any decisions I make because, at the end of the day, I'm the one who has to live with myself and my choices.

"So, Elliot's bachelorette party is this weekend, and I was thinking maybe we could do a spa night at home?" Maggie says, and my ears perk up, listening intently for any indication that Jack may be there. "We could order a pizza, watch some chick flicks, and maybe even have a massage therapist set up at my place?"

"That sounds amazing!" Elliot claps, "Maggie, will you please make the special brownies? Just a small batch this time? Oh, and can we watch *Horrible Bosses*? I know we've seen it like fifty times already, but it's my favorite!" she screeches, and my left eye waters in response.

The pregnancy hormones just keep coming for me.

"This weekend? As in tomorrow night?" I swallow the pickle lodged in my throat, washing it down with the sweet frozen drink.

"Yeah, is that okay for you?"

"Of course. It just snuck up on me, that's all. The time really has flown by. I feel like I've missed so much of the wedding planning process."

"It's not your fault you were stranded on a deserted island, Gwenny. I'm just glad you're home safe."

"Me, too," I say the words I know I'm supposed to say, but deep down, I feel this island-shaped hole in my heart, and I'm not sure I'll ever be able to fill it back up. I've just got to move forward and take one day at a time, and hopefully, one day, the scar will fade, and I'll feel like myself again. I just don't know who that person is anymore.

My eyes burn as I hold back the tears threatening to fall when I think of how lonely I am without Jack. Though I'm in a booming city, and everywhere I go, I'm surrounded by crowds of people, I feel like the loneliest person in the world.

I stare down at the phone in my hands, wishing he'd write back, wishing he'd take back the last message he sent me, wishing he would say anything to make my aching heart feel better or at least finish the job. I feel so angry, but deep down, I know it's not true anger, it's heartbreak, and I don't know how I'll ever recover from it.

I drain the rest of my fake Pina Colada and play back the memories over and over again. Maybe I'm a glutton for punishment, but the memories are all I have now, so I let myself dream of how good things were and what might have been in another life.

CHAPTER THIRTY-SIX

JACK

I throw back two Tylenol and guzzle half a bottle of water as my pounding head throbs from last night's bender. Sam's been a good sport keeping me preoccupied in the evenings with soccer games and booze as I finish this last week of antibiotics.

"Oh, Jack, someone's here to see you!" Sam singsongs behind the door, and I let my head fall back, smacking the headboard. I know the exact visitor he's referencing, and I'm in no mood for her insults or abuse.

"Yes, Jack. Come out here, and let me remove your pic line ... Unless you want me to come in your bedroom and take it out?" Tatiana taunts from behind the door.

Of all the nurses in the godforsaken city, Sam had to arrange for Tatiana the she-devil to be my home health nurse. The woman gets off on my pain, and after that catheter removal, I'm actually shaking, thinking of her removing a pic line from my artery.

I shiver and contemplate crawling under the bed and

hiding, but it's no use... She's too strong. She'd probably just lift the bed with one arm while she pulled me out—kicking and screaming—with the other. Hell, she'd probably enjoy that even more.

I close my eyes, count to three, and muster up the courage before I open the door. I see her face a mere inches away when I crack the door ever so slowly. Her mustache and curly eyebrows glisten with sweat in this sweltering heat, and it takes everything I have not to piss myself from fear.

"Let me just grab some pants, and I'll meet you in the living room," I say through the crack.

"There is no part of your body I have not seen, but do what you wish. I will wait."

I find my backpack in the corner of the room and remove all my equipment. It's the first time I've held my camera since my accident, and it feels strange in my hand. I don't know if I want to throw it across the room for leading me into such a dangerous passion or cling to it as a lifeline. This camera has led me to places I never expected to see, and somehow, it feels like an awkward extension of my body. Maybe I am more like Captain Hook than I realized, only instead of a hook, I have a camera.

As I chuckle at the memory of Sam and I wasted on the couch, planning my new forever-future Halloween costume, something tickles my memory. He said something weird that night that caught me off guard, but I can't quite put my finger on it...

"Jack! I'm waiting!" Tatiana's muffled voice calls from the living room, and I flinch before carefully placing the camera back in my backpack.

I find a pile of clean clothes in the nearby dresser and grab a pair of shorts tucked away at the bottom. The last thing I want is for Tatiana to be upset with me for stalling... whether or not it's true.

I carefully slide on the shorts. I'm getting better at balancing without the crutches as my leg gets stronger and stronger every day. Sam and I have been playing this new game where he sits on the couch in the evenings and I have to refill our drinks... without the help of my crutches. Let's just say things get a little more interesting as the night goes on. I've got so many new bumps and bruises from busting my ass on this tile floor, but to his credit, I am getting stronger.

I make my way to the living room, where Tatiana has all her nursing shit splayed out on the coffee table, and I suck in a breath.

This is the last thing keeping you stuck here. So buck up and let her do her thing, and you can move on from this whole experience and lick your wounds in peace.

"Come and have a seat, Jack. You've kept me waiting long enough. I have a hot date to get to after this, so be still. I'd rather not have your blood on me at dinner." She cracks her knuckles, and I swallow my cry for help.

Somehow, I feel like I should warn the poor soul who's agreed to date this devil of a woman, maybe use my blood to write a warning message or something?

The cool sensation of alcohol interrupts my thoughts and is quickly followed by the all too familiar ripping of hair.

As to be expected, Tatiana holds nothing back.

It's been a few hours since the pic line removal, and I haven't mustered up the strength to move from the fetal position on the sofa. Between the ripping flesh and hair of the medical tape... and the actual removal of the pic line... I've had catheter flashbacks all afternoon. I think I'll make an appointment with Benjamin's therapist when I return home.

"How's it going over here?" Sam asks as the familiar hiss of a can opening sparks my attention.

I sit up and give him a warning glare, but he notices my judgmental gaze and holds the can up in defense. "Relax, it's just sparkling water. I'm still nursing my hangover from last night, too. I wouldn't do that to you, man."

My muscles ease, and I lie back down, only this time turning to face him. "So, now what? Tatiana's had her evil way with me, and there are no other forms of torture I'm aware of. When can we go back home ... er, to Chicago?" I correct.

He studies me for a moment and takes a long sip of his water. "I guess that depends on you, Captain. What are you thinking?"

Captain. It's the new nickname Sam's been calling me, and I have to admit I don't hate it. There are worse things than being compared to the most famous pirate in history. I lay my head back down and rub my aching arm as I think.

"Have you heard from Gwen?"

"She's back at work. She's staying with Maggie for a while until she can find a new place big enough for her and the baby." He shrugs. "That's all I know."

My heart skips a beat, and my breath catches in my chest at the word "baby." I sit up in a rush and shake my head. Surely I didn't hear him correctly.

"What did you say?" I choke out.

"She's back at work?" He looks at me with confusion.

"No, not that part. The other thing... did you say 'baby'?" The word gets stuck in my mouth.

"Oh, yeah. She's looking for a bigger place." He shrugs and takes another drink of his water.

"Gwen's pregnant!?" I force out the words that taste like vinegar on my tongue. "When? Who? How long?" I have so many questions, and I want to throat punch Sam for looking so calm at a moment like this.

"What are you freaking out about, dude? You told me she told you." He looks at me like I've grown another head, and I jump up to stand, only to topple over on the coffee table.

"Fuck!" I groan as my ribs ache beneath me.

"What the hell is wrong with you?"

I push myself up, this time remembering I only have one leg to stand on, and hop across the living room to the decorative table where I threw my phone.

"Please don't be broken. Please don't be broken," I say as I slide the table to the side, revealing my shattered phone. I click the power on, and it lights up, indicating a low battery. "Fucking help me out, will you!" I scream and cradle the delicate metal in my palms as if any rogue breeze will cause it to crumble to pieces.

"Uh... sure." Sam sits his water down on a coaster before getting up. "I'll be right back."

"Take care to remember the coaster when your best friend's entire life is at stake!" I call after him. I know it's not Sam's fault, but there appears to have been a major misunderstanding, and he's the only one here I can blame. Therefore, I default to this being his fault.

"Careful. Here, let me help you." He comes over and offers me a hand. Normally, I'd wave him away, but in this moment of need, I'll take all the help I can get.

He pulls me up, throwing one of my arms over his shoulder to help me hop back to my spot on the couch. I'm afraid my ass has made a permanent indentation. I've spent so much time here that it's practically an extension of me by now.

He passes me the charging cable, and I plug it in as I wait the longest three minutes of my life until the phone lights up.

I cut my finger on the broken glass as I swipe to reveal the only text messages on this device.

> So you're just going to leave without saying goodbye?

> Are you mad about the accident? You know I'd take it back if I could.

> I hope this doesn't change anything …

GWEN

> Of course, this changes things. I need some time to figure out what I want.

> Take all the time you need because I'm out.

I stare at the messages in disbelief as my mouth goes completely dry. "Sam... what the fuck is going on here? Are we both talking about the same thing? Does Gwen know about my leg? Because I sure as fuck didn't know she was... pregnant."

I find Sam staring at the wall, next to me on the couch, his mouth agape and eyes wide as saucers. He swallows a gulp and shakes his head. "I... um... I thought."

"You son of a bitch!" I swing, and my fist makes a satisfying contact with his cheekbone.

"Whoa, fuck! Ouch!" He curls into a ball as I pelt him with blow after blow. "Hold on, how the hell is this my fault! I told you I didn't want to be involved!"

I gasp a heaving breath as I pause for a moment. "Why the fuck wouldn't you tell me about this? You saw how distraught I've been over the last few weeks." I strike him again, this time in the chin, and my hand aches in the best possible way.

Fucking finally, I'm starting to feel something again.

"Shit, dude, can you just stop hitting me and let me talk."

He wipes the blood from his mouth and gives me a death glare. "Gwen told Maggie to stall, so she had time to think. I assumed you knew when you got that text. What was I supposed to do, insert myself into your adult problems?" He shakes his head and dabs his swollen lip with the hem of his shirt.

"So, all this time, Gwen's been pregnant?" I look down at my blood-stained knuckles as I try to process this information. "And by the looks of these texts... she thinks I'm out because I don't want anything to do with her and the baby?"

Sam sighs and pulls out his phone. "It seems that's the most likely conclusion."

I fall back onto the cool tile floor as my mind spins.

"What am I going to do, Sam? How the fuck am I going to fix this?"

I hear Benjamin's voice answer through Sam's phone. "Hey, Ben, um... we've got a big problem over here, and we need your help. Jack's really fucked himself this time."

"I was wondering when he was going to call me. Jack, it's so nice to see you've pulled your head out of your ass. What can I do to help?"

"I need to know everything I've missed. Catch me up while I think of a plan."

Benjamin sighs. "Hey, guys, can you give me a minute? I need to take this call," he says to whoever he's meeting with. I hear the door click shut and the squeak of his desk chair before he finally speaks. "Okay, here's what I know. I hope you're ready to take notes..."

CHAPTER THIRTY-SEVEN

Gwen

My phone buzzes on my desk, and I turn it over, not wanting the distraction to break my concentration. I've been working on this press release for Pheobe Thorstein for the last week, and I've almost worked out all the details. We've spun her little mishap with the cult leader into a tell-all memoir, and I've managed to get her a book deal out of this shit show.

We're rebranding her as the first in her family to seek outside help and how she overcame her crippling people-pleasing tendencies and learned to stand in her truth. Of course, the whole joining a cult and becoming its matronly symbol will be the B story, just another example of how people prey on the innocent.

I stretch my aching neck from side to side. All my muscles are stiff from sitting at this desk for hours on end. I need to schedule an appointment with my masseuse ASAP.

Sandra not so subtly suggested that the VP promotion will

finally be mine when this is all wrapped up with a pretty red bow.

I balance my pen between my fingers as I wait for the rush of excitement, but nothing happens. If anything, I feel more annoyed that she's continued to dangle the carrot in front of me—even after surviving a plane crash on the company's behalf. Though I suppose I never finished the job. It's not like there's much of an image to repair when he's all but disappeared from the internet. That's the thing about being in the public eye; once you disappear, someone else comes along demanding attention, and everyone forgets about you and your problems. I laugh at the realization. Maybe our strategy should be to disappear for three months, and when you come back, no one will be the wiser. People are too caught up in their own lives to pay attention to Jack or anyone else's problems.

My phone buzzes, again and again, rattling the surface of my desk.

Jesus, it must be a full moon tonight with all the chaos I've been slammed with.

An email from Sandra pings in my inbox with the subject line, ***URGENT!!!* I roll my eyes.

Everyone thinks their life is so important, but I've learned the difference between real problems and the made-up ones that the media deems urgent.

It's all bullshit.

"There you are!" Sandra bursts through my door. "I've been trying to get in touch with you. Is your phone not working!?" She's breathless, heaving actually, as she stands in my doorway.

"Have you not seen the news?" She clicks on the TV mounted on the wall across from my desk.

Immediately, a clip of a scrawny, bearded Jack flashes across the screen with the words, "Wombat Willy YouTube survivalist makes the documentary of a lifetime..."

My heart sinks in my chest when I see the footage of him on the life raft. It's not something I ever expected to see. Then as I catch my breath, an image of myself wearing a bright red bikini and holding a fishing pole flashes across the screen.

"Everyone's talking about the massive news Wombat Willy dropped on his final episode of his YouTube channel. Not only did he lose his leg during his epic rescue attempt, but he's resigning from his massively popular YouTube channel, which currently has over a million subscribers and counting. It's the most viewed episode in YouTube history, and it only dropped four hours ago. I think Wombat Willy needs to rethink his business strategy—"

Sandra turns off the TV, staring at me in stunned silence before finally speaking. "You did it! I don't know *how* exactly you did it, but somehow you've managed to twist this into the biggest media event of the century! The phone's been ringing off the hook; clients are pouring in; everyone wants the chance to work with you. In my forty professional years, I don't think I've ever been so surprised. I've got to go. It's all hands on deck. We've got to capture as much business as we can. At the rate we're going, we'll double our revenue by the end of the quarter."

She turns to leave, but not before saying, "As much as I'd like to celebrate, I hope you're in for the long haul tonight! I'll need my right-hand woman by my side. Congratulations, Gwenneth. I'm naming you the new VP of Éclat! Now, don't celebrate just yet. We've got a lot of work to do if we want to capitalize on this. I've scheduled a press conference at four. They'll want to speak to you, of course." She cracks the door, still talking through the crack. "Prepare something magical to say and woo them all! Make sure they know it was your expertise that drove the narrative. I'll be right there!" she calls over her shoulder before closing the door, leaving me with a kaleidoscope of emotions.

Heart racing, I open the Youtube link and click play, preparing myself to relive something so terrible, so impactful, that I never thought I'd actually see.

My breath hitches when I see Jack, with his face clean-shaven face and with short-clipped hair, sitting in front of the camera. My eyes catch on his missing appendage.

"No..." I whisper. How could he have kept this a secret from me? Surely I would have known...

"Hey, Dubbies. Before you watch this footage, I just want you to know that this community means the world to me. Everything I've done in life that is good has come from pursuing this dream." He sucks in a breath. "So, when my girlfriend and I," he pauses, scratching the back of his head, "Well, I don't know if I get to call her that anymore... Anyway, when we crash-landed on an island in the middle of the Caribbean Sea, I thought we were as good as dead. The entire experience changed my outlook on life. It showed me what's really important. I hope you enjoy the footage I was able to capture. We certainly faced our share of adversity on that island, but somehow we were miraculously saved through no survival skill or technique on my part." He sucks in a hiss. "I hope I haven't given you any false confidence in making these videos. It was never my intention to steer you wrong or entice you to chance fate. So I hope you can learn this hard lesson from me and maybe even laugh about some of the shit we got ourselves into." He pauses, swallowing hard. "I apologize for any harm my videos may have caused, and I know that the life I've led isn't the norm. Sometimes we have to grow up and stop living with our heads in the clouds and take responsibility for our actions, so this is me saying, Goodbye, Dubbies. We had a good run. This is Wombat Willy signing off."

A gut-wrenching sob cracks through me, and I can't hold back the tears as I watch his resignation video. Jack's face looks so sullen and broken. The dark circles under his eyes tell me he hasn't been sleeping. He looks absolutely miserable. There's no trace of his trademark sunshiney glow, and he's just going to quit... After everything he's been through?

A knot twists in my stomach, and suddenly, I feel like I'm going to be sick.

This isn't what I wanted from him. I never wanted him to change who he was for me.

I suck in a breath and push through, playing the rest of the video, and my heart breaks all over again as I watch us fall in love, fighting and bickering in the beginning. I see the footage of me learning to swim, and I can't help but belly laugh when I watch as I throw a bloody tampon over my head in an attempt to save myself from the non-violent shark. Then he's teaching me to fish and swim.

My heart swells as I catch glimpses of him eyeing me with stars in his eyes. I was so oblivious in the moment, but watching it all back, there's no doubt in my mind of the shared feelings, feelings that Jack caught way before I came around.

My chest caves in when I listen to his goodbye messages to his viewers but mostly to me. He really sacrificed his own life for the slight chance that someone would find him, dead or alive, and through his videos, eventually find me. I shake my head as my tears flow. He loves me. I knew it before, and I know it now, but something doesn't add up.

I flick open my phone screen and stare at the text messages I've burned into my memory.

Is it actually possible he didn't know about the baby? Just like I didn't know about his leg?

I drop the phone with a gasp when his face fills the screen. He's lying on the raft we built together in the middle of the ocean.

"This is my message in a bottle. If these are the last words I ever speak, I hope you'll play them over and over again, so everyone knows the love I have for Gwenneth Pierson. Baby, you changed me in the best way. Before I met you, I was living life for only myself, and hell, I was having a damn good time. But I would trade it all, anything I have to give, for one moment with you. In the short time on that island, I felt love in a way I thought only existed in fairy tales. I hope you know you were the very last memory to cross my mind at the end, and I wouldn't have changed anything about our short love story... Well, except for your rescue anyway. I love you, Gwen."

The tears fall down my cheeks like waterfalls, and there's no use even trying to wipe them away. I'm puffy and wrecked from watching the footage, and all I can think about, all I long for, is to be in Jack's arms again. I have to talk to him, and I don't care how far or long I have to travel to do so.

I check my watch, and it's right on time. I stand up from my desk and march downstairs to the press conference, just as Sandra gives her opening remarks.

"It is my absolute honor to introduce my most prized employee, Gwenneth Pierson, the new VP of Éclat. She's prepared something brilliant in regards to her first-hand experience working with the internet sensation you all know as Wombat Willy. Let's all give her a warm welcome!"

I walk up to the podium and take the mic, not bothering to wipe my makeup or fix my disheveled clothes.

"Good afternoon, everyone. My name is Gwen Pierson. Three months and three weeks ago, I was assigned to help repair the public image of the man you all know as Wombat Willy.

We chartered his private plane and set out to film content in Costa Rica, and as you all know by watching his video, that plane never reached its destination.

Instead, Jack crash-landed the plane somewhere in the middle of the Caribbean near a deserted island where we–" I force a smile through my flowing tears, "fought like cats and dogs for weeks." I laugh at the memory.

"Together, we built a raft that Jack would later use to try to find help, but the ocean didn't care about our plans." I suck in a breath, not caring that I've got a heap of snot and mascara mixing on my face. "He documented our failures and successes along the way... all the way up to the end." I wipe my face with the back of my hand and draw in a long calming breath. "This entire experience has changed me, as you can imagine how any near-death experience changes someone. I set out in an attempt to help Jack not to lose any sponsors, but what transpired on that island had the complete opposite effect on me." I turn, so I'm facing Sandra as I deliver my last punch.

"I learned that there's more to life than being appealing to everyone. Jack taught me that character is how you behave when no one is watching, and he has more honor in his pinky finger than anyone I've ever met," I laugh. "If anything, we should all be learning from him how to live life in a way that's right for us... No matter how silly that may seem. With that being said, I'm stepping down as the newly named VP of Éclat in pursuit of literally anything else that lights my heart up." I place my hands over my lower stomach. "I'll take no further comments on Wombat Willy or any affiliation I have with him. Sandra, you can take that promotion and shove it up your ass."

I step away from the platform with what feels like a two-ton weight lifted from my shoulders.

For the first time in my life, I'm finally free.

CHAPTER THIRTY-EIGHT

JACK

"Come on, step on the gas, man! What are you, like eighty or something?" I call to Sam from the passenger seat as I swipe through the mountains of tweets about Wombat Willy's latest video. We've just landed in Chicago, and I'm trying like hell—no thanks to Sam's old-man driving—to get to Gwen before it's too late.

I knew my resignation video would make a wave, but nothing could've prepared me for the mass chaos hitting my inbox about the announcement. I can't keep up with all the sponsorship offers, death threats, kudos, and basically everything in between. I let my head fall on the back of the headrest as I think of Landon and his high blood pressure. The poor man is probably ready to strangle me for not running this stunt by him before I posted it, but I'm a man fueled by desperation, and I had to do something to get her attention.

The hashtag WombatWilly is trending on Twitter, so I've spent the last twenty minutes since our plane landed scrolling through in search of anything that would give me real-time information about Gwen. My finger hovers over the screen when I see a video clip of her at a podium. "There we go." I click play and catch a ten-second clip of her telling her boss to shove the promotion she worked so hard for—the thing she bitched about the entire time we were on that island—up her ass. I can't help the giant grin that spreads across my face. I don't even care if Gwen forgives me or anything that happens next. Knowing she stood in front of the press, and God knows who else, and told her boss to fuck off is like music to my ears.

God, I love that woman, and I hope she can forgive me for being such an arrogant prick, for assuming the worst of her when she's given me zero reasons to do so. Now, I just need to find her and tell her how I feel.

"I'm literally driving ninety. I don't know what more you expect!" Sam yells as he grips the steering wheel with white knuckles. I have to hand it to the guy; he helped me with the video launch and even booked our flights first thing this morning. I want to be mad at him, but I know he was just trying to stay out of it and let us handle our problems. Of course, that seems to be where everyone went wrong. Everyone assumed everyone knew because they were scared to spill our secrets.

Fucking Gwen is just as hardheaded as I am, and it goes to show we've both met our match.

My palms are sweaty, my heart is racing, and I just need to see her, touch her, know she's okay, apologize, and assure her I'm nothing like her father, that I would never abandon her and our child. I feel sick just thinking I could've been anything like what she experienced from men growing up.

"I see it. That's Éclat just ahead, the tall white brick building!" I point out to Sam as if the GPS he programmed hadn't already told him that much. Hey, maybe I'm old school, but old habits die hard.

"I've got it." He swerves into a parallel parking spot across from the building, and I tighten my grip on my crutches as I wait for his assistance. It kills me that I can't jump out and o find her before we've even come to a stop, but I know my limits. Sam throws the car into park, and I leap out, tightening the grip on my crutches, and I stumble across the street, navigating oncoming traffic.

Car horns blare as I wobble across the street, making my way to the crowd outside the building. I squint, scanning the crowd for Gwen's white blonde hair, but I have no luck.

Though I spot Sandra standing near the front as a slew of reporters shove microphones in her face. I smile and make my way toward her. I figure she's my best bet until I can call Maggie or Elliot and figure out if they know where Gwen's run off.

"Excuse me!" I wave to Sandra.

Her eyes widen when she notices me, and I take that as a cue to approach her. "I'm looking for Gwen Pierson. I believe you know her?"

She rolls her eyes and looks up, not making eye contact with me. "Mr. Willy, I assure you, if I had any idea of where Gwen is, I wouldn't tell you if my life depended on it," she scoffs. "Now, why don't you hobble along and leave me to clean up this gigantic shit storm your *girlfriend* created for me."

My heart skips a beat when she says the word *girlfriend*... So maybe there's a chance she'll forgive me.

"With the utmost disrespect, I feel like you're getting exactly what you deserve for stringing her along all this time." I laugh. "Maybe if you didn't dangle that promotion in front of her face for the last, I don't know, five years, she wouldn't have felt so taken for granted." I shrug. "But what do I know? I'm just a silly YouTuber." I turn and make my way back to Sam's parked car.

"Change of plans. She's not here. I need you to get Maggie

and Elliot on the phone right now and see if they know where she's gone."

"Already on it." Sam's phone screen lights up with Maggie's number, and she answers on the second ring.

"Please tell me you know what the hell is going on right now!"

"Listen, Maggie. We're looking for Gwen. Have you heard from her?"

"No, she hasn't called me, but I just found out she quit her job on Twitter. What the hell is going on?" she shrieks.

"I have Jack, and we're looking for Gwen. Is there any way you can find her? Do you think she's with Elliot?"

"No, she wouldn't have gone to Elliot's..." She's quiet for a moment. "Oh! I can track her phone! I forgot I set it up when I gave it to her... You know. after the accident, you can never be too careful–"

"Where is she!?" I scream before she can finish her sentence.

"Oh, um... hang on... let me just... Ok, it looks like she's heading toward Rockford International–"

"Go!" I scream as Sam pulls out onto the busy street.

"Whoa, what's going on over there? Do you need me to do anything? Is Gwen okay?" Maggie bombards us with questions over speakerphone.

"Don't worry about it, Maggie. Just stay by the phone. If you hear from Gwen, tell her to wait where she is, I'm coming to get her."

"Okay, but I really feel like–"

I end the call before she can finish her sentence because I don't need anyone else's opinions about what I should do anymore. I'm in full-on survival mode, and I feel like every second I spend away from Gwen makes me want to explode, and I still need to apologize.

"Hold on. This is going to be a bumpy ride!" Sam calls from the front seat.

I grip the Oh Shit handle and smile. "Let's go get my girl."

<hr>

We pull up to the terminal, and Sam drops me off so he can park. "Hey, man, good luck," he says just before I close the door.

"Thanks, Sam. I really appreciate all of this, and I promise I'll cover that speeding ticket back there."

"Oh, I know you will," he laughs. "Now, go get your girl."

I slam the car door shut and brace myself on my crutches as I look up at the gigantic airport before me. Gwen's in there somewhere... I've just got to find her.

I grip my crutches and limp my way to the front desk to buy a random ticket and make my way through security.

"Whoa, whoa, whoa. Hold on a second, buddy. What's the rush?" The security officer pulls me aside for a random check.

"I'm trying to catch my flight just like everyone else in this line," I retort. The second the words come out of my mouth, I know I've just fucked myself.

"We've got ourselves a smart-mouth, do we?" The security officer smack's his gum as he scans me from head to toe.

Jesus, Jack, why the fuck did you pick this particular instance to lose your cool?

"Hey, I know you. You're that Wombat Willy character, aren't ya?" The security officer clenches the taser on his belt buckle. *Are you fucking serious right now?*

"That's me." I hold my hands wide and wiggle my fingers, hoping to ease some of the tension. "Do you want an autograph or something? I'm down for a selfie or whatever, but I really need to get going to—"

"You got a lot of nerve, buddy." He pulls out his billy stick and points it in my face.

"Whoa, whoa, what's the problem?" I hold my hands up in surrender.

"The problem? The problem is my son doesn't have half of his arm cuz of you!" A spray of spittle soaks my face as he screams at me.

If there was ever a more inconvenient time to run into an angry parent, it's now. I should've known this would come back to haunt me. I force a laugh and point to my own missing appendage. "It seems karma is real now, doesn't it? I'm sorry about your son's arm. I really am, but there's a girl, and I really need to get—"

"Oh, no, you don't." He grins. "Why should I help you when you made my son look like a fool?" he hisses.

I cock my head to the side and try to contemplate what he said, but my pent-up rage gets the best of me. "Your son made himself look like a fool. Maybe next time he won't be such a dumbass and think the rules don't apply to him." I shrug.

"That's it. You're gonna pay for that, you prick!" The officer spins me around, slamming my face against the wall as he pulls the cuffs out from his belt.

"This is fucking awesome!" some kid in line behind me calls, and I have zero doubt that he's filming me. I hang my head in defeat because this rent-a-cop's got something to prove, and I've just given him the perfect bait. There's no way I'll make it to Gwen in time.

That's when the idea hits me... I just need to create a bigger scene since I'm already trending on Twitter...

"Since we're doing this... there's something else I think you should know about your bouncing baby boy—"

He tightens the cold metal cuffs over my wrists. "Don't you talk about my son—"

"Did you know that he and his buddies had drugs on them during the entire trip?" I laugh. "Yep, he was so strung out, I imagine he didn't even feel it when the caiman ripped his arm off."

"Liar!" the security officer yells, and I know I'm getting closer. I can actually *feel* him shaking with rage.

"Yep, what college does he attend again?" I pretend to think. "Oh yeah, Princeton, is it? I wonder what would happen if they found out a person with such low character was representing their school?"

"You son of B-word!" the officer screams, and I have to bite my tongue to keep from laughing.

He jerks my cuffs and slams me against the wall, and I take a page out of the old soccer handbook, collapsing on the ground.

"Oh shit, I'm sorry, officer!" I yell as the crowd gathers around me, everyone's phone held out in front of them as they record the show. "Ow, my leg! Listen, man, I'm just trying to get through security to find my girlfriend and tell her I'm such a dumbass."

"Excuse me, what's going on here?" Another security officer steps in.

"This fella is way outta line!" the first officer says. "He's saying bad things about my boy. Don't worry, I've got it handled–"

"Gwen, if you're watching this, please don't get on that plane! I'm sorry about what I said. You know I didn't mean it. Fuck, I'm so excited to be having a baby with you that it's all I can think about. I don't know what this means for us or what happens next, but I know I want to figure it out. I want to write our own story, and I believe we can make this work. I'll get a normal job. I'll put on a suit and tie every day. Hell, I'll be a stay-at-home dad and support your career. Please, let's just try–"

"Okay, lover boy, get up. You have the right to remain silent–"

"Jack! Jack! I'm over here! Stay right there. I'm coming to get you!" I hear Gwen's sweet voice scream over the crowd.

"Stay back, lady, this man's being arrested for... uh... resisting arrest."

"If you're arresting him, then you may as well take me, too." She holds her hands in front of her as the security guards look around in confusion.

"Ma'am, it doesn't work like–"

"Jack! Are you alright! I'm so sorry! I want all of that, too." She rushes to me, ignoring the security guards.

"Ma'am, please back away from the man..."

"You can either cuff me now, or I'll give you a reason. Take your pick!" She eyes the security guard, letting her eyes drift to his groin.

"Uh, Sheila, go on and cuff the crazy lady, too," the first guard says. "Ok, folks, that's enough of that. There's nothin' to see here. Let's just keep this line moving along."

It's there, with my face pressed against the rough airport carpet, that I fall in love with Gwen all over again. "I love you so much. As soon as I get out of these handcuffs, you're not going to be able to keep me off of you."

"I love you, too, Tarzan."

CHAPTER THIRTY-NINE

Gwen

"Are you ready to find out the sex of the baby?" the doctor says as she rubs the ultrasound wand over my small baby bump.

I look at Jack, who's practically reeling with excitement. He's been talking about this appointment for weeks, making pro and con lists for all the reasons to find out or not about the baby's sex. His decision changes daily, but today, it seems like...

"Yes!" He grips my hand, and a warm wave of comfort washes over me.

"Are you sure?" the doctor teases. She knows how excited he's been, probably because he's left her approximately one hundred voicemails over the last three months.

He sucks in a long breath and nods his head. "Tell us, doctor. We're ready."

She laughs and rubs the instrument around my belly. I must say, this experience is far more comfortable than the dildo cam I received in the hospital. I'm learning pregnancy is not for the weak.

"Okay, let's see here... It looks like you're having a little... girl!"

Jack lets out a shriek so shrill that my eye actually waters, and I can't keep from smiling as my heart fills with so much love I feel like I could burst.

"We're having a little girl!" He kisses me on the cheek, then tucks his face into the crook of my neck and whispers, "You've made me the happiest man in the world. I can't wait to raise our daughter with you."

Hot tears flow down my cheeks as I kiss him like we're the only two in the world. I close my eyes, and it's like it's just all alone on that island again.

"I'll give you two some privacy. You can meet me in my office after you're done celebrating." The doctor laughs.

The door clicks closed, and Jack pulls away as he digs for something in his pocket.

"I've been waiting for the perfect moment to do this, and I don't think I'll find a better time than right now." He helps me sit up, scooting me to the table's edge.

"Jack, what are you—"

I gasp when he lowers himself, very slowly, down on his knee. A flush of heat rushes to my cheeks because the man knows how sexy I think his one-legged squat is.

"Gwenneth Pierson, from the moment I laid eyes on you in that dark bar, I knew there was something special about you. You challenge me in the best ways, and I can't get enough of you. Even when we fight, there's no other person I'd rather make up with." He smiles at me adoringly, then opens a small light pink velvet box revealing the most beautiful pearl ring I've ever seen.

"I found this pearl near the coral reef that day on the island, and even though I had no idea what would come of any of this, I took it as a sign from the universe that I'd one day give it to you when I asked you to marry me. So, baby, what do you say? Will you marry me and make me the happiest man in the world?"

"Jack... I..." I gasp as I take the velvet box from him, studying the gold-banded pearl ring. It's so delicate and unique and completely perfect. "How did you keep this... all this time?"

"I stowed it in my camera bag," he says. "I'm really glad you made Maggie go back for it."

"Of course, I'll marry you!" I say as I help him up, pulling him into a hug. "I can't imagine a life without you, and I don't want to try."

"She said YES!" Jack yells as the door opens and all our friends come rushing in.

I throw my head back in laughter when I see Sam holding a video camera.

"Are you seriously live streaming this right now?" I pin Jack with a glare, and he shrugs. "Baby, this is the happiest day of my life... so far. Why wouldn't I want to share it with all two million of my fans?"

I shake my head and laugh because it's such a cocky Jack move, and I wouldn't expect anything less.

I look around at my best friends huddled together in the small examination room as tears flow down my face. In my wildest dreams, I never could've predicted anything about this moment, but somehow, it's better than anything I ever imagined. I've learned so much about what's important in life. Jack's shown me how to slow down and have fun, to enjoy the little moments just as much as the monumental ones, and for the first time in my life, I don't care what anyone thinks of me. I'm happy to be figuring it all out with Jack by my side.

Who knows where any of this will lead? All I know is I'm in love with a wild man, and we're open to whatever adventure life brings us next.

EPILOGUE

Gwen

Three years later...

"Stay right there. Don't move." Jack calls behind the small camera he's just set up in front of us. My muscles strain as I try to hold a wiggly Archie up for our Sunday family photo. It's something Jack started as soon as our oldest child, Indie, was born, and he's extremely proud of our streak.

Whether it's rain or shine, we're living with or without internet, sick, mad, sad, or otherwise, Jack Manning will take a photo of his family every single Sunday without fail.

Sparky, our mini Australian Shepherd, runs between my legs, chasing a blowing leaf around my feet.

"There we go," Jack hits the automatic timer and scoops up Indie in his arms, tickling my favorite giggle out of her. I hear the faint shutters click, indicating he took a photo burst—good, because my ankles are killing me, and it's hot as sin out here in the Costa Rican sun.

I rub my swollen belly, stretched so tightly I don't know how I'll make it another month without popping.

"Perfect! That's a good one, definitely in the top fifty Sunday family photos!" Jack slides the camera off the tripod and strides up to me, planting a gentle kiss on the top of my head. "You look so beautiful pregnant. You know that, don't you?"

I laugh. "Who knew the man had such a breeding kink?" I joke.

"Baby, it's not a breeding kink. Though I'm not going to lie and say I don't enjoy breeding." He waggles his eyebrows. "It's a Gwenneth Manning kink." He rubs his large palms over my swollen belly, and his tender touch feels so good on my poor, stretched skin. "I'm obsessed with you." He kisses me again, this time on the lips.

Archie kicks his legs to get down, and I finally relent, setting his chubby barefoot feet on the warm sand. A breeze blows, sending my hair flying in every direction, and Jack takes the opportunity to tuck a wild strand behind my ear.

We're living in Costa Rica now, mostly full-time, traveling back to Chicago to see our friends every chance we get.

I knew that life with Jack would be amazing, but nothing could've prepared me for all the adventures we'd share. It's comical, really, thinking about how much my life has changed. As soon as I left Éclat and begged Jack to start a production company with me, we took our talents international.

There was a whole new wave of inspired survivalists after Jack's video. I convinced him to submit his video to an indie documentary festival, and we won first place. After that, everything changed. Jack and I started our own Youtube production company, signing new content creators and coaching them on how to scale their platforms with Jack's proprietary method.

Together, we teach people how to connect with their audience and monetize their platforms—of course, that's where I come in.

After leaving Éclat, I realized I could make a bigger impact by using my skill set to help small creators get their videos in front of the right sponsors. I've used Elliot's company, Clutch Media, to partner with and take on a few private-coaching cohorts each year. When I finally let go of my desire for control, things just got easier. I never realized you could chase a dream and work toward a goal with ease. If it weren't for Jack's things-will-work-out-for-the-best attitude, I would've spent the rest of my working life spinning myself into a ball of nerves.

We may travel eight months out of the year, but since I'm so close to my due date, we'll spend the next six months or so in Costa Rica at our home base.

Jack still doesn't like the idea of being tied down to any one place, and that's the part of him I love the most.

We know we need plenty of sunshine, an ocean close by, and our kids—and Sparky—running around at our feet. Everything else is just a bonus.

"How about I get dinner started, and you prop your feet up and watch the sunset?" Jack pulls me into him, and I tuck my face in his neck, breathing in his wild masculine scent.

A sudden squeal of excitement from Indie and Archie jolts me to attention, and I pull away, scanning for the source. My eyes land on a brightly colored red and blue bird sitting in a palm tree only a few feet away.

Jack sneaks behind Indie and pulls her up on his shoulders, then grabs Archie and carries them both to get a closer look.

"Now, this is a toucan. It's your mother's favorite."

"She's so pwetty!" Indie claps.

Jack laughs, looking right at me. "Well, this bird is actually a boy! Isn't that silly?"

Indie's eyebrows pull together in confusion. Then the bird lets out an ear-piercing squawk. "Why is he such a loud bird?" She plugs her ears with her fingers.

I grab the camera when Jack's not looking, framing the three of them in the center of the shot.

"He's just showing off, looking for his mate." Jack laughs. "Sometimes boys have to go to great extremes to get a girl's attention." His eyes twinkle with mischief, and he lifts his hand, offering it as perch for the loud bird.

I watch as the bird steps onto his hand, and both Indie and Archie squeal in disbelief. Jack tells them all the facts he knows about the bird, and all I can think is how lucky I am for this man to be my partner in life and the father of my children.

Who knew it'd take a near-death experience being stranded on an island for me to finally let myself release my death grip of control and finally live a life worth chasing.

The End.

ACKNOWLEDGMENTS

I'd like to thank my husband, my therapist, and my best friend for supporting me during the grueling months it took to finish this manuscript. Without their support this would never have been possible.

Really though, these people are the Sam to my Frodo, wiping the sweat from my brow as I fumbled my way—not so gracefully—through the writing/revision process.

They listened to my whine and complain, offered me advice on how I could make the story stronger, and encouraged me to keep going even when I wanted to quit.

I don't know why this story was so hard to write, I think there's a weird thing that happens to your confidence when you release your second book. Like there's some invisible pressure that only you are aware of... or maybe that's just me and my anxiety talking.

I'd also like to thank my very best Beta reader, Casey, for helping me whip this story into tip top shape. Your eye for storytelling is fantastic and I am so grateful that you took the time to help me. I know Wild For You is better because you had your hands in it.

And lastly, I'd like to thank my children—specifically my 12-year-old daughter, for being the biggest hype-girl a mom could ask for. I don't know what I'd do without you promoting my book to all your middle school teachers! It's a special thing to feel so supported and I never imagined my daughter (who isn't allowed to read my books until she's at least 18) would be my biggest fan.

I am so grateful for every single one of you and only hope that I can someday return the favor.

AUTHOR'S NOTE

Thank you so much for reading my book! I really hope you enjoyed reading it as much as I enjoyed writing this story.

I'm not going to lie, this book was a challenge but being able to disappear into Gwen and Jack's world was absolutely delightful. I had so much fun with these characters and the more time I spend with the whole friend group, the more I wish I could live amongst them.

I love Gwen and Jack so much! My goal with all my books is to create characters that readers can connect with. So if you didn't connect with Elliot's anxiety, maybe you can connect with Gwen's workaholic nature. I think many people–especially women–understand feeling like they have to hustle for their worth.

I wanted to dig into what it would look like for someone who's been on the "right track" in their career to have to decide what success really looks like. Does it always present itself in the most traditional sense? How hard would it be to abandon a lifetime of programming and change your mindset? What external forces could trigger such a shift? I think we could all benefit from asking ourselves this question in some way or another.

I wanted to create two imperfect characters that would only be able to overcome their circumstances by working together and embracing each of their gifts, ultimately bringing out the best in each other. Obviously I wanted Jack to annoy the snot out of Gwen because if there's anything I know about being stressed and scared, it's that all of those emotions are enhanced when you're around someone who simply doesn't allow themselves to worry.

My husband is like this in many ways and though it's enraging when I'm in a stress-spiral, I find it fascinating that he can *choose* to not allow himself to feel stress.

Maybe we can all learn from Gwen and Jack to let ourselves challenge our beliefs that no longer serve us and that we get to decide how we want to live out the rest of our lives... even if it doesn't make sense to our families or anyone else.

Thank you for reading Wild For You, I look forward to bringing you more stories in the very near future.

If you loved this story, please consider leaving a review and telling a friend!

XOXO
Jeré

1. Gwen is the kind of woman who knows what she wants and when she wants it. How do you think that personality trait served her in her life? How did it blind her?
2. Gwen's work environment was intense, some could even say toxic. Have you ever worked for a boss like Sandra? Do you think there's any good that comes from working in that environment?
3. What do you think were Jack's positive qualities? What were his flaws?
4. Jack and Gwen could not be more opposite. Do you believe that opposites really do attract (and work) in the real world?
5. Gwen struggled with trusting people–especially men–due to her parent's emotional neglect growing up. How can you relate to this in your own life?
6. How would you describe Gwen's character in the beginning? What was the major change that took place over the course of the story? How would you describe her in the end?

7. If you were stranded on a deserted island, would you adopt a positive make-lemonade-out-of-lemons attitude like Jack? Or would you be more cynical like Gwen? What kind of person would you want to have as a survival buddy?

8. How did Jack's injury affect his identity? Have you ever had a challenging injury or diagnosis, whether physical or mental (ie: bipolar, ADHD, Autism, Autoimmune disease) that has challenged your own identity? How did you overcome it and learn to accept your new truth?

9. How were you surprised by the unfolding of the story's theme of trust through Gwen and Jack? What did each character need for them to be able to fully truth each other and themselves? Is trust something that comes easily to you? Why or why not?

10. Strong friendships are a central theme of this book and are what helped Gwen and Jack in their journeys. How has friendship helped you overcome hardships?

ABOUT THE AUTHOR

Jeré Anthony (pronounced like hooray with a J) writes steamy, swoony, and hilarious romantic comedies with depth.

She is a mental health advocate, a lifelong anxiety warrior, and is ADHD AF. Her quirks bleed out into her stories making for an exciting group of characters. Because of her undiagnosed ADHD, growing up she always felt different from everyone around her. Now she strives to create stories that give readers an escape from reality while also helping them feel seen.

She loves a strong cup of coffee and thinks beer + buffalo wings are a delicacy that is unmatched.

Jeré currently lives in NW Arkansas with her husband, three children, dog, and two cats. When she's not writing, you can find her reading, driving her kids all over for travel soccer games, watching cat videos on her phone, or trying to convince her husband to go on another family adventure somewhere new.

Connect with Jeré:
NEWSLETTER: https://mailchi.mp/87e346b13331/jere-anthonynewsletter
INSTAGRAM: @author_jere_anthony
TIKTOK: @author_jere_anthony
WEBSITE: JereAnthony.com

9 781736 819531